THE SPECIALIST

NORCROSS SECURITY #3

ANNA HACKETT

The Specialist

Published by Anna Hackett

Cover by Lana Pecherczyk

Cover image by Wander Aguiar

Edits by Tanya Saari

ISBN (ebook): 978-1-922414-23-6

ISBN (paperback): 978-1-922414-24-3

WHAT READERS ARE SAYING ABOUT ANNA'S ACTION ROMANCE

Heart of Eon - Romantic Book of the Year (Ruby) winner 2020

Cyborg - PRISM Award Winner 2019

Edge of Eon and Mission: Her Protection - Romantic Book of the Year (Ruby) finalists 2019

Unfathomed and Unmapped - Romantic Book of the Year (Ruby) finalists 2018

Unexplored – Romantic Book of the Year (Ruby) Novella Winner 2017

Return to Dark Earth – One of Library Journal's Best E-Original Books for 2015 and two-time SFR Galaxy Awards winner

At Star's End – One of Library Journal's Best E-Original Romances for 2014

The Phoenix Adventures – SFR Galaxy Award Winner for Most Fun New Series and "Why Isn't This a Movie?" Series

Beneath a Trojan Moon – SFR Galaxy Award Winner and RWAus Ella Award Winner

Hell Squad – SFR Galaxy Award for best Post-Apocalypse for Readers who don't like Post-Apocalypse

"Like Indiana Jones meets Star Wars. A treasure hunt with a steamy romance." – SFF Dragon, review of *Among Galactic Ruins*

"Action, danger, aliens, romance – yup, it's another great book from Anna Hackett!" – Book Gannet Reviews, review of *Hell Squad: Marcus*

Sign up for my VIP mailing list and get your *free box set* containing three action-packed romances.

Visit here to get started: www.annahackett.com

CHAPTER ONE

The man was a tyrant.

Harlow Carlson grumbled under her breath as she climbed out of her Uber and hurried down the sidewalk.

San Francisco was draped in darkness. It was almost nine o'clock at night, and here she was, heading back into the office.

Because her boss was a workaholic control freak who never slept.

She mentally added arrogant, demanding, and bossy to Easton Norcross' personality faults.

Harlow had been his executive assistant for two weeks. The man had a mind like a steel trap, and never stopped. It was probably why he was a gazillionaire.

She sniffed. She usually worked for Tenneson Industrics, a Norcross Inc. subsidiary, and loved her boss, Meredith Webster. When Easton's usual assistant, Mrs. Skilton, went on leave due to the birth of her grandchild, the imposing woman had selected Harlow to stand in for her.

"Easton needs someone who can keep up with him. Someone smart, with a spine." The older, gray-haired woman had rolled her eyes. "And who won't throw herself at him."

"As if I'd do that," Harlow muttered. The man might be sex in a suit, but usually, she just wanted to stab him in the eye with her stylus.

She approached the front door of the gleaming office building. Norcross Inc. was housed on two of the upper floors, with killer views of the city and San Francisco Bay.

Harlow pulled out her access card from her glittery, red Roger Vivier clutch. She'd bought it at a little second-hand boutique she'd discovered on Chestnut Street. The bag made her smile every time she held it, and it matched her little red dress perfectly.

Easton's text telling her to get back to the office to find the missing paperwork he needed for an early-morning call with London had interrupted her date.

She swiped the card. The reader beeped and the glass door slid open.

It had been the most boring date she'd ever been on, so her overbearing boss had done her a favor, but she wasn't telling him that. Her heels clicked on the marble floor.

She and Michael had sparked about as much chemistry as a couple of wet sponges. Harlow sighed. It'd been so long since any man had been near her lady parts that she'd suffered through the dinner longer than she should have.

Note to self: no more blind dates set up by her mother.

Harlow shrugged off her coat. The security guard at the desk stood. "Good evening, Ms. Carlson."

She threw her coat over her arm. "Hi, Joe."

The older man's eyes widened. "You look like a million bucks tonight."

She smiled. "Why, thank you." Her red dress had long sleeves, a deep *V* neckline, and hugged her curves. It was also short.

"What brings you back tonight?" Joe asked.

"I was on a date before the Grand Master snapped his fingers."

Joe's lips twitched. "He works late a lot. Don't let him keep you too long."

"I won't." The elevator doors closed. One thing she'd learned—it paid to stand toe-to-toe with Easton Norcross, or he'd run right over you. The man radiated "I'm in charge" vibes every second of every day.

Growing up, she'd thought her dad had the same "man in charge" aura, but Charles Carlson was nowhere in Easton's league.

Thoughts of her dad made her stomach tie up in little knots.

Two days ago, he'd left her a worrying, cryptic message.

Her father was a successful local businessman, who, even though he was retired, still kept busy with a few investment projects. Her mom kept busy lunching with friends, going on yoga retreats, and sitting on lots of charity boards. Eleanor Carlson had never met a charity she didn't want to support.

That niggle of worry in Harlow's belly grew. Something was going on with her dad. He'd left her a message saying that he had some trouble, but then he'd told her not to worry. He hadn't sounded like himself.

Since then, she couldn't track him down. He hadn't returned her messages, and her mom said he was working late. Harlow got the feeling he was avoiding her.

Charles Carlson had fully expected his daughters to attend college, launch fantastic careers, and marry socially acceptable men.

So far, he was exceptionally disappointed. Neither Harlow, nor her younger sister, Scarlett, were anywhere close to married.

Harlow had suffered through a boring law degree, before realizing she wanted to be an executive assistant. She loved organizing, solving problems, juggling issues, and finding effective, efficient solutions. She thrived on it and it fed her soul.

She'd been organizing her family for as long as she could remember. As a teenager, she'd helped her father with his work as a side job. And her sister was ten years younger than Harlow, so she'd helped her mother a lot when the new baby had arrived.

When she'd first told her father that she wasn't going to practice law, he'd lost it. "No child of mine will be a lowly assistant."

Harlow snorted. She was well aware good assistants kept the business world running. Her father's included.

The elevator slowed and she straightened her shoulders. She knew a brilliant executive assistant was worth their weight in gold. She was well-paid, and that helped with her ultimate goal—buying her own house.

She felt a giddy little feeling. Harlow wanted to own a lovely San Francisco home all of her own. She wanted to renovate. Decorate. She was a closet reno-show addict. She had a burning need to knock down some walls and gut some bathrooms.

She grinned to herself.

She was so good at her job that she had earned the dubious prize of working for Easton for the foreseeable future.

The elevator doors opened. The main office level was shadowed, the lights on low. Pushing worry for her dad away, she strode forward. She'd pin him down eventually.

The carpet muffled the sound of her steps. There were lights on in Easton's office.

Maybe the man was part machine?

She passed her own desk. It was exactly how she'd left it several hours earlier. Mostly clear, with a few neat, organized piles.

She paused in the doorway.

Against her will, her belly tightened. The man might be a tyrant, but she was female enough to admit he was a mouthwatering one.

Especially like this.

Usually, Easton wore perfectly tailored suits. He was always pressed, looking gorgeous and intimidating.

Right now, he was in off mode. Or as off as he got.

His dark suit jacket hung over the back of his executive desk chair. He still wore the white shirt he'd had on today, but now the sleeves were rolled up, and the top two buttons were undone. All of that revealed the ink that was usually kept hidden.

Harlow's pulse skipped a beat, her mouth suddenly dry. Intricate, black designs coiled around his muscled forearms, and there was the hint of more on his chest.

Oh, no. No. No. *No.* She wasn't giving this any air time.

For now, Easton Norcross was her boss. She couldn't, *wouldn't*, entertain any attraction to him.

She hadn't made a noise, but his head lifted. Instincts honed from his time in the military.

Harlow lifted her chin. It would have been really nice if the universe could have made his face less gorgeous. His Italian-American heritage was stamped all over his features. He was a little too rugged to be strictly handsome. A strong jaw, clean-shaven in the morning, was now covered in a dark, five-o'clock shadow. His eyes were a deep, cobalt blue, and his ink-black hair was just a little longer than what you'd expect from a successful businessman.

That sharp gaze roamed over her, then flicked back to her face.

"A little overdressed for the office, Ms. Carlson."

Ignoring the deep drawl, Harlow strode in and dumped her coat and clutch on one of the guest chairs in front of Easton's lake-sized desk of polished teak.

"I'm not supposed to be in the office," she said sharply. "I'm supposed to be finishing my date, but I'm employed by a workaholic."

Dark brows drew down. "Date?"

"Yes, you know, man, woman, dinner."

His gaze dropped to her legs. "And a little more than dinner if that dress is anything to go by."

"There is nothing wrong with my dress." She strode around his desk. She wasn't letting him intimidate her. "And my date is none of your business." She started scanning the desk for the missing files. "I left those reports right on your desk. What have you done with them?"

He looked up at her. She caught a faint whiff of his cologne—crisp and sexy, with a spicy undertone.

Dammit. Focus, Harlow.

There were no files on his desk, just one hot boss leaning against it.

"Ms. Carlson." His fingers wrapped around her arm.

The heat of his touch ran through her. She sucked in a breath.

"Anyone who works for me is very much my business."

EASTON WATCHED Harlow's blue-green eyes fire.

She didn't pull back. No, one thing he'd learned about Harlow Carlson over the last few weeks since she'd become the bane of his existence, was that she rarely did the expected.

She leaned closer, rifling through the papers on his desk.

"You might think you're in charge of the world, Mr. Norcross, but you aren't."

Fuck. Easton finally confronted the fact that anytime this woman called him Mr. Norcross, he got hard.

She was dressed like a man's fantasy. Her gorgeous curves were packed into a fire-engine-red dress. Her silky, blonde hair was piled up on her head; strands of it escaped to tease the slender line of her neck.

"I'm in charge of my little piece of the world," he drawled.

She cocked her hip. "You aren't in charge of *people*."

He sat back in his chair, not examining why trading barbs with Harlow woke something up inside him.

Since he'd left the Army, Easton had thrown himself into business. It had given him purpose.

And kept the dark memories at bay.

He worked hard, played when he had the time, and put in extra effort to control his little part of the world.

"I'm in charge of a lot of people," he countered. "You seem to be the only one who has trouble with my orders."

She smiled. "Which is why you keep me around."

"I'm going to fire you and send you back to Meredith, as soon as I find a competent replacement."

Harlow made a sound, completely unconcerned. Of course, he'd threatened to fire her multiple times a day ever since she started with him. Nothing rattled the woman.

Except the message she'd gotten two days ago. She'd been pale, upset, and refused to tell him what was going on.

It was eating at him. He'd find out. He always got what he wanted.

Although, she seemed fine tonight, and far too edible

in that red dress. He scowled. He hated that she's worn it for some schmuck.

"I left the files right here." She slapped the desk and her gaze narrowed. "Did you move them to mess with me?"

He raised a brow. "Yes, I wanted your delightful company at—" he looked at his Rolex "—9:25 at night."

She made a harrumphing sound and moved to the sleek credenza against the wall. Her curvy form was silhouetted by the lights of San Francisco through his floor-to-ceiling windows. She leaned over the credenza, her dress hugging her ass.

Easton's hands clenched on his pen, and his hard cock throbbed.

She *worked* for him. Even if it was only temporary, she was off limits.

And besides, she drove him crazy. She'd do the same in bed.

Or bent over his desk.

Shit.

"Here." She lifted a file triumphantly.

"The cleaners were in here when I left to grab some dinner," he said.

Harlow slapped a hand on her chest...which made him notice the swell of her breasts.

Fuck. Get a grip, Norcross.

"You stopped work to eat?" she said. "It's a miracle."

He shot her a look. She was a first-class smartass. He took the file from her.

"I'm sorry I had to call you in." He wasn't really.

She sighed. "It's okay. The date was a bust anyway."

She circled the desk and grabbed her coat and bag. "Right, good luck with your meeting in the morning." She shuddered. "I wouldn't wake up at 4:30 AM for anything, even to make millions of dollars."

"Tens of millions of dollars."

She rolled her pretty, blue-green eyes. He still hadn't decided if they were blue or green, since they seemed to change colors.

Easton's head filled with a few ways he'd happily wake her up that early. He gripped the edge of the desk. He had to get this incendiary desire under control.

"Okay, Mr. Heart-Attack-Waiting-to-Happen, I'm out of here."

He rose. "How are you getting home?"

"Uber."

"No."

"Yes," she called back.

"No."

She spun and rested her hands on her hips. "I've gotten Ubers for years. I've also been an adult for years, too. That means I make my own decisions."

"I'm leaving now. I'll drop you at home."

She dragged in a breath. "No."

Easton grabbed his own jacket and shrugged into it. He looked up to find her staring at his chest. While she was distracted, he took her coat and held it out for her.

She shot him a disgruntled look, then turned and slipped into her coat. "You are so annoyingly bossy."

"Yes."

"You're not even sorry."

He paused. "Not really." He stepped closer and her

perfume hit him. It was a blend of something musky and sexy, with an undertone that was pure Harlow. "I'm dropping you off at home. I dragged you in here, it's the least I can do."

"Fine. But only because I love your car." They headed toward the elevator.

They zoomed down to the parking garage and he led her to his gunmetal-gray Aston Martin Superleggera. When he opened the door, she slid in, flashing a lot of long leg.

He stared at the concrete ceiling and prayed for a break. Then he circled the car and slid in. The engine started with a purr.

He looked over. She was snuggling into the seat, stroking the leather.

Releasing a sharp breath, he imagined her stroking other things. With a mental curse, he roared out of the underground parking

"Do you know where I live?" she asked.

"Yes."

"Of course, you do. Control Freak Norcross doesn't leave anything to chance."

His hands flexed on the wheel. "I like control. It's better than chaos."

She made a rude noise. "You can't control everything, Mr. Norcross. Life doesn't work like that."

"Easton. I think you should start calling me Easton when you berate me."

He felt her looking at him.

"Fine. Easton."

"And I've been in lots of uncontrolled situations...

people died." Shit, why had he said that? He looked straight ahead through the windshield.

She was silent for a moment. "You're talking about the Army?"

Easton gave her a tight nod, then dragged in a breath. "I know I'm not in a war zone anymore."

"Do you?" she asked quietly.

He turned a corner, the sports car hugging the turn. He headed to Haight-Asbury where Harlow's apartment was.

"Yes," he replied. "But if you can control your environment, it's better. Safer. More likely to give you the results you want."

Shocking him, she reached out and touched his thigh. "You don't have to be 'on' all the time, Easton."

The touch was electric. His hands flexed on the wheel. But she was wrong—he did. He didn't know how to switch off.

He pulled onto her street.

"You can drop me at the corner," she said.

"I'm walking you to your door."

"No, you're not." Her chin lifted. "I'm going to help you loosen up that control. Drop me at the corner."

Easton scowled. *Fuck that.* He'd drop her off, then shadow her until she made it inside.

CHAPTER TWO

Harlow relished the cool night air on her heated skin. She needed some distance from Easton and his sexy car.

Damn, it sucked having a hot boss.

She hurried toward her apartment building. It wasn't fancy, but the place was an open plan, with wooden floors, and a pocket-sized balcony where she loved to drink her morning tea.

With her head down, she wondered if Easton's hands were flexing on the wheel of his sleek Aston.

Dammit, she wasn't supposed to be thinking about him, or his hands.

Ahead of her, a shadow moved and Harlow jerked to a stop.

The shape of a large man detached from the darkness, powering right toward her.

She'd barely drawn in a breath before the man grabbed her arms.

"Hey!" she cried.

His fingers dug in painfully. He wore black clothes, with a knit cap pulled down low over his head. She got the impression of rough features.

"You're coming with me," he growled.

What? Her heart thundered.

"No!" she yanked backward, her coat falling open.

"Daddy's fucked, and so are you."

The man lunged forward and grabbed the neckline of her dress.

As Harlow struggled, she heard fabric tear. The man's elbow cracked into her cheekbone. *Ow.*

Then suddenly, a second dark shadow lunged past Harlow, and slammed a fist into her attacker's face.

She smelled Easton a beat before she recognized him.

Her attacker grunted, then violently shoved her away. She flew back and hit Easton's hard body. His arms closed around her.

"Harlow?" His voice was a deep growl in her ear. "You okay?"

She swallowed, trying to clear the panic from her head. "I think so."

Her attacker ran and she felt Easton's arms flex.

"You want to chase him," she whispered.

"I'm not leaving you."

Thank God. She swallowed. "I—" Her legs gave out, turning to Jell-O.

Easton swept her into his arms like she wasn't five foot eight and curvy with it.

He strode to the front of her building. "I've got you."

Trembling started. *Dammit.*

"Keys?" he said.

She had them in her hand and lifted them.

He took them and opened the door. As he strode inside, he headed straight for the elevator, and Harlow leaned into his warmth to try to get a grip on the residual fear thrumming through her.

"Fourth floor," she murmured as they entered the elevator.

Moments later, they stopped and Easton maneuvered her down the hall. He stopped at her door and opened it.

Inside, he hit the light switch, then set her down on her gray couch.

The apartment was very white, except for the blonde wood floors. She'd spent time adding her stamp on the place. A colorful rug in a swirl of jewel tones covered the floor, and she'd added a ton of matching throw pillows on the couch. A funky, metal mirror rested on one wall, while a gorgeous, black-and-white print of the Eiffel Tower hung above the couch.

Easton strode to her kitchen and she heard water running. He returned and held out a glass.

"Here."

She sipped the water. As he sat beside her, the couch dipped.

She felt the weight of his gaze on her. Then she looked down and her muscles froze.

The asshole had ripped her dress. The neckline gaped open, and she was currently giving her boss a perfect view of her favorite red bra. It was made of gossamer-like lace, so her nipple was front and center.

Before she could move, he reached out and flicked her coat over her chest.

"Thanks." She drained the water and set the glass on the coffee table. Her hands were shaking.

"You know that guy?"

"What?" She looked up. "No. I figure he was just a garden-variety, asshole mugger, right?"

But tension snuck in like a thief. *Daddy's fucked, and so are you.*

She shivered. She had no idea what that meant. It had to be just some criminal's ramblings. It had to. She really wanted it to be that.

Easton's far-too-perceptive gaze zeroed in on her face. "You sure?"

She tossed her tumbled hair back. "Yes. I'm okay."

He reached out and nudged her coat aside a little. "The bastard hurt you. You've got bruises forming on your shoulder already."

"I bruise easily." She touched her cheekbone where he'd elbowed her and knew she'd probably get another one there.

As Easton's fingers brushed her skin, she sucked in a breath. Her skin tingled.

"I really am okay," she said quietly. "Thanks to you."

He touched her chin.

"This is your chance to say I told you so," she added.

"I told you so." There was no heat in his words. "You should report this to the police."

"What are they going to do? He didn't take anything, and I didn't really get a good look at his face."

Easton's jaw worked. "I know you're not telling me the entire truth."

"I am."

"You aren't. I *will* find out what's going on with you."

She rose. Her knees were wobbly, but she locked them. "I'll be fine. You should go now. Go home and do more work, or sip expensive cognac, whatever it is you rich men do."

He shook his head, his lips quirking. The man had yummy lips—the bottom one full, sensual.

"This isn't over."

Crap. Harlow hurried to the door. "Thanks again, Easton."

"You sure you're okay alone?" He stopped in the doorway.

"Yes. As soon as you're out of here, I'm triple locking this door."

He eyed her. She made herself meet that strong gaze.

His fingers brushed her jaw line. "Tough. Sleep well, Harlow."

He sauntered out and she forced herself not to watch him go. The man had this way of walking that captured every female gaze in the vicinity. She closed the door and locked it, then leaned her back against the wood and squeezed her eyes closed.

Then she pushed away, her anxiety ratcheting back up. She snatched up her phone. It was later than she'd normally call her parents, but she had to check if her dad was okay. And find out what the hell was going on.

The call went straight to her dad's voicemail.

Harlow sighed. "Dad, call me as soon as you get this." She dropped onto a stool at her high kitchen counter. "A man tried to snatch me off the street tonight. I'm okay...

But he said something. Dad, I think it has something to do with you. Call me."

She ended the call and worry nipped her like little bugs all over her skin.

Harlow decided she needed a hot shower, maybe a glass of wine, or a day at the spa, or a vacation in Tahiti. She could still feel Easton's touch on her jaw.

Easton Norcross wasn't a man who gave up easily. He'd keep pushing her to find out what was wrong.

She just wished she knew.

After a scalding-hot shower, Harlow pulled on her favorite, oversized T-shirt and fluffy, gray socks. One had a hole in the toe, but they were so soft and comfy.

She climbed into bed, thinking that worry for her dad would keep her awake.

Instead, it was thoughts of Easton's sexy tattoos that danced in her brain.

How many did he have? And how much of that hard body did they cover? She groaned.

Boss. Boss. Boss.

"He's your boss, Harlow Maree Carlson. Totally one-hundred-percent off-limits." She pulled her pillow over her head and willed herself to get to sleep.

SUN BLARED INTO HER FACE.

With a groan, Harlow rolled over in bed. She'd forgotten to close the curtains last night. She flopped onto her back.

She'd had a rough night. Not because of her attack, no, she was blaming it solely on Easton Norcross.

Her demanding boss was even taking over her dreams, damn him.

She shifted on the sheets. She'd woken twice in the night, both times hot and flushed, picturing those strong hands on her skin.

In one, his sexy car had featured too, with Easton spreading her out on the hood.

Heat pooled between her legs. She sat up, pushing her hair back.

A cold shower was the first order of the day.

Her phone beeped. It had to be her dad. She lunged for the bedside table.

She was wrong. It was a text message from a contact she'd saved as Tyrant.

Did you sleep well?

Speak of the devil. She tapped her phone.

No.

Are you okay?

Fine. Still waking up. Unlike certain workaholics, I don't get up to make millions before breakfast.

I worked out as well.

You need help.

Harlow wrinkled her nose. Her workouts involved

the odd Pilates class when her friend, Christie, dragged her to one, or power walking to the coffee shop for a latte.

Do you need a day off?

She gasped and typed furiously.

No.

Sure?

She wasn't sure she could deal with a considerate Easton Norcross.

Yes. Stop being nice.

Okay. See you in the office, Ms. Carlson.

Don't mess up my desk before I get in.

She showered—she only managed lukewarm, because despite the hum of inappropriate desire, she couldn't do a cold shower. She had a few finger-shaped bruises on her shoulder, and a faint smudge along her cheekbone. Thankfully, that could be hidden with makeup. She moved her arm and felt a twinge. She might pop some Advil as well.

She dressed in a fitted, black skirt and a sensible white shirt before she blow-dried her hair. She pulled it back into a sleek ponytail.

Her phone beeped again.

She shook her head. No doubt Easton couldn't find something.

She glanced at the phone and her stomach clenched. It was a message from her father.

Meet me for breakfast. Sweet Maple.

Damn. Harlow pressed a hand to her cheek. He hadn't even asked her if she was okay. *What the hell are you mixed up in, Dad?*

She shot off a quick text to Easton.

Change of plans. I'll be a little late.

Then she grabbed her bag and dashed out the door. Her phone beeped as she entered the elevator, but she ignored it.

A few minutes after eight, she walked into her favorite neighborhood breakfast place, the laid-back Sweet Maple. They did the best French toast. It took a second to spot her father. He sat alone at a table, nursing a coffee mug. He was staring out the window.

Her heart clenched. Her normally well-dressed, well-groomed father looked disheveled. He wore a creased suit, and his hair looked like he'd run his hands through it a hundred times.

"Dad?"

His head jerked up, and he shot to his feet. He had dark circles under his eyes.

"Princess." He pulled her close and hugged her. "Are you all right?"

"Yes. Luckily, my boss dropped me off last night and scared the guy away."

Charles Carlson bobbed his head and sat. He toyed with his mug nervously.

Harlow dropped into a chair. "Dad, what is going on? You left a message saying you're in trouble, then you avoid me, now this man saying—" Harlow couldn't swear to her dad "—you're screwed, and so am I."

Her dad drew in a choppy breath. He looked so tired. "I'm so sorry, Princess."

Not tired. Dejected.

She pressed her hand over his. "Talk to me, Dad. Let me help."

The air shuddered out of him. "It started last year. I had a real estate deal go bad."

Okay. That didn't sound so terrible. Her dad unfortunately had deals not work out before.

"Then another business deal fell through. I..." He shook his head. "I lost a lot of money."

"I understand. It happens."

Weary, worried eyes met hers. "*A lot* of money, Harlow. I was going to lose the house."

She sucked in a sharp breath. Her mother loved that house in Presidio Heights. Harlow and Scarlett had grown up in the large, light-filled home.

"But then I met an investor. I made some new deals."

"Dad?" She didn't like the tone of his voice.

"He's not a great guy. The deal wasn't what I'd hoped. I kept trying to find a way out." Desperation soaked his voice. "I just needed *one* good deal, then I could clear all the debts."

She closed her eyes. "But it wasn't good."

"No." A quiet whisper.

"Dad..."

"I'm in debt to a very bad man, Harlow."

Her stomach dropped away. "Okay, we just need to

find a solution." She set her shoulders back. This was what she did. "We can—"

"He's going to kill me if I don't pay him back."

Harlow felt the world lurch and she grabbed the edge of the table for support. "What?"

"I told you, he's...not a good man."

She swallowed. "He's a criminal."

Her father's blue-green eyes met hers. They roiled with emotion. "He's never been charged with anything."

"*Dad*," she breathed. "How could you get involved with someone like that?"

"I was desperate." His face turned miserable. "I messed up, Princess."

He was perspiring. Anger swelled inside her. She couldn't believe he'd done this. Risked everything.

But this was her father. The man who'd hugged her when she'd needed it, taught her to drive, and while he wasn't perfect, she knew he loved her.

She grabbed his hand again. "What can we do?"

He squeezed her fingers. "Harlow..." He swallowed. "I need some money."

"I have some savings. We can pay this man off."

Her dad ran a hand through his hair. "I owe him more than you'd have."

Harlow wasn't drinking anything, but she still choked. "What? How much?"

"I'm not saying. But a down payment will buy me some time."

Visions of her own place to renovate evaporated. "I have fifty thousand saved." Saved from years of hard work.

Her dad squeezed her hand. "Thanks, baby girl, I can always count on you. Can you transfer it today?"

She nodded dully. A mix of anger and sadness welled inside her. "Does mom know?"

"No," he said quickly. "And I want to keep it that way. This would kill her. You know how she is."

Yes, Eleanor Carlson was...delicate. She coped with stress by avoiding it, ignoring it, and heading to bed with a headache.

He patted Harlow's hand again. "This money will help me get some time to make things right. And get things in order before Scarlett's next college payment is due."

Harlow pulled in a breath. Scarlett was finally loving her studies and doing well.

"Thanks, Princess." Her dad hugged her again, his arms tight, and a little desperate.

"Dad?"

He rose, his chair squeaking on the floor. "It's all going to be okay." He patted her back.

"The man who tried to grab me—"

"I'll talk to Armand right away, and give him the money. He'll leave you alone."

Her nerves were dancing. She *hated* this.

"I'm so sorry, Harlow."

She nodded and stood. "I need to get to work."

"Right. Um, you'll transfer the money right now?"

She nodded. "I'll text you when it's done."

"Thanks. Bye, Princess."

She watched him hurry out of the cafe and then

pinched the bridge of her nose. Her phone pinged and she pulled it out. She had a bunch of messages.

What the—? They were all from the Tyrant.

Why will you be late?

Where are you?

Harlow, what's going on?

Call me.

"Crap." She tapped the app for an Uber. She'd be at the office soon, and she needed to transfer all her savings to her dad. The tyrant would have to wait.

CHAPTER THREE

Easton rapped his knuckles on his desk.

Where the hell was she?

First, she'd said she was fine, then that she'd be late. He scowled. He wanted to see for himself that Harlow was all right.

He saw a flash of movement outside his office and heard someone at Harlow's desk.

He strode across his office, and when he saw her, something in his chest eased.

"Ms. Carlson, you're late."

She looked up. She was perfectly put together as always, but her eyes looked sad. He shoved his hands in his pockets.

"My office. Now." He turned around and strode back to his desk.

"I haven't even sat down and it's orders, orders, orders." Harlow slammed his door and the walls rattled. "Yes, Master? You want to fire some grumpy, abrupt things at me?"

Easton swiveled, then closed in on her.

She stiffened.

He cupped her cheek. He saw the bruising she tried to hide with makeup around her left eye. He gently stroked it.

The scent of her wound around him. He swore her perfume was designed specifically to drive him crazy. "You smell good." *Fuck.* "Forget I said that."

"You smell good, too," she said. "Forget I said that."

Their gazes meshed, and a pulse of something moved between them.

She stepped back and his hand dropped.

"Are you all right?" he asked.

She cleared her throat. "I told you I was."

"I can tell something's wrong."

Her eyelids dropped, like she was hiding from him. "Everything's fine."

"Harlow." He reached for her.

She pushed his hand away. "It is."

"You know I was in the Army Rangers, right?"

"I...knew you were in the Army. The Rangers are special forces, right?"

He nodded. "I was a specialist in certain areas."

She shifted. "Okay."

"In interrogation." Old memories pushed up, and as he was used to doing, Easton shoved them back down. "I'm trained to read minute facial cues and other physical body language. I know you're lying."

Her lips parted.

Damn. His gut coiled. She'd painted them a luscious red today.

"It's none of your business," she said.

"I'm making it my business." He'd begun by calling his friend Hunt. Detective Hunter Morgan was a good Army buddy of his brother Vander's, and now worked at the San Francisco PD. Hunt spent a lot of time helping Vander and his company, Norcross Security, out when they got into scrapes. Hunt had told Easton that there were no reports of muggers in Harlow's area. That didn't mean there weren't any, but Easton's instincts were humming.

Something was going on. "Harlow?"

For a second, she looked so sad, then she straightened.

"Everything's going to be fine." She looked at the slim, silver watch on her wrist. "You have a meeting with Felix Enterprises in the main conference room in five minutes." She pulled away. "I'll check to see if they're here."

She sauntered out. She was wearing one of those long, tight skirts that accentuated her curves.

Something was going on, and he was going to get to the bottom of it.

Easton grabbed his tablet off his desk and heard the murmur of Harlow talking to someone.

"I have a report for Mr. Norcross," a breathy, female voice said.

"Leave it on my desk," Harlow replied. "I'll see he gets it."

"Oh, I thought I could...give it to him myself."

Easton paused in the doorway and saw a young woman in a sleeveless dress. She tossed her cloud of streaked blonde hair over her shoulder. Shit, she looked like she was lucky if she was old enough to drink.

Harlow skewered the woman with a look. "Leave it on my desk."

The young woman pouted and set the file down. Then she strode off like she was opening fashion week.

He heard Harlow mutter under her breath, then she turned back to her computer screen.

"Ready?" he asked.

She jolted, then tapped the screen so it went to sleep.

But not before he saw that she was on a banking website.

"Ready." She rose, gathering her things.

Easton followed her to the conference room. She sailed in, moving to the side table, to check the drinks and snacks.

The door opened.

"Easton," Larry Miller boomed. The man was in his late fifties, with a wide, easygoing smile. "Good to see you."

Then the man spotted Harlow and his eyes and smile widened. "I see you traded in that bossy, old dragon lady of yours. Well done."

Easton felt a flash of annoyance. "Mrs. Skilton is on leave. This is Ms. Carlson."

"A pleasure," Miller drawled.

Harlow gave him a small, professional smile.

Easton sat at the head of the table. "Let's talk business."

The meeting went long. Miller talked a lot, but he

was a savvy negotiator. Another assistant brought in lunch.

Harlow bent over, arranging the food.

Miller let out a low, appreciative noise and leaned closer to Easton. "Is your lovely, new assistant single?"

"Yes, but you're not," Easton bit out. "How is your wife?"

"Happy when I leave her to her own business." Miller laughed.

Easton kept his face blank. *Asshole*. "Let's get these final contract points decided." Then Easton could get Miller out of here.

They ate their lunch and finished their business.

"Always a pleasure doing business with you, Norcross." Miller eyed Harlow again.

"I'll see you out," Easton said.

"I'm going to say goodbye to the delectable Ms. Carlson."

Easton gritted his teeth together. "No, you aren't."

Miller's grin slipped a little. "Norcross—"

"You're not going near her."

The older man nodded and winked. "Ah, I see you've got your eye on her yourself."

"Just go, Miller, before I change my mind about doing business with you."

The businessman left looking disgruntled. Easton didn't give a shit.

"Right." Harlow bustled up to him. "You have a call with New York shortly. Zane Roth."

Easton nodded. He enjoyed working with the finance billionaire.

"And lawyers from Cartwright, Dolan, and Bird sent some contracts over. Legal has marked some things for you to take a look at. It's all on your desk."

"Thanks."

They crossed the floor, and reached her desk.

"You also have a two o'clock with Eva Morales from FlexDash. I'll let you know when she arrives."

God, she was more organized than Mrs. Skilton.

"There's also fresh coffee on your desk. And a dark chocolate and pistachio cookie."

His favorite. His gaze narrowed. "Firstly, how did you know about the cookies? And second, how did you organize that?"

She winked. "A good assistant never reveals her secrets."

And yet, Easton wanted hers. He studied her face. "You're really okay after last night?"

Her smile dimmed. "Yes."

"When you were late this morning—"

"I met my father for breakfast." She turned to face her computer.

She sounded normal, but every one of Easton's instincts, honed sharp by the Army, itched.

She slid a wireless headset on. "This is Harlow." She glanced over her shoulder. "Mr. Roth is on the line."

Easton nodded and headed for his desk.

One thing a good interrogator needed was patience.

HARLOW SIPPED her Earl Grey tea and burned her lip.

Ow.

She set the mug down on her desk and massaged her temples. She'd had too much coffee today and had switched to tea. She heard the rumble of Easton's deep voice in his office. He'd been on this latest call for over an hour.

Her phone rang and she saw it was her bestie, Christie.

"Hey," Harlow said.

"You still breathing?" Christie drawled. "Or has Mr. I-Own-the-World Norcross done you in?"

"Ha ha. If I don't make it, it's because he's made my head explode."

"Well, at least you'll go out with a killer view." Christie hummed. "Anytime that man visits our office, my heart takes off like my feet when I hear there's a shoe sale on."

Harlow snorted. Christie worked at Tenneson Industries. Harlow was well aware of the stir in the office when Easton visited her boss Meredith.

"Is it true that he has tattoos under those delicious suits?" her best friend asked.

"Yes."

"God. Hang on, how do you know?"

"At the end of the day, he sometimes rolls his sleeves up."

Christie made a sound. "Sorry, having a little orgasm."

"Stop it. You're happily married, remember?"

"And I love Charlie, but my darling hubby doesn't even own a suit."

No, Charlie was a landscape designer. He favored boots and shorts.

"You're as bad as all the women who stop by to give Easton a file or a report. I have to beat them off with a stick."

"My money's on you. You're mean when riled." A pause. "You aren't tempted by the sexy bod, the tattoos, and that face?"

"Working for him for about thirty seconds cured any heart eyes." Oh boy, she was lying to her bestie now.

"We should get together for a coffee soon."

"With Easton's schedule, that'll probably be next September."

"Easton, huh?"

Harlow shifted in her seat. "That's his name."

"So, have you narrowed down any horrible house wrecks to buy and flex your reno skills on yet?"

Harlow's stomach plummeted and she struggled to keep her tone even. "Not yet."

"Why did your voice go funny?"

Damn, she hated her best friend sometimes. "What? No, it didn't."

"Spill, Carlson."

"I haven't found the right place."

"Hmm." Christie sounded dubious. "How was your date last night?"

"A dud."

"Ugh. I don't miss the dating merry-go-round."

"The tyrant actually saved me. He needed me back at

the office. Then when I got home, a mugger grabbed me on the street."

"What?" A screech. "Why didn't you call me and Charlie?"

"I was fine. Easton scared him off." She couldn't tell Christie about her dad. Harlow nibbled her lip. She wouldn't drag her friend into this mess. She'd deal with it.

"Easton, again. So, your sexy boss played hero?"

"He dropped me home."

"You sure you're okay?"

"I promise." Harlow's cell phone rang. "I have to go, babe. Coffee soon?"

"If your hunky boss lets you out. Oh, and Charlie and I are heading down to San Diego for a week, remember?"

"Lucky duck. Bye. Love you." She snatched up her cell phone and saw her sister's name.

"Scarlett."

"Hey, big sis."

A flood of love hit Harlow. "Hi, little sis."

"I haven't got long," Scarlett said. "I'm about to head into a lecture. I just wanted to say hello."

"How's school?"

"S*o* awesome." Her sister's voice lit up. "I've finally found my thing Harlow. Like you did. Another year, I'll have my degree, and I have *so* many plans."

Harlow smiled, but her hand curled around the phone. Her sister was so happy. After several years of being so miserable doing a business degree, she'd switched to studying teaching at UCLA.

Harlow couldn't let that get ruined. "Do you need anything? I can organize for—"

Scarlett let out a huff. "I'm a big girl now, Low. I can do things for myself. I know you love to keep us all organized, but you need to chill."

"I just want to help."

"I know." Her sister's voice softened. "But I'm not a little girl anymore. And Mom and Dad depend on you too much. I know you organized the new gardener at the house, and booked their upcoming cruise, and made dad's doctor's appointments. They're adults."

"I like helping."

Her sister sighed.

It was an old argument that Harlow usually sidestepped. "You keep studying hard."

"I will. You don't work too hard. Hey, on my next vacation, I'm coming home. I can help you knock down some walls when you get a place."

Harlow's belly knotted. "Sure."

"Or I can paint. I'm good at painting."

"I have to go, Scarlett."

"Sure, me too. Love you."

"Love you, too."

When Harlow ended the call, she dropped her head into her hand. Then she looked up and logged onto her bank website.

Her savings account showed a big fat zero.

The money was gone.

Well, she hoped her dad was safe now.

"Find a problem, solve the problem." This would all be sorted out soon.

"Harlow?"

She jolted, spun, and threw the pen in her hand. Easton caught it before it hit him in the face.

He frowned. "You okay?"

She felt heat rising in her cheeks. "You just surprised me."

He eyed her like a scientist studying a sample. "I overheard you talking with your sister."

"You shouldn't eavesdrop. Shoo, I have reports to finish and meetings to schedule." She waved her hand. "Go buy a Rolex or something."

Easton pressed his hands to her desk and leaned across it. Her pulse spiked.

"I know something's not right with you. You work for me, so you belong to me. I protect those who are mine."

His face was only inches from hers and her heart did a funny jerk. "I don't even know where to start with that."

"Talk to me." His voice was low and smooth, like melted chocolate.

"I'm not dumping my personal problems on you."

"Others do."

Yes, she noticed way too many popped by to share their problems, which he could solve with a check. "Well, I'm not others, and you need to learn you can't control everything."

Suddenly, there was a ripple of whispers through the office. She looked up and saw a man walking toward them. Her spine straightened.

Vander Norcross looked a lot like his older brother. They both had coal-black hair, muscled bodies, and blue eyes. Although Vander's eyes were deep, midnight blue, so dark they almost looked black. Easton's were a prettier cobalt that she got lost inside.

The middle Norcross brother was slightly leaner than Easton, harder, and even though he wore a suit, he didn't have the same elegant, classy edge Easton radiated.

No, Easton looked like he could stride into a boardroom and initiate a company-wide takeover without breaking a sweat. Vander looked like he could defeat an army before breakfast, dismantle a biker gang at lunch, and then take over a small hostile nation at dinner time, maybe followed by a little global assassination for dessert.

Harlow locked her knees. Vander was the definition of hot badass, but he also scared the bejesus out of her.

"Harlow," he drawled.

"Hi, Vander. If you've come to see your brother, he has a tiny gap in his workaholic, make-a-billion-dollars-before-dinner-time schedule."

Vander's lips quirked, and damn if it didn't make a little curl of heat pulse in her belly.

Easton shot her a look. "Hi, Vander. Ignore Ms. Smart Comeback and come in." He waved his brother into his office. Then he looked back at Harlow. "We'll *talk* more later."

She didn't miss his emphasis on talk.

She rolled her eyes.

As the brothers disappeared into Easton's office and closed the door, Harlow dropped back in her chair.

A notification popped up on her screen.

She had a new email. She clicked it, and her heart clenched.

It was a sale alert on a gorgeous, rundown Victorian

home. A diamond in the rough. The house had wonderful curb appeal, but needed new paint, and inside, it needed a complete gut.

She closed the email and deleted it.

Time to stop daydreaming and get back to work.

Her cell phone rang. It was her father.

CHAPTER FOUR

Easton closed the door.

"How are things?" he asked his brother.

"Busy."

Easton sat behind his desk, while Vander strode to the windows. His brother had always been intense, even as a boy.

Vander had joined the Army, and soon ended up leading a Ghost Ops team. A covert special forces team made up of the best of the best across all the special forces in the military. Their younger brother Rhys had also been Ghost Ops. They'd all fought for their country. Seen too much. Done too much.

"We have loads of work going on," Vander said.

"That's good."

"Not making billions like my big brother, though." Vander's lips moved into a grin.

Easton rolled his eyes. "Don't start. I cop enough smart-ass sass from my assistant."

"Your sexy new assistant who you watch like she's your favorite candy."

Easton felt an instant jerk of annoyance. He didn't need Vander noticing that Harlow was sexy.

Vander's dark gaze was on him and his grin widened. "You got a thing for tight skirts and sexy heels?"

Easton made an annoyed noise. "No."

"No? I suspect for you those are just icing on the sharp mind, and the fact that she's a woman who doesn't bend under the force of Easton Norcross."

"Did you make time out of your busy day just to come here and give me shit?"

"No." Vander moved over to Easton's desk. "You asked Saxon to run a background check on Harlow."

Easton straightened. "You found something."

"You sure you want to wade into this?"

Easton growled.

Vander nodded. "You want to wade in. Don't blame you."

"Vander, get to the point."

His brother pulled an envelope out from the inside pocket of his jacket. He dropped it on Easton's desk.

"Her father's in debt. Big time."

"Shit."

Vander sat in one of the guest chairs. "You know her dad?"

"Not personally. Charles Carlson. Local businessman."

Vander nodded. "He had some deals go bad. He got desperate."

Easton met Vander's dark blue gaze. "And?"

"He got really desperate. Made some shady deals with some shady people."

Easton clenched his teeth. "Who?"

"Antoine Armand."

"Fuck."

"Yeah, fuck," Vander agreed.

Armand was bad news.

"Armand has some semi-legit businesses, but he's got his fingers in a lot of ugly spaces."

"Not legal ones, I assume?"

"Right," Vander said. "Drugs, laundering, prostitution."

Easton leaned back in his chair. "Charming."

"Carlson invested in some real estate deals. Anyway, things went bad. He took loans from Armand."

"Shit." And Carlson was dumping this on his daughter?

"Armand isn't known for being generous. He has a cousin who likes to use a knife. If Carlson doesn't pay up, he'll end up dead with his throat slit."

Easton leaned forward, pulse pounding. "Someone tried to snatch Harlow off the street last night."

Vander's face hardened. Easton's brother detested violence against women. He'd seen some horrible things during his missions.

"That matches Armand's MO. He usually threatens the family."

Easton thrust a hand through his hair. "So, she's in danger."

"There's more."

Shit. Easton knew he wasn't going to like this. He

rose and looked out the windows at the Transamerica Pyramid and the city below. He was used to being in control. He liked it. Preferred it.

"This morning, Harlow transferred all her savings to her father," Vander said. "Just over fifty thousand dollars."

Easton closed his eyes.

He'd thrown himself into business after he'd left the Army. He'd been driven. Needed to find purpose. Something to keep him busy. He'd made a lot of money, and fifty thousand dollars was change to him, but he hadn't grown up wealthy. Ethan and Clara Norcross had been hard-working people—their dad was a retired firefighter, and their mom a dedicated homemaker. They'd both instilled a strong work ethic into their kids, and the importance of saving money.

Easton knew just how hard Harlow would have worked to save that money.

A muscle ticked in his jaw. He wanted to chew out Charles Carlson. "He tried to buy himself some breathing room."

Vander nodded. "Armand isn't known for being magnanimous."

Easton turned. "So, you do think she's in danger?"

"It's a strong possibility."

"Fuck."

"I can spread the word that she has our protection."

Easton gave a sharp nod. "Do it."

"How much do you think Harlow knows?" Vander asked.

"No idea. I can see her handing over her savings to her father without blinking an eye."

"I'll get back to the office. Make some calls."

"Thanks, Vander."

His brother grasped Easton's shoulder. "We'll take care of your girl."

"She's not mine."

Vander grunted.

"She's my employee."

"Temporarily. It's sticky, but not impossible to navigate. You have a big, cunning brain, bro."

Easton smiled. "I'm pretty sure there was a compliment in there."

"Don't ruin it."

Easton's smile dissolved. "The first thing is to get her safe."

Vander nodded. "Whatever you need, you just let me know."

"Thanks." It didn't matter what they faced, the Norcross siblings stuck together.

Easton strode to the door. He needed to talk with Harlow and get some answers. "If anything else comes up, let me know."

Vander tossed him a salute. "Will do."

Easton opened his office door, eager to see Harlow.

Her desk was empty.

His muscles tensed.

He strode out, and saw her computer was asleep. Her desk was neat and tidy as always.

He cursed.

Then he spotted one of the other assistants nearby.

"Gina, do you know where Harlow is?" *Be in a meeting. Be in a meeting.*

Gina froze like a deer in headlights.

Easton always worried the woman was going to have an aneurism when he talked to her.

"Um, she got a call, Mr. Norcross. She said she had to go out for a while."

Easton fought for some control.

"I think she was meeting with her dad," Gina said.

Easton met Vander's gaze.

Fuck.

HARLOW HURRIED ACROSS THE STREET, a little out of breath.

After the quick, panicked call from her dad, she'd power walked from the Norcross building to meet him.

Her father had sounded scared.

Her mouth was dry and her pulse was jittery. She scanned Rincon Park. The waters of the Bay were choppy and gray today. They matched her mood. She barely spared the Bay Bridge a glance.

As she crossed the street, a cold wind tugged at her red coat and tried to tear her hair out of its tie.

She spotted her father at the railing, his shoulders slumped.

Swallowing, she hurried over. "Dad?"

He spun. "Harlow." His face was drawn, gray. "Princess." He grabbed her hand. His weren't steady.

"Did you meet that man?" she asked. "Did you give him the money?"

Her dad nodded. "We met for lunch at Saison."

Harlow kept her face blank. She'd forked over her life savings, and yet her father was having a fancy lunch with a criminal. "And?"

His eyes met hers. They were miserable. His fingers clenched on hers hard enough to hurt.

"He said it wasn't enough. He said if I couldn't pay it all, I'd pay with my life."

"*No*," she breathed.

"Then he got a call. I used the restroom and managed to escape."

God. *God*. Her chest was so tight. This couldn't be happening.

"And he said if I messed around, then my family wouldn't be safe."

The words were like a punch to Harlow's gut. "Mom. Scarlett."

Her father shoved his hand through his already messy hair. "I sent your mother away yesterday. A week-long yoga and spa retreat in Napa."

Harlow blew out a breath. "And Scarlett?"

"Antoine's reach shouldn't extend to Los Angeles, but I'll call her. Ask her to go away for a week."

"Then what, Dad?" Panic felt like bony fingers closing around Harlow's throat.

"I'm going to fix this," her father said.

Harlow couldn't see a solution. She couldn't find a safe way out for all of them.

Yesterday, her life had been awesome. A job she loved, and plans to buy her own house.

Today, everything had splintered apart.

"Harlow, I need you to lay low for a few days. Let me sort this out—"

"How, Dad?" She grabbed the end of the ponytail, trying to keep the strands from blowing in her face.

His jaw tightened. "I'll find a way."

She turned to look at the water, her belly churning.

"Harlow?"

"I love you, Dad, but I'm so angry at you right now." She turned to face him. "I *can't* believe you've dragged us all into this."

"I'm sorry.

She grabbed his arms. "You need to stay safe, as well."

He pulled her close and hugged her.

"Well, well, well."

The masculine, accented voice made Harlow jerk back.

Her gaze fell on the man standing nearby. He looked about forty, and was wearing a dark-blue, woolen coat. He had a sharp face, with pale-blue eyes, and well-cut, blond hair. There was a faint smile on his thin lips. Everything about him was sharp—chin, nose, his clothes. He was flanked by two guards in suits—one burly, and one short and wiry.

"Charles, where have you been hiding this beauty?" He had a French accent.

Her father stepped in front of her. "She's not a part of this, Armand."

Armand. This was the guy her father was in debt to. She lifted her chin.

The man smiled at her. "She looks like she has more spirit than you, Carlson. I'm going to assume she's your daughter and not your girlfriend. She has your eyes."

"From what I hear," Harlow said. "You're a criminal and an asshole."

Her dad made a choked noise.

Nerves winged through her, but she was sick of feeling helpless and afraid.

"I've never been charged with a crime," Antoine drawled.

She rolled her eyes. "Right. You just do shady deals. Suck people into ventures that lose money. And you threatened my father and family."

Antoine held up his gloved hands. "I'm simply a businessman, Ms. Carlson." His voice iced over and he looked at her dad. "And when people don't pay me my money, I get very, very unhappy."

A shiver ran down her spine. Antoine managed a perfect combination of creepy and charming, with a dash of sleaze.

"Lovely," she said. "I see you have a winning personality, as well."

Antoine stepped closer. His cologne hit her and she wondered briefly how a bad guy could smell so good. He moved even closer, invading her personal space, and Harlow stiffened. She held herself still, even when she wanted to step away.

The man might smell all right, but he creeped her out.

"You are quite delicious," he murmured. "What's your name?"

Ew. "You're a creep."

"Your name?" he repeated.

His two bodyguards stepped forward. The small, wiry one swept his suit coat open and flashed her a glance of the holstered gun at his hip. Her pulse spiked. He shot her a grin that wasn't quite...normal.

"Let me teach her a lesson, Antoine."

"Quiet, Hugo." Antoine raised a brow.

"Harlow," she spat.

"Harlow. Lovely."

"Still a creep."

He stared at her intently for a long moment, then broke into laughter. "I like you, Harlow."

"I'm sorry I can't say the same."

Something moved through the man's eyes. He turned to her father. "I've come up with another way to clear your debt."

Hope flared in her father's eyes. Harlow clutched her handbag more tightly in her fingers.

"I'll take your daughter, instead."

Her father gasped.

Harlow's mouth dropped open. "*What?* You can't *buy* people."

Another sharp smile. "Sure, you can."

"No!" her father cried.

She lifted her chin. "I am *not* for sale."

"Everyone has their price." Antoine reached out to touch her hair, but she knocked his hand away.

"I don't know you," she said. "And I don't like you."

"I could change your mind."

"No. And believe me—" *think of something to throw him off* "—my boyfriend would *not* be happy."

Antoine waved a hand negligently. "I don't care about your boyfriend." He cocked his head. "And I suspect you'd do anything for your father."

Her heart clenched.

"No," her father said again.

Harlow's skin crawled at the thought of letting this man anywhere near her. In that second, she felt so incredibly alone.

"I'll get your money, Antoine," her father pleaded. "I just need more time."

"I've already given you enough time."

"I can—"

Antoine held up a hand, his gaze met Harlow's. "Dinner."

"What?" she said.

"To buy your father forty-eight hours, you'll have dinner with me tonight."

Oh, God.

Her father grabbed her arm. "Harlow, you don't have to—"

"Just dinner?" she asked.

Antoine smiled. "If that's all you want."

"Harlow—" Her father tugged on her arm.

She nodded. "Okay."

Antoine's smile widened. "I'll send you details and have a car collect you."

"Send me the details, and I'll meet you there."

"Harlow," her father said again.

"Go, Dad. I'll call you later. I need to get back to the office."

With one searing glance at Antoine, she strode away.

She couldn't think and her skin felt slimy. The office was closest. Most people would've left for the day by now. She needed to collect her things, and get herself together.

She hoped Easton was gone. She was pretty sure he had a business dinner this evening.

She trembled, goose bumps forming on her arms and legs, and headed toward the main door on autopilot. This was all a nightmare. Dinner with a criminal. She shuddered. She'd get through it. And if it bought her dad time, it was worth it.

Although she had no idea how he could come up with the money. She wondered just how much he owed.

She swiped herself into the Norcross building.

When she reached the office level, it was thankfully empty. She strode to her desk.

Correction, it was empty, except for Easton's office.

She heard the rumble of several male voices.

"Find her," Easton barked.

"We're working on it," Vander replied.

"I've got Ace on it," a third voice said. "It'd be easier if he could see her phone. He'll be able to track her more easily."

Harlow stepped into the doorway.

Easton leaned against his desk, with his arms crossed over his chest. His face looked like a thundercloud. Vander and another man—a tall, handsome man with blond-brown hair stood beside him. Saxon Buchanan was

Vander's best friend and right-hand man at Norcross Security. He was also engaged to Easton and Vander's sister, Gia.

"What's going on?" Harlow asked.

The men spun fast. Easton straightened, his gaze burning into hers. "Where the hell have you been?"

CHAPTER FIVE

Easton fought down the knot of emotions in his chest. He grabbed Harlow's arm and towed her out of his office.

"Hey," she cried. "Easton—"

"Quiet." She was safe. He reminded himself of that.

He shoved open the door to the conference room and pulled her in.

"Let me go," she snapped.

"Where the hell did you go? Are you all right?"

She strode to the long, glossy table, then spun. "I'm not yours to worry about."

He stalked toward her and she backed up two steps. He pinned her against the table.

He knew he was coming on too strong, but that hour she'd been gone... His jaw worked. She had no idea of what people like Armand were capable of.

"You don't get to manhandle people." Her eyes sparked. "Even if you are Easton Norcross."

She twisted, her body brushing against his.

He felt his body respond and clamped down on that reaction. "Harlow—"

"Easton," she snapped back.

He gripped her hips. "I want to help you." *Keep you safe.*

She stilled, shadows in her eyes. "No one can help me. I'll fix this."

"It's your father's mess to fix."

She stilled, her eyes widening. "You know." Her voice was a whisper.

He didn't respond, fighting the urge to slip his fingers into the waistband of that maddening skirt and touch her skin.

"Of course, you know," she said, resigned. "You're Easton Norcross."

"I asked Vander to do some searching."

Her lips pressed together and she looked at the floor. "So, you have all the ugly details."

"I know your father made some stupid mistakes, and he's in debt to a bad person."

She laughed, but there was nothing humorous in it.

"I want to help," Easton said.

Her gaze met his, her chin lifted. "I'm fixing it."

His gaze narrowed. "How? Do you know who Antoine Armand is?"

A faint grimace crossed her face.

"Let me enlighten you, Harlow. Armand was born and raised in the South of France. He was the son of a wealthy businessman, and eventually took over the business. It's said he poisoned his father to speed up that process."

She jolted.

"He built up the business to include gambling, smuggling, prostitution, money laundering, drugs. You name an illegal way to make money, and Armand does it."

Harlow's teeth sank into her bottom lip.

"He made enemies, bigger, more powerful ones, than him. So, several years ago he moved here. He's rebuilding his little empire from scratch. That's who you're dealing with. He won't hesitate to slit your throat. How are you going to deal with that?"

"I have to try," she said quietly. "For my father."

Frustration burst in Easton. "Harlow—"

"This isn't your business." She pressed her hands to his chest and pushed. He didn't budge. "I promise this won't spill over into my work."

Easton growled. "I don't give a fuck about work. I want you safe."

Her big, blue-green eyes glimmered. Shit, he could almost feel himself falling into them. What was it about this woman?

Her fingers curled in his shirt. "It'll be over soon. I'm not dragging others into this, especially not my boss."

"Forget about me being your boss," he growled.

Her gaze met his, her lips parted. "I can't... If I do..."

Desire—a hot flood of it—poured into him. His fingers dug into her hips. She leaned closer, her gaze on his mouth.

"You drive me crazy," he murmured.

"Oh, you've driven me way past crazy," she murmured back.

Easton wasn't sure who moved first, whether it was her or him.

Their mouths collided, her breasts pressed against his chest.

His mind just stopped functioning. Harlow was in his arms. Her mouth his to claim.

With a short growl, he forced her lips open. She moaned, her hands sliding into his hair. Her tongue stroked his.

Easton ravished her mouth, pulling her closer. She tasted like every dark promise he'd ever wanted.

His cock was hard in an instant. He lifted her onto the conference room table. She gasped, then tugged his tie loose.

He couldn't get close enough. "These damn skirts." He shoved her skirt up, baring thigh-high stockings with lace circling her upper thighs. He groaned.

She yanked him closer. She had two buttons of his shirt undone, her fingers touching his ink.

Easton shoved her legs apart and closed the gap between them. The hot core of her, covered only in tiny black panties, pressed against the bulge in his pants.

She moaned and he muttered a curse. She undulated against the hard ridge of his erection.

Hunger rose, eroding his control. The control he lived and breathed.

Harlow kissed him, clutching his head, her luscious body moving wildly.

He drove his tongue in to find hers, pulling her closer.

He needed her closer.

He needed her safe.

A phone beeped.

Easton ignored it. He needed Harlow more than he'd ever needed anything.

But she stiffened.

She fumbled with her bag and lifted her cell phone. Whatever the message was, it drained the color from her face.

She pushed against him, her legs falling away from his hips. She sat there on the conference room table where he did business daily, looking thoroughly disheveled—from his hands and mouth.

Her gold hair was tangled around her face, her lips swollen, and her skirt still hiked up to show those damn stockings and her long legs.

"Harlow?" Easton straightened. He was well aware that his suit pants did nothing to hide his raging hard-on.

She shook her head, like she was waking from a daze. She blinked, her cheeks flushed. "This shouldn't have happened." She slid off the table and yanked her skirt down. "God, you have dozens of women throw themselves at you every day. I'm not joining that party."

"You didn't throw yourself at me." He worked his jaw. "And while you're working for me right now, you still report to Meredith."

Harlow's eyes met his. "I'm not going to sue you for sexual harassment, Easton."

"I know. I just...I don't want you to feel pressured. I am in a position of power."

She made a scoffing sound. "This didn't happen—" she waved at the table "—because I felt coerced." She glanced at her phone again and her spine straightened.

She glanced at her watch and a panicked look crossed her face. "I have to go."

"Harlow, you could be in danger."

"I promise I'm okay." She swallowed. "Armand gave my dad a bit more time."

Male voices echoed outside the conference room. Vander and Saxon.

"I've got to go." She slipped out of the room.

Easton pressed a hand to his hip and ground his teeth together. He wanted to throw her over his shoulder and take her back to his place, and not let her out.

Vander and Saxon appeared in the doorway.

"She okay?" Vander asked.

Saxon raised a brow. "She looked like someone just kissed the hell out of her."

Easton just glared. "She said she and her father are fixing the issue."

Both men scowled.

"Armand doesn't give second chances," Vander said.

Frustration rode Easton hard. "She said she was safe." For now, he'd have to trust that. He looked at his Rolex and cursed. "I've a business dinner to attend."

And he was going to need a little more patience where Harlow Carlson was concerned. He wasn't sure where he'd find it, especially when he could still taste her on his lips.

HARLOW FINISHED PUTTING her makeup on, her belly tied up in knots.

She had thirty minutes to be at the Acquerello restaurant to meet Antoine.

She pulled a face in the mirror, then touched her lips.

And thought of Easton's mouth. On hers. Heat curled low in her belly.

She'd kissed the hell out of her boss on a conference room table with her skirt hiked up around her waist.

Harlow groaned, and dropped her chin to her chest.

She couldn't succumb to Easton's panty-melting—and clearly brain-scrambling—hotness. She needed her job. She needed the money now more than ever.

And a fling with her boss was the last thing she needed on top of all the current complications in her life.

She couldn't think of Easton right now. She hated that he knew all the gory details of the shit that was swirling around her and her father.

At least he didn't know that Antoine had blackmailed her into dinner.

She finished with her lipstick—a soft pink. Minimal and natural. She was trying to look as plain as she could. Her hair was in a simple twist and she wore the plainest dress she owned. It was black, and had a high neck, long sleeves and ended at mid-calf.

It did hug her body, but at least it covered her skin more than anything else in her wardrobe.

"Shoes." She pondered her admittedly large shoe collection. She didn't own any ugly shoes.

It would have to be the Louboutins. She'd be keeping the sexy red soles firmly on the ground.

Harlow felt a little nauseated as she walked into the gorgeous Italian restaurant in Nob Hill five minutes late.

She dragged in a deep breath. *Suck it up, Harlow. You agreed to this.*

She strode in and stopped at the hostess desk. "Armand table."

"This way," the elegant woman said.

The woman led Harlow through the restaurant, with its old-world elegance and low, romantic lighting. A huge vase of fresh flowers dominated a central table. Nearby, Antoine saw her and rose, a smile on his face that made her skin crawl.

"Harlow, you look beautiful."

She moved to the chair opposite him and sat. "I agreed to come. I did not agree to be nice."

He sat and eyed her with a half smile.

"I don't like you," she said. "And never will, and until I know you'll leave my father alone, I won't trust you."

A server appeared, hovering and uncertain.

"A bottle of the Bruno Giacosa Borolo Riserva," Antoine said.

Harlow didn't react. Her father had mentioned the Bruno Giacosa Riserva. The wine went for almost a thousand dollars a bottle.

"I promise you, Harlow, I'm not the monster you think I am."

She thought of what Easton had told her. "Nothing you say will change my mind." She grabbed the glass of water off the table. No way she'd drink wine and lower her defenses tonight.

"You should be nicer to me. We both know your father can't come up with what he owes me in two days."

Despair flared in her belly. "How much?"

A slimy smile. "That's between me and your father. But you'd be worth any price."

"I told you, I'm not for sale."

The sommelier appeared and showed Antoine the wine. The man poured the red and Antoine tasted it. Harlow tried to get a grip on her out-of-control emotions.

Their server appeared and they ordered their meals.

The sooner this was over, the better.

"So, what do you do, Harlow?"

He was talking like they were out on a date. "I'm an executive assistant."

Antoine held his wine and swirled the red liquid around the glass. "You like it?"

"I love it."

"Taking care of other people's needs?" He sounded dubious.

She sniffed. "I love being organized, efficient, and damn good at my job." She scanned the restaurant. She'd always wanted to come here, and now Antoine had ruined it for her.

Out of the corner of her eye, she watched a small group enter—three men in suits, and a woman in a sexy, fitted black dress that Harlow had seen in the Chanel collection and coveted.

The woman laughed, a husky sound. She was tall and slender, and the dress was fabulous on her. She smiled at the man beside her.

The man was sauntering through the tables like he owned the place. A liquid way of moving, in complete control of his body.

Harlow froze. She knew that walk.

Easton turned his head, gracing the woman with a smile.

Damn. With everything that had happened, she'd completely forgotten his business dinner with the team of lawyers from Peregrine Corp was here. How the hell could she have made this mistake?

The woman looked like she'd be happy to do anything for Easton.

Much like Harlow had on that conference table.

Her hands clenched on her glass. *Screw it.* She needed a sip of wine to make it through this.

She grabbed the wine glass and gulped. She covertly watched Easton's party get seated. Not too close, but not as far away from her table as she'd like.

If he saw her...

God, clearly, she was being punished by the universe.

Easton was sitting in profile to her. She slumped a little in her chair.

"Why do I get the feeling you aren't listening to me, lovely Harlow?" Antoine's voice was a silky drawl.

She glanced back at Antoine. "Because I'm not."

His cold eyes flashed. "I like a little sass and feistiness, Harlow, but don't push it."

A skitter of ice ran down her spine. "Well, I'm not going to ask you what you do. I've no interest in criminal activities."

"I'm a businessman."

"I work for people in real business. You're no businessman."

Antoine sat back in his chair. "I also enjoy art, black-and-white movies, and collecting antique weapons."

She looked out the window. "This is not a date."

"I recently purchased a gold-encrusted sword that once belonged to Napoleon."

She remained silent.

"What do you enjoy when you aren't working?" he persisted.

"Spending time with my family, who I hate seeing threatened."

His brows pulled low, and she knew she was definitely trying his patience. She blew out a breath. "Watching renovation shows."

He arched a brow. "Renovation?"

She guessed criminal masterminds probably didn't get involved in renovations. "Yes. Rehabbing old homes."

"You'd like to do that one day?"

"Yes." She risked a quick glance at Easton's table.

The female lawyer had her hand on his arm, leaning in close.

Oh yes, Mr. Norcross. Whatever you want, Mr. Norcross. Harlow's hand clenched hard on the stem of her wine glass.

"But you gave your father all your money."

Her gaze flashed back to Antoine.

He smiled. "I could help make that dream a reality. And make your father's debt disappear. All you have to do is agree to be mine."

His slave. To sell herself. Let him put his ugly hands on her.

"No, thank you."

Their meal arrived, but Harlow wasn't hungry. She

didn't think she'd be able to swallow a mouthful of the pasta.

As Antoine talked with the server, she looked away.

And her gaze collided with a furious blue one.

She sucked in a breath.

Easton glared at her across the restaurant, his gaze shifting to Antoine, then moving back to her. Harlow felt the punch of his anger across the distance between them.

CHAPTER SIX

Easton's hands balled into fists under the table. He heard Helena, the lawyer from Peregrine, droning on.

But his full attention was on Harlow.

Rage welled in him. She was sitting there, looking beautiful, with Antoine fucking Armand.

"Easton?" Helena said.

"Sorry, go on," he muttered.

He glanced back at Harlow. He saw panic on her face before she hid it.

Armand said something to her, and Easton watched repulsion cross her features. When she rose and headed for the restrooms, Easton stood abruptly.

The lawyers he was with all startled.

"Restroom," he said. "I'll be back."

He strode across the restaurant, intent on his target. He walked into the narrow hall leading to the restrooms. There was no sign of her.

He spotted a small, darkened alcove nearby. He

leaned against the wall and waited. While he did, he tried to keep a lid on the volcanic temper writhing in his chest.

Usually, he was a cool, controlled man. Harlow seemed to bring his temper to boil faster than anyone he knew.

He waited, and finally the door to the ladies' opened.

Harlow stepped out. Easton guessed she thought she'd dressed down. She had no idea just how that deceptively simple black dress hugged her body, loving every sweet curve. Need was a vicious twist in his gut.

Her hair was pinned up, a few strands tickling along the line of her neck.

She saw him and her eyes widened.

Easton strode to her, tugged her a few steps to the side, then spun her into the alcove. Now they were hidden from anyone using the restrooms.

"Easton—"

He shook his head. "Don't talk. I'm too angry."

Her eyes sparked. "I already have to deal with one asshole tonight, don't make it two."

He shook her a little. "You know what he is. How dangerous he is. Yet, you're sitting there with him, drinking wine. Is this how you're dealing with the situation?" His voice was a contained roar.

She stiffened, like she was going to fight back, then she slumped into him. "Easton, I'm holding on by a thread. He threatened my father, and said if I had dinner with him, he'd give my father a few extra days to get more money." There was a glimmer of tears in her eyes.

"Don't you dare cry."

She scowled at him. "Quit with the orders. I'll cry if I want." She sniffed.

She looked brave, but vulnerable. *Dammit.* She woke up every one of his protective instincts.

Easton yanked her to him. She was stiff for a second, then her arms slid under his jacket and around his body. She pressed her face to his chest and held on tight.

"I want to help you," he said.

"I know. But you have so many people coming to you for help, or money, or something else. In the last few weeks, I've seen so much of it. I'm astounded at the gall of people. I don't want to add to that."

His hands tightened on her. "The difference is that I'm offering."

She looked up. "I know. Give it a couple more days. My father said he has a plan."

Easton stared at her face. "You don't believe him?"

She sighed. "I just don't see how we can make this right." She stepped back, pulling herself together.

Easton missed the warmth of her. *Hell.*

"I have to go back," she said. "Finish this dinner."

His reaction was knee-jerk. "No."

"Yes." She lifted her chin.

Easton wanted to bite the stubborn line of her jaw.

"You go back to the fawning, eyelash-fluttering lawyer," she said acidly.

He ignored her jab and instead, gripped Harlow's chin. "I'll be watching. Until you're out of here safely."

She trembled. "Thank you."

It was fucking hard for him to watch her walk away. He stayed in the shadows, fingers flexing, breathing deeply. For a second, he was back with his Rangers, on a mission, waiting for the right time to strike.

Forcing himself to relax, he walked out and rejoined his group. They started talking business again.

"Easton," Helena murmured. "I was hoping you might come back to my place after. For a drink."

He looked past her to Harlow and Antoine. The man was talking, but Harlow was silent, picking at her food.

The asshole had blackmailed her. Used her love for her father against her.

"Easton?" Helena's smile slipped.

"No, thank you. I can't. This is business."

The lawyer sniffed, but nodded.

"Well, this has been a productive and enjoyable evening." The managing partner stood, and held out a hand. "I'm looking forward to our joint venture, Easton."

Easton nodded and shook hands with the man.

They all started out of the restaurant.

"I have something I need to do," Easton said. "Thanks again and good night."

He crossed the restaurant and strode to Harlow's table. She saw him coming and her eyes widened.

Antoine glanced up, his gaze darkening.

"Harlow, time to go," Easton clipped out.

"Easton Norcross," Antoine drawled. "We haven't had the opportunity to meet before."

"I'd prefer to keep it that way." Easton gripped the back of Harlow's chair. "Harlow, let's go."

"Ah, this is the unhappy boyfriend you alluded to," Antoine said.

Boyfriend? Easton glanced at her.

She moved her eyes, like she was trying to communicate something. He got it. She'd been trying to throw obstacles at Armand.

"Harlow won't be seeing you again," Easton said.

She started to rise.

"We haven't finished our dessert." Armand leaned back in his chair, his gaze like a hawk. "If she leaves, our deal is off." His voice turned Arctic cold.

Harlow froze, then a resigned look hit her face. She dropped back into the chair. "Go, Easton. I'll be fine."

Fuck. He wanted to punch Armand in his smug face. "I'll wait outside." He speared a look at Armand. "You know who I am. Who my brother is. You hurt her...you'll pay."

He saw Harlow's eyes widen. Then he turned and strode out.

Dammit, he wanted to pull Armand's arms out and break every bone in the man's body.

Old memories stirred, a bad taste rising in his mouth. He'd done horrible things to the enemy in the past. Knew ways to extract information that no man should ever do to another.

You're not at war anymore, Easton.

Even now, some of those things haunted him. He shouldn't be anywhere near Harlow, let alone touching her with his stained hands.

He reached the street. The temperature had dropped, and he pulled on his coat. He closed his eyes for a second. He liked the cold air on his face; it helped clear his head.

He wasn't letting Harlow have any more cozy dinners with Antoine Armand, that was for damn sure.

"Easton?" A feminine drawl.

He opened his eyes to find a smiling Helena standing in front of him.

He frowned. "Why are you still here?"

She moved closer, a sexy smile on her face. She touched her hands to his chest.

"I sensed you didn't want to mix business and pleasure." Her smile widened. "Our business is over now, so we can deal with the pleasure part of the evening."

Easton sighed. He was used to dealing with forward women. Power, wealth, and good looks attracted most of them. Few were actually really interested in him. The man.

"Helena—"

The doors behind them opened, and he heard Antoine's smarmy accent.

Easton was about to step back when Helena pressed into him and kissed him.

THIS WAS ALMOST OVER.

Little pricks of relief stabbed at Harlow as she walked out of Acquerello beside Antoine. She was careful to keep a decent distance between them. She did not want to touch the man.

She watched the doors ahead get closer.

It helped to know that Easton was waiting for her.

She'd gotten so used to being self-sufficient. She'd always sucked at asking anyone for help.

They stepped outside and the cold air hit her. Winter was well and truly on the way.

Then Antoine gave a low laugh. "I guess your boyfriend lost patience waiting for you."

Frowning, she glanced up.

Shock was a hard punch to her gut. Easton and the slim lawyer were kissing on the sidewalk.

Harlow sucked in a breath. Damn, this hurt so much.

Stupid. Easton was a rich, powerful, and gorgeous man. He could have whomever he wanted, whenever he wanted them.

Easton stepped back, a dark scowl on his face.

Harlow turned away, her chest tight. "Are we done?"

Antoine stared at her. "Our dinner is over. I wasn't an ogre, was I?"

"I'm leaving." She wanted to get home and shower this night off, then climb into bed and pull the covers over her head.

No criminals. No hot bosses. No fathers in trouble.

"Harlow." Antoine grabbed her arm. "My offer still stands. Be mine, and I can make all your troubles go away." He glanced past her.

She followed his gaze and saw Easton bearing down on them.

"If you were mine, I wouldn't be kissing another woman."

It was a twist in her gut, but she was well aware that this man was a manipulative bastard who disregarded rules and laws. He took what he wanted. He wouldn't know loyalty if it smacked him in the head.

"Don't touch her." Easton slid between them and took her other arm.

"You're a fool, Norcross."

Harlow yanked free of both of them. "I'm going home."

"Harlow—"

She met Easton's gaze. "Go back to your friend."

His jaw tightened. "You're coming with me."

She straightened. "Believe me, I want to be alone right now."

"No."

"Leave me alone, Easton!"

She spun and started down the sidewalk as fast as she could walk in her heels. She wanted to escape, put some space between her and him. Then she'd call an Uber and get the hell out of here.

Seeing another woman kissing him shouldn't hurt this much. God, she was an idiot.

A dark SUV screeched to a halt beside her.

She slowed, her brows drawing together. The doors flung open and two men leaped out.

"That's her," one muttered.

What the hell?

Before Harlow could say anything, one of them grabbed her. "Hey, what do you—?"

The other grabbed her hair, yanking it back hard.

Harlow screamed. The men started shoving her toward the idling SUV.

Shouts echoed down the sidewalk. *Please let Easton still be there.* He'd come for her. He'd help her.

If these men got her in the car...

She had to stall them.

Harlow stomped her heel down on one man's foot. He cursed.

She elbowed the other one, and he yanked her hair harder. His elbow collided with her cheekbone and she saw stars.

"*Ow.*" Her eyes watered. Anger exploded inside her, and she turned her head and bit the man's forearm.

He yelped and shoved her. Then he punched her hard in the stomach.

Harlow flew back and landed on her ass. God, that really, really hurt. She wrapped an arm around her middle, fighting back the need to vomit.

Easton sprinted into the fray.

He landed a hard punch to the man who'd hit her. The man's head jerked back. With a low roar, he charged at Easton.

Harlow's heart was beating so hard that her chest hurt. Easton's face was set, hard like stone. Almost as scary as Vander.

Easton's next moves were so fast and brutal.

He landed a punch to the man's gut, dodged the guy's fist, then rammed a vicious elbow into the man's face.

The second man rushed in.

"Easton, watch out!" she yelled.

Without missing a beat, Easton pivoted and kicked the second man hard. The man flew back and collided with the concrete. He let out a low groan.

Oh, God. *God.* Harlow rose on shaky legs, watching the fight with her heart in her throat.

Easton was a *badass.*

The first guy reached under his jacket and pulled out a gun.

All the air rushed out of Harlow. She tried to scream.

Easton turned and kicked the handgun out of the man's fingers. The guy stumbled, and Easton kicked the gun away, sending it skittering well out of range.

"Fuck," one man bit out.

"You got more?" Easton asked darkly.

The SUV's engine gunned.

Suddenly, the two men sprinted for the vehicle. They dived inside and as it roared away, its tires screeched.

Oh, God. God.

She watched the taillights disappear into the darkness.

Easton strode toward her and Harlow flew at him.

Then she was in his arms.

"God. *God.*"

"Are you okay?" He held her to him, his arms tight.

"Yes...I think so."

She was now. He was so warm and hard and strong. She clung tighter.

"I've got you." He stroked a hand down her hair. It had fallen free and was tumbling around her shoulders.

"That guy hit you hard." Danger vibrated in Easton's voice. His hand slid under her coat, one big hand spanning part of her rib cage. He probed gently.

She winced.

"Just bruised," he murmured.

"Easton?"

His blue eyes met hers, churning with something she didn't quite recognize.

"Yes?"

"Can you please hold me a bit longer?" Her body was trembling, and she couldn't seem to control it.

He tugged her closer, her face pressed against his shirt.

It felt so good. Like she'd been looking for this very spot for so long.

"Better?" His voice rumbled under her ear.

She nodded and gripped him tighter.

Footsteps echoed behind her.

She tensed, and felt Easton do the same.

"You made a big mistake with that stunt, Armand." The tone of Easton's voice made her jerk.

He was furious.

CHAPTER SEVEN

Easton struggled to hold on to his control. With his blood still pumping through his veins from the fight, and the volcanic anger that Armand had tried to take Harlow—like she was a fucking commodity—and the fact that she was trembling in his arms, he was close to the edge.

He eyed Antoine. The man looked relaxed, his two guards hanging back. Easton wanted to plant his fist in the middle of the asshole's face.

"I assure you, Norcross, this has nothing to do with me."

Harlow turned, glaring at the man. "You said if I had dinner with you, that my dad would get forty-eight hours' extra time."

Easton ground his teeth together. Blackmailing her. *Fucking scum.*

"Those were not my men, Harlow," Antoine insisted.

Easton frowned. From what he could tell, Armand

wasn't lying. Easton was sure the guy lied as easily as he breathed, but nothing he said now gave off a lying vibe.

In fact, the asshole looked concerned.

"Don't worry," Antoine continued. "I'll find out who's responsible and—"

"No," Easton growled. "You aren't coming near Harlow again." He wrapped an arm around her and picked her up. She gasped, leaning against his chest, but didn't fight him.

The shorter guard lunged forward. "Don't fucking talk to him like that. He wants the bitch, I'll get him the bitch."

Armand threw an arm out, spewing out some French. The guard vibrated, scowled, then stepped back.

"I apologize for my cousin Hugo. He's...spirited."

Easton strode past Antoine. "She doesn't exist for you anymore, Armand." Easton stopped where he'd parked his Aston. He set her down and bleeped the locks.

"Easton—" Her voice wasn't quite steady.

"Get in, baby."

Her gaze met his, then she slid into the car.

He stomped around the other side and got in. He pulled onto the street, his hands tight on the wheel. He scanned their surroundings, looking for anyone watching them. He glanced in the rearview mirror to see if anyone was following them.

He thumbed a button on the wheel.

"Yeah." Vander's deep voice.

"Armand blackmailed Harlow into dinner."

Vander cursed and Harlow sank deeper into her seat.

"Afterward, two guys tried to snatch her off the street and shove her into a black Suburban."

"Fuck. You know who they were?"

"No. Armand insisted it wasn't his goons."

"Who else wants her?" Vander asked.

"I don't know," Harlow said. "Before today, no one did. I'm nobody special."

Easton glanced at her and she turned away to look out the window, her face pale.

"I got a partial plate off the SUV." Easton said. "6WDG."

"I'll run it. You keeping her safe?"

"Yes."

"Good. I'll talk to you tomorrow."

"Easton, I'm sorry," Harlow said. "I said I wouldn't drag you into this—"

He reached out and rested a hand on her thigh. "You didn't."

She touched his hand, then gasped. "Your knuckles!"

He flexed his hands. His knuckles were torn and bloody. It'd been a while since he'd been in a fistfight. "They'll be fine."

"Where are we going?" she asked. "This isn't the way to my apartment."

"You can't stay at your place, Harlow. Armand is interested, and now some unknown player is after you, as well. It's too dangerous."

"God." She wrapped her arms around herself. "What else could possibly go wrong? An earthquake? A volcanic eruption? Maybe the entire West Coast will fall into the ocean."

His lips twitched. She wasn't beaten down. Harlow's spirit was shining through. "Let's hope those things don't happen."

"Where are you taking me?"

"My place."

"Your place?" Her voice rose to a squeak.

"Yes. You're staying with me."

She turned in the seat. "I can't stay with you, Easton. You're my boss."

"I don't care. You're in danger. I have a security system, guards who do drive-bys, and a brother who owns a security company."

"This is crazy. I can't stay the night at your place—"

He shook his head. "Not just a night. You're moving in with me until this is all over."

She sucked in a breath. "We can't."

"Why?"

"Because..." She fidgeted and plucked at her dress.

"Because we're attracted to each other?" he prompted.

She made a sound. "I was going to say because we wanted to bang each other's brains out, but sure, let's go with attracted."

Easton almost swerved into the oncoming lane. He muttered a curse, his cock pressing against the zipper of his pants. "I don't have a problem with that."

"Easton—"

"I'm a man who, when I see something I want, I go after it with everything I've got." And he was finally accepting that he wanted Harlow Carlson.

He liked flirting with her, liked watching her work, liked fighting with her.

"I can't process that right now."

He squeezed her hand. "You don't have to. Right now, I'll get you safe. That's the most important thing."

He drove into the Pacific Heights neighborhood, turning onto Broadway.

"Of course, you live on Billionaire's Row," she muttered.

"There are seven places in San Francisco claiming to be Billionaire's Row."

She snorted. "This is the main one. Everyone knows that."

He slowed and turned. He thumbed the remote on the dash and his garage doors opened.

Harlow looked out the window.

"Oh my God, I knew you were rich, but—" She shook her head, taking in his four-story, cream stucco mansion. It took up a spacious corner block. "It looks like an apartment building and a Tuscan mansion had a love child."

Shaking his head, he drove into the garage. Lights clicked on automatically, and the door closed behind them. He parked beside his black Audi R8 Spyder.

Harlow got out, spinning around and taking it all in. "You have a four-car garage. And a second sports car."

"There's a gym and wine cellar down here, too." He pulled his coat off and slipped his keys into his pocket. "Come on."

He led her to an elevator and pressed the button for the third floor. They ascended. When the doors opened, he waved her out.

"Oh, wow." Her heels clicked on the wooden floor. She moved toward the central circular staircase, taking in the black iron railings as the staircase circled downward and upward to the top floor. "Wow."

Easton gripped her elbow. "This way." He led her into the kitchen and casual living area.

She paused, taking in the large island covered in white stone, the large, double Sub-Zero fridge, and the dark-metal range hood over the Viking stove.

"God, these appliances." She stroked the island.

There was also an oval-shaped wooden table, and a comfortable living area with built-in shelves around a flatscreen TV. A sleek, gray couch faced it.

A wall of French doors opened onto a grassed area walled in by a tall, green hedge for privacy.

"How many bedrooms?" she asked.

"Six."

"Bathrooms?"

"Nine. Two are half baths."

She choked out a laugh. "Oh, well then." She spun. "Just how rich are you?"

"Really rich." His gut tightened. Would she look at him differently?

She shook her head. "You should totally chill out more. It's not like you need more money."

Easton leaned against the island. To be honest, he wasn't sure how to slow down. He needed the challenge of his work, the purpose.

Her gaze went to his hand, her face changing. "Do you have a first aid kit in this giant house of yours?"

"Yes."

"Good." She dumped her bag and coat on the stool. "We need to clean your knuckles."

HARLOW RIFLED through the large first aid kit, pretending not to notice Easton loosening and removing his tie, then unbuttoning the top buttons of his shirt.

She really pretended not to notice his tattooed, strong forearms as he rolled up his sleeves.

It was so unfair. The man was good-looking in a masculine, rugged way, smart and rich, and he also had a hard, muscular body.

No doubt he spent time in the gym he'd mentioned.

She glanced around the living area and kitchen. It wasn't so intimidating in here. It was gorgeous, but the fancy kitchen aside, it was clear that this was the heart of this home.

She noted the books on the coffee table in front of the big, gray couch. They weren't for show—a crime thriller, and a true crime book.

He set something down on the counter.

She eyed the pills. "What are those?"

"Ibuprofen. That cheek and your ribs will start to throb." He moved to the refrigerator and pulled out a bottle of water.

Harlow took the pills. "Sit," she ordered, waving at the stools that stood beside the California-sized kitchen island. "Let me see those knuckles."

"Have you always been this bossy?" he asked.

She snorted. "I'm organized, and I'm damn good at arranging things, not bossy." She took his hand, ignoring the tingles that touching his skin generated. She just had to accept that touching this man lit a fuse inside her.

She rested his fingers on the marble and started dabbing antiseptic wipes over his torn knuckles. "You're the one that has bossy down to an art form."

Seeing his torn skin and blood made her remember just what he'd saved her from.

She shivered.

"Hey." He pressed a finger under her chin and made her look at him. "You're safe, Harlow."

"Thanks to you. If those men had gotten me into that SUV..." She took a deep breath.

"I wasn't going to let that happen."

She met his blue gaze. It was intense, lit with an inner fire.

"There is no way I want to train a new assistant," he added.

The dry comment surprised a laugh out of her.

His lips quirked. She set to work, cleaning his left hand. It wasn't quite as bad as the right.

"Did one assistant really strip naked on your desk?"

He grimaced. "Yes. It was a bit of a shock after I came back from a meeting." He shook his head. "I didn't even know her name. We'd never spoken. Yet she expected—" he shook his head again. "Some people only see the dollar signs, or the power, or what you can do for them."

Oh, Harlow was sure the woman had seen Easton Norcross in all his handsome glory. But she understood what he was saying. The woman had been there solely for her own needs, not his.

"Poor Mrs. Henderson from HR had to come up and deal with it," he said.

Harlow shivered. "That woman would do well in the Army."

"She'd make a good Ranger."

They smiled at each other. Heat unfurled in Harlow's belly, glowing bright.

"Who do you think tried to take me?" She kept her tone neutral, trying to stay away from the enticing feelings inside of her. She opened a tube of antiseptic cream and spread some on his knuckles. "Do you think Antoine is lying?"

"I wouldn't put it past him, but he didn't seem to be."

Her stomach did a sickening turn. *So, who the hell* else *was after her?*

Easton grabbed her hand. "You aren't to be anywhere near Antoine Armand alone again."

She cocked her head. "Is that an order, Mr. Norcross?"

"If you knew what you calling me Mr. Norcross in that snotty tone did to me, you wouldn't do it."

She froze. *Oh. God. Ignore it, ignore it.* She quickly finished attending to his knuckles. "Who else could possibly be after me?"

Easton's face hardened. "I don't know, but we'll find out. We need to talk with your father tomorrow."

Harlow slid off the stool, and paced across his living area. Just the thought of her father and this mess made her feel sick. Fathers were meant to protect, not put their family, their children, in danger.

"I can't stay with you" she said.

"This again?" Easton swiveled on the stool, looking like a king on a throne. "Why?"

"You're my boss."

He raised a brow. "So?"

"It's not appropriate. People will talk."

"So? They talk all the time. Half the time they make shit up."

Tiredness hit her. It was late, and she'd been running on caffeine and anxiety all day.

She dropped onto the couch. "I don't know how to fix this, Easton. I'm usually really good at fixing things." She stared at the lovely gray rug on the floor.

He came and sat beside her, and took her hand. "Sometimes you can't do it alone. Sometimes you need to ask for help."

She glanced at him. There was a deep note in his voice.

What had Easton needed help with?

"I can't stay with you," she said again. "If I do..." *I'll be no better than that misguided assistant when I strip naked on your bed.* She wondered what his bedroom looked like.

No, Harlow. Not seeing his bedroom.

"Harlow, I don't give a fuck about what people say."

"They won't say nasty things about *you*."

He growled. "I won't let them say shit about you, either."

She looked at him, eyebrow arched. "Sorry to burst

your billionaire bubble, but you can't control what everyone thinks or says." She flopped back on the couch. It was surprisingly comfy. "I can't believe this all happened." She felt a tight knot in her chest. "My dad. Antoine. Whoever the hell those kidnappers were." Everything was caving in on her. Then she felt a horrifying prickle behind her eyes.

No. She wasn't going to cry. It wouldn't make anything better, and she wasn't a crier to begin with.

"Don't cry," Easton bit out, sounding a little desperate.

"I'm not." A traitorous tear slid down her cheek.

"Harlow—"

She sniffed. "I can't help it. It's been a really shitty day."

He made a sound and yanked her into his arms.

She was too weak to push him away. He smelled good, felt good. So strong and solid. She wrapped her arms around him and held on.

But soon, her emotions morphed into something else.

Something far hotter and steamier.

Harlow swallowed. She needed to let go. She needed to get away from him and leave his million-dollar house. She'd go somewhere, and find a hotel for the night.

She gripped him tighter.

His hands slid up her back, then into her hair.

She didn't let herself think, just feel. She turned her head and kissed the side of his neck.

He made a sound and tugged her head back.

Then his mouth was on hers.

Harlow moaned. Tongues stroked. He tasted like

wine and dark, sexy things. She pushed closer and he devoured her lips.

Gasping, her head fell all the way back. "See, this is why I can't stay here," she panted.

"This?" He nipped her neck. "Or this?" One big hand cupped her breast.

She pushed into that electric touch. "Yes. *Yes.*"

Then his mouth was on hers again. She matched each nip and stroke of his tongue. They kissed like they'd both been deprived for far too long.

Then suddenly, he pulled back. They were both breathing heavily.

Easton rested his forehead on hers. "You've had a rough day. You need some sleep."

She sucked in a breath. "You're being noble?"

His gaze bored into hers. "I won't take advantage of you. You're vulnerable, emotional, tired, and coping with a lot of crap."

Damn him for being nice.

"When I finally make love to you..." He nipped her lips, making her gasp. "When I finally slide inside you, you'll be focused on nothing but me."

Her belly contracted and her panties were soaked in a second. "I'm adding arrogant to your list of faults. Bossy, arrogant, autocratic."

He raised a brow. "It wasn't on there already?"

"I'm also adding nice."

He grimaced.

"I mean that in a good way, Easton. Not a boring way."

"Shut up." He pulled her against him and leaned back on the couch. "Let's just lie here for a minute."

Harlow kicked her heels off, and settled against him.

Mmm. This felt really good. She soaked it in, his strength, his scent, his warmth. She'd let herself switch off for a bit before she had to face the mess of her life again tomorrow.

CHAPTER EIGHT

Easton woke up, and for a second, he wasn't certain where he was.

He wasn't in his bed.

He blinked. His face was buried in a cloud of blonde hair. He was flat on his back on his couch, with a sleeping Harlow stretched out on top of him.

Damn.

He stayed still and appreciated the feel of her. She wasn't quite snoring, but she was making cute little snuffling noises. He found them outrageously attractive.

He'd had plenty of women in his life. Beautiful, elegant, and accomplished women. But he'd never slept on the couch with any of them.

Harlow stirred. She lifted her head, and her eyes were heavy with sleep. "Hey." Then she stiffened, her eyes going wide.

Before she panicked, he clamped an arm around her to hold her in place. "Good morning."

She stayed silent, but he could practically hear the wheels turning in her mind.

"What's going on in that head of yours?" he asked.

"I'm wondering if I ignore you, if you'll disappear. Like a figment of my imagination."

"How's that working out for you?"

She groaned and shifted. Her body brushed against his.

Which had his wakening cock jabbing into her belly.

Those eyes got wider.

Shit. "I really want to kiss you."

"No. No kissing." She rolled off him and stood. She thrust her hands into her hair. "I can't believe we slept together."

"Fully clothed. On my couch."

"I don't—"

Easton reached up and grabbed her arm, then tumbled her back on top of him.

"Easton!"

He kissed her. She resisted for about half a second, then she fisted a hand in his hair and kissed him back.

Fuck. He wanted to tear that dress off her. He reached down and bunched the fabric, and started pulling it upward. She moaned into his mouth, then bit his bottom lip.

"You should come with a warning label," she complained.

He dragged his hands up her thighs. "Oh?"

"Yes. Hot, potent, and causes women to make bad decisions."

"You want to be bad, Harlow?"

A cell phone rang.

She froze. "That's mine!"

She leaped off him, and he narrowly avoided a knee to the groin. As she dashed to her handbag, he tried to get his aching cock under control.

"Shit, my battery is almost dead." She thumbed the screen. "Dad?"

"Harlow." Charles Carlson's flustered voice came through the speaker.

Easton sat up.

"Are you okay?" There was slick panic in Carlson's voice. "Where are you?"

Harlow flicked Easton a glance, worrying her bottom lip. "I'm fine, Dad."

"I went to your apartment and you weren't there."

"Um, I stayed with a...friend."

"The dinner went all right?"

Her nose wrinkled. "It was bearable. Dad, we need to talk about the next steps."

"There have been some developments," her father said.

"For me, too. Some men tried to grab me off the street, Dad. And Antoine swore it wasn't him."

"*No.*" Her father's voice was a harsh croak.

Easton frowned and moved closer. Her father's voice showed signs of stress. Easton looked at Harlow. He hated seeing the worry lining her face.

"Princess, meet me at your place in thirty minutes. We'll talk then." The line went dead.

Harlow fished around in her bag and found a hair tie, then pulled her hair up in a messy knot. "I need to get to my apartment. I need to shower and change, and meet my dad."

Easton nodded. "Let me change first. Help yourself to something to eat."

He went upstairs to his master suite. Today, he didn't take in the breathtaking views of the Bay, with the Golden Gate Bridge and Alcatraz Island in prime position.

In his large master closet, he stripped off the clothes he'd slept in, then headed into the bathroom. After a quick shower, he brushed his teeth, and pulled on a clean shirt and suit. His hair was still damp when he rejoined Harlow.

She pushed a mug of coffee at him. Beside it was a plate holding a bagel.

"Coffee, black with one sugar. Bagel with cream cheese and smoked salmon, and a few capers."

Just how he liked it. "Thanks. You didn't have to." He pulled out his phone and called the office.

"Mr. Norcross' office."

"Gina, it's Easton. I'm going to be late. Can you cancel my calls for the morning, and reschedule the Buxton meeting to this afternoon?" He listened to Gina throw questions at him, watching Harlow look at the shelves beside the TV. "Harlow's going to be late, too, so that's why I need you to do it. We'll be in the office in about an hour or so."

Harlow turned and whisper yelled, "*No*. She'll know we're together."

"Thanks, Gina." He ended the call. "We *are* together."

"God, office gossip won't be a wildfire, it'll be a nuclear explosion." Harlow threw her hands in the air.

He drank his coffee, then bit into the bagel. He chewed and swallowed. "It'll be fine."

She glared at him.

Easton quickly finished his breakfast. As they headed to the elevator, he saw her looking around his place. She peered into the formal living area that he rarely used and her eyes widened.

"Oh, my God. Your views." Large windows framed the Bay.

"They're better from my bedroom upstairs."

She stepped into the elevator. "Please tell me you didn't just say that." She nervously played with the strap of her handbag. "No more talk of bedrooms. We need to meet my father."

She was quiet on the drive to her place. Easton studied the lines of worry bracketing her mouth.

"Relax. We'll get this sorted." Vander would find out what the hell was going on.

She made an unhappy noise.

Easton found a parking space a few streets away from her building.

"You don't have to come up," she said.

He got out of the car and shot her a look across the hood of the Aston.

She sniffed. "Bossy."

When they stepped out on her floor, there was no sign of Charles Carlson. Harlow let them into her place. She plugged her cell phone in to charge, and then disappeared into her bedroom.

When she came back, she paced across her living area, while Easton took a seat on the couch. She kept glancing at her watch. Her father was late.

"I like your place," Easton said. There were lots of pops of color. Her personality was stamped on the apartment.

"My apartment would fit into your kitchen." She shrugged a shoulder. "My dream is my own slice of San Francisco. I'd love an old Victorian or Edwardian place to renovate and flip." She looked at her watch. "I'm going to take a quick shower and change. Can you let my dad in when he rings up?"

"Sure." Easton watched her disappear again, and spent the next few minutes not thinking about her naked in the shower, water sluicing down—

He cursed under his breath and readjusted himself.

When she'd talked about renovating a house, her face had lit up. And now her savings account was zero, thanks to her father.

She was quicker than he'd expected. She wore a fitted, black dress with a thin metallic belt at her waist. She held a small, gray jacket in her hands. Her golden hair was pulled back in a messy twist.

"He's not here?"

Easton rose and shook his head.

Her face fell. Then she marched to her phone and stabbed at it.

"Dad, I..." She made a noise of frustration. "It went straight to his voicemail. Dad, where are you?" She slammed the phone down on the counter. "What if something happened to him? What if—?"

"Hey." Easton cupped her shoulders. "Let's not start second-guessing. Let's wait until we hear from him."

She nodded.

"You're not alone, Harlow."

Her gaze met his, and it was drowning in misery.

"I'm right here," he murmured.

"I don't think he's coming. We'd better get to work before I cry or have a meltdown."

Easton lifted her jacket, and she turned and slipped into it. The damn thing hugged her body and accentuated her curves.

He wanted to back her into her bedroom, and take the damn jacket and dress off her.

"I'm ready." She lifted her chin. "Dad will call soon. I'm sure of it."

SITTING AT HER DESK, Harlow tried to focus. When they'd reached the office, Easton had gone straight into meetings, and she had a stack of messages and emails to deal with.

Between those and worrying about her dad, she had no time to wonder if people were looking at her and Easton funny.

She'd slept with Easton.

Okay, not *slept* slept, but she'd spent the night wrapped up in his arms. She hadn't stirred once during the night. She'd slept like a rock.

She blew out a breath and checked her phone. Nothing from her dad.

Where was he?

A sick feeling was growing in her stomach. She'd left her father another voicemail, and several text messages.

"Hi, Harlow."

The female voice made her spin in her chair and whack her hand against her desk.

Ow. She pulled it to her chest and saw Saxon Buchanan and a beautiful, petite woman with a mass of dark hair set in loose curls.

Gia Norcross. Easton's sister.

"Hi, Gia. Saxon."

The tall, handsome man kept an arm around his fiancée. "I called Easton," Saxon said. "He's expecting us."

Just then, Easton's door opened. His gaze met Harlow's. "Did you hear from your father?"

She shook her head, worry churning in her stomach.

He strode out and touched the back of her neck. Then he spun and hugged his sister.

"Hello, big brother," Gia drawled, watching them with interest.

"Saxon, you have anything?" Easton asked.

"Not as much as I'd like." The men walked into Easton's office.

"I don't know all the details," Gia said, "but I know you've got troubles. As someone who recently had some of her own unfun troubles, how are you holding up?"

There was sympathy in Gia's brown eyes.

Harlow liked dealing with things herself. She'd always been too busy to have loads of girlfriends to unload with. She caught up with friends occasionally, especially Christie, but she didn't have lots of people that she bared her soul to. She liked keeping her soul to herself.

But the understanding in Gia's face broke Harlow down. "I'm hanging on by a thread here. My father's in debt to a really bad guy. Said bad guy blackmailed me into having dinner with him." Harlow swallowed. "And don't tell Easton, but Antoine—"

"The bad guy?" Gia hitched a hip up on Harlow's desk.

Harlow nodded. "He offered to wipe out my father's debt..."

"In return for?"

"Me."

"*Ew.*" Gia nibbled her bottom lip. "Yes, best not to tell my overprotective big brother that bit."

"Then, to make matters worse, some unknown men tried to grab me off the street last night."

"Oh no." Gia's eyes widened. "Are you okay?" She pressed a hand to Harlow's shoulder.

"Easton beat them up."

"He looks elegant, but make no mistake, there is an Army Ranger under the Armani." Gia squeezed her shoulder. "He'll keep you safe, Harlow."

"I feel terrible that I've dragged him into this mess."

Gia snorted. "Easton doesn't let himself get dragged anywhere." She smiled and leaned closer. "You strike me as super smart and competent, so I'm guessing you haven't missed how he looks at you."

Harlow's heart did a little flip-flop. "Like he wants to choke me?"

"That, but mostly like he wants to get you out of that super-sleek dress I'm coveting, and do very naughty things to you. And I'm being nice here, because I dislike thinking about my brothers doing naughty things. Believe me, having three hot brothers is a cross to bear."

Harlow laughed, but her smile dissolved. "He's my boss, and I just can't go there. Especially not with all my unfun troubles." Harlow clenched her hands together. "I was supposed to meet my father this morning and he never showed. He isn't answering his phone."

Gia squeezed her shoulder again. "I'm sorry, Harlow. Lean on Easton. He has very broad shoulders. And Vander, Saxon, and Rhys will help."

Harlow let out a shaky breath.

"Harlow?"

Her head jerked up. Easton looked grim.

She shoved to her feet. "What? Is it bad?"

"Come into my office."

Her chest locked.

His face softened. "There's no word on your dad."

The air rushed back into her lungs. "Okay."

She headed around her desk, and Gia stepped in behind her.

Easton eyed his sister with an arched brow.

"I'm coming for moral support," Gia said.

Easton closed the door. Saxon was in the guest chair in front of Easton's desk, and Gia perched on the arm. He slid one muscled arm around her.

The couple touched each other a lot. They were clearly in love. Harlow felt a funny burn under her ribcage.

Easton pressed a hand to Harlow's back and led her to the other chair. Then he leaned back against his desk.

"Saxon tracked the Suburban's partial plate."

Her pulse leaped. "Okay."

"It's registered to Incise Incorporated. Which is a shell company."

Harlow frowned. "So, there's no way to trace it?"

"We traced it," Saxon said. "The Norcross Security tech guru, Ace, followed the trail. It led them through a bunch of companies, and ended with Pierced Enterprises." Saxon leaned back. "It's owned by Rhoda Pierce."

Harlow glanced at Easton. The name meant nothing to her, but he didn't look happy.

"She's in her late forties, smart, sharp, and savvy," Easton said. "She owns some private clubs, and an online casino, and runs an illegal gambling operation. High-stakes games for anyone with the money to buy in."

Harlow frowned. "I don't understand why she's after me. I don't gamble. I don't even play poker or roulette, or whatever the hell people play at illegal gambling spots. I don't know a Rhoda Pierce."

"Does your father play?" Easton asked.

"What?" She shook her head. "He saves his gambling for business. I've only ever seen him play cards at a charity casino night my mother ran once."

"Okay, well, Vander and I will make contact with Pierce," Saxon said. "See what she has to say."

Harlow slumped. "Everyone's getting involved in this—"

Easton touched her jaw. "Hey. Keeping you safe is the most important thing."

Her phone vibrated, then rang.

She gasped. "It's my mom." She felt a wild rush of relief. "Maybe Dad went up to see her. Hi, Mom."

"Harlow?"

Her mother sounded distraught. "Mom?"

"Harlow, I can't track down your father. He missed his doctor's appointment this morning, and the medical center called me. He isn't answering his phone."

No. Harlow's throat tightened. "Mom, try not to worry. He must have gotten caught up with something."

"Harlow, he's been upset for weeks. He always calls me at breakfast time when I'm away. He didn't today."

Harlow closed her eyes. "Okay. Relax. I'll find him. You just enjoy your retreat."

"Thank you, Harlow. I don't know what I'd do without you. Call me when you find him."

"I will," Harlow replied woodenly. She looked at Easton. "My mom. Dad missed an appointment and she can't get in touch with him."

Easton cupped her face. "Don't worry."

"Easton—" All she could do was worry.

"I'll find him." His voice was laced with promise. "For you, I'll find him."

CHAPTER NINE

Harlow couldn't believe she was in a swanky bar, sipping martinis in the middle of the afternoon.

"I should be at the office."

"No, you shouldn't." Gia sipped her drink. "You're stressed and worried. Besides, Easton isn't there."

No. He was out with Saxon, looking for Harlow's dad.

"My life is a mess."

"Oh, honey." Gia squeezed her hand. "It's going to be okay. Drink up."

Harlow sipped her drink. She was on her second one. She turned her head and looked at the stone-faced man sitting with them. Her bodyguard.

Easton had commanded Gia to stay with Harlow until someone from Norcross Security had arrived at the office. That someone had been Rome Nash. Big and muscular, with delicious dark skin and a square jaw, Rome was a man of few words.

The handsome man had given Gia a look. "No trouble."

"Who me?" Gia had winked, then demanded Rome take them to the bar at ONE65, the six-story, French venue. The bodyguard hadn't been thrilled about it.

"I once dragged Rome into a coffee shop confrontation," Gia said. "He still hasn't forgiven me."

Rome's amazing green eyes flicked to Harlow. "I'm here to protect you. I'm not rescuing any babies."

Harlow raised a brow and looked at Gia. "Sounds like there's a story."

"There sure is, and ignore Mr. Grumpy Pants. He'd totally save a baby."

A brunette entered the bar and rushed over to them. "Sorry I'm late. I was finishing up with a new exhibition."

The woman wore a sleek, pink dress, her long brown hair framing her pretty face.

"Harlow, this is Haven. My best friend and my brother Rhys' best decision."

With a smile, Haven sat and shook Harlow's hand. "It's a pleasure to meet you. Sorry to hear about your dad and everything."

"Thanks."

"I had my own problems a little while ago." Haven ordered a martini, then launched into a story about a missing $100-million-dollar painting, a toxic ex, nasty bad guys, and trying to avoid falling in love with Rhys Norcross.

Gia swirled her drink. "Haven failed miserably on that last one. She was so busy swearing off men after her ex, she was totally blind to the fact that my brother had his eye on her."

Haven smiled. "And then he kind of steamrolled me with his bossy, alpha-male hotness."

Harlow made a sound. "Norcross men are good at that."

"Rhys also kept me safe, rescued me, and loves me more than anyone ever has before."

Harlow could practically see hearts in Haven's pretty eyes. Harlow definitely wasn't going anywhere near the *L* word.

"I'm so worried about my dad."

Rome leaned closer. "Easton and the others will find him. Vander can find anyone."

Harlow nodded. She wanted to believe that.

The women chatted about work—Gia owned a successful PR firm, and Haven was the curator at the Hutton Museum, which Easton's company owned.

Glancing around the bar, Harlow spotted a woman with a fabulous pair of Jimmy Choos on. As she watched, the woman stopped talking midsentence, her mouth dropping open.

Harlow turned her head to follow the woman's gaze, and her heart did a crazy dance against her ribs.

Easton, Vander, Rhys, and Saxon were walking across the bar.

She didn't blame the woman for being rendered speechless.

They sure were an assault on the senses. Saxon—tall and elegant, with a gold gleam to his hair, and a blue shirt that set off his golden skin.

Rhys Norcross had his jacket off and slung over one shoulder. The top buttons of his white shirt were open, and he had messy, rock-star hair. He spotted Haven and a smile broke out on his handsome face. *Wow.* It was a doozy. Sexy, with a dash of charm and cheek. She was pretty sure all the women in the bar sighed at the sight of it.

Vander was next. His black hair was a little past needing a cut, framing his expressionless face. It was the kind of expression that taunted a woman to get to know the man beneath it. He wore a black suit that did nothing to hide his muscular body.

And Easton.

Her chest tightened and she felt a tingle in her belly. He was just hot. Handsome, and radiating power and authority.

His gaze found her, and she felt like the center of his universe.

"Wowser, those two are generating some heat," Haven murmured loudly to Gia.

"Tell me about it. My bro is toast."

Harlow ignored them.

Rhys and Saxon claimed their women for kisses. Vander nodded at Harlow, then turned to Rome for an update.

Easton gripped Harlow's shoulders. "We haven't found him yet."

She slumped. God. *Where are you, Dad?*

"But he was spotted at a few places. He's alive, Harlow, and seems to be laying low."

She jolted. "He's avoiding us on purpose?" She felt a spark of annoyance.

"I'm guessing he's avoiding the people after him, not you."

"And putting us through hell worrying about him." She pressed a hand to her forehead. "How could he do that?"

Easton cupped her cheek. "Calm down, baby."

"I need another martini."

Then he shocked her by running his thumb across her lips. "You'll deal. You're tougher than you think."

"I'm going to cry later and you'll change your mind."

He just shook his head, a faint smile on his lips.

"Any luck with Rhoda Pierce?" she asked.

Vander turned to them, his face hardening. "Talked to her right-hand man. Wouldn't put me through to her, but she's agreed to meet me tomorrow."

"This could all be a misunderstanding?" Harlow asked hopefully.

"No," Vander said.

"Damn." She needed a moment alone, plus she needed the restroom. Her bladder was full of martini. "I'm heading to the ladies' room."

Easton frowned.

"It's just over there." She pointed to the hall with a discreet restroom sign. "Rome checked it already. There's no way out of there, unless you can shimmy through a tiny window and scale the building."

"All right."

Harlow crossed the bar, suddenly full of anger at her

dad. She couldn't believe he was avoiding her and her family. Her mom was so worried. "Dammit, Dad."

She accidentally bumped into a man.

"Sorry," she said automatically.

Then she glanced up and saw heavy brows over dark, angry eyes. She gasped. It was Hugo, Antoine's cousin.

"Hey, pretty bird."

Her skin crawled. "I'm with friends." She looked back and saw Easton watching them with a frown.

"I know you have protection. Norcross protection." Hugo spat the words. "Those fuckers think they own the city."

"Leave me alone." She sidestepped him.

He just leaned closer, his voice dropping to a whisper. "If I get you for Antoine, I bet he'd reward me real good. Snatch you away, where no one can find you."

Her pulse tripped, and she saw Easton start toward them.

Hugo moved closer, invading her space, and his hot breath brushed her cheek.

"And he might even share." Hugo made an ugly, sucking sound.

Her heart was pounding so fast she could barely breathe. A trio of laughing women moved closer, and Hugo moved away.

Harlow turned and she couldn't spot him anymore.

Easton reached her. "What's wrong?"

"That was Antoine's cousin."

Easton glanced back and waved Vander over.

"What did he say?" Easton demanded.

She gave him a quick summary.

Dark anger fired in Easton's eyes. "Anything else you aren't telling me?"

She sighed. "Antoine might have agreed to wipe out whatever my father owes him, in return for...me."

A muscle ticked in Easton's jaw, and he looked at his brother as Vander reached them.

"Hugo Durant, Armand's asshole cousin, just threatened Harlow."

"Fuck," Vander muttered. "Let's find him."

The men stalked out of the bar. Rome stayed behind, but from his scowl, it looked like he'd prefer to be out on the hunt.

Harlow was really busting to go to the toilet now. "I'll be in the ladies'."

She walked in. Everyone was trying to keep her safe. Easton was like a shield, protecting her.

She moved quickly into a stall and took care of business. When she strode out and washed her hands, the vanity in front of her seemed to wobble, and she blinked. Then, the room spun, and she felt a little woozy. She gripped the sink. *What the hell?* How many martinis had she drunk?

The room swirled, her legs faltered, and her skin flushed.

A door opened, and she looked up to see a redhead stride out of another stall.

The woman smiled. "It's her."

"What?" Harlow tried to get her brain firing.

A man came out of another stall to join them.

"Hey, you can't be in here," Harlow slurred.

The woman pulled something out of her large bag. A red wig that matched the exact shade of her vibrant hair.

She yanked it on Harlow's head.

"No. Stop it."

The man wrapped his arms around Harlow. She tried to push him away, but couldn't move. All she wanted to do was close her eyes and go to sleep. They wrapped her in a black coat.

The woman pulled on a blonde wig, adjusting it in the mirror. "Ready?"

The man holding Harlow nodded, and then half carried her out. They headed into the bar, the man holding her close, like they were a couple.

Rome or Gia would see them. Harlow's stomach turned over. They'd spot her.

Then before she knew it, they were outside.

Where was Easton? But Harlow could no longer form any words because darkness closed in, and then there was nothing.

EASTON STRODE BACK INTO ONE65, frustrated as hell.

Durant had vanished like the rat he was.

Vander's cell phone pinged. "Ace with info on Durant." Vander flicked through his screen, his face darkening. "Scum has several charges against him in France for sexual assault and battery."

"Fuck." Another asshole to keep away from Harlow.

"I want to get this shit fixed, Vander. Find Charles Carlson."

"I'm on it. Right now, we have too many damn questions with no fucking answers."

And Easton knew that Vander liked answers. He kept his finger on the pulse of everything happening in San Francisco—legal, and not so legal.

Back inside the bar, Gia and Haven were still sipping drinks under Rome's watchful gaze.

"Harlow?" Easton asked.

"Ladies' room," Rome rumbled.

Gia frowned. "She's been gone a while."

"Haven't seen her come out," Rome said.

Shit. What if Hugo Durant was still in the bar? Easton strode to the restrooms, Vander and Rome falling in behind him.

He shoved open the door to the ladies'. A middle-aged woman was refreshing her lipstick. "Hey, just because you boys are hot, doesn't mean you can just barge into the ladies' room."

"There a blonde woman in here?" Easton asked.

The woman shrugged. "Just me, darling."

Easton strode in and checked each stall.

"I'll check the men's room." Rome disappeared.

A hot rush of panic hit Easton. *Shit. Where was she?*

They met back in the hall. Rome's face was thunderous. "I'm sorry, Easton, she isn't here. I've no idea how the fuck someone took her. I was watching, and I didn't see her come out."

"Security tapes." Vander swiveled and strode to the bar.

It took a few menacing looks, and a couple of threats from Easton, but the bar manager agreed to let them watch the tapes.

They squashed into a small office in the back of the bar. Saxon joined them, while Rhys stayed with a worried Gia and Haven.

"Shit quality," Saxon muttered.

They watched the comings and goings of the bar. The quality wasn't very clear, but there was a camera right outside the entrance to the restrooms.

Easton felt Rome vibrating with rage. The man was damn good at his job, and Easton knew he'd be enraged that someone had gotten Harlow on his watch.

Easton was just worried about Harlow. If anyone hurt her, he'd burn down the city.

"There." Vander froze the image.

It was a couple. A woman with bright red hair, leaning heavily against a man.

"I saw them go in just before Harlow," Rome said.

Of course, Rome would have noted everyone's movements in the bar.

A moment later, the couple left, and then a blonde sauntered out of the restrooms.

But she wasn't Harlow.

"Wait." Easton waved a hand. "Rewind."

Vander froze the image on the couple again.

"She looks unsteady," Saxon noted. "Had a few too many drinks."

"Her shoes. Those are Harlow's shoes." Easton had watched her put the damn things on. "The redhead is Harlow."

"Fuck," Rome exploded. "And the blonde must be the redhead who went in."

Vander pulled out his phone and thumbed it. "Ace, I've got pics of a man and woman I'm sending your way. Looks like they drugged Harlow, then took her out of the bar. I need you to find them."

Drugged? Easton stared at the image, at the way the woman had stumbled against the man, and the way the man appeared to be holding her upright. His hands balled into fists, his torn knuckles stinging.

Vander stepped in front of him. "I'll find her."

"Shit, Vander—"

"We don't know who's got her. There are no signs that she is in immediate danger."

"There aren't any signs that she's safe, either." Easton turned and punched the wall.

"Do I need to lock you in my office?" Vander asked.

"No. I want to help find her."

Vander lifted his chin. "Let Ace work his magic. We'll find these assholes, and then we'll find Harlow. Meanwhile, I need to make a few calls."

They headed back into the bar. Gia's face was pale and pinched. Haven had an arm wrapped around her.

"Harlow?" Gia asked.

"Working on it."

"Oh, Easton." His sister hugged him. "She's tough. I get the impression she could organize a war and not get flustered."

"Yeah, but I think her entire freaking family leans on her. They let her take care of everything." He ground his teeth together. "I promised her that I'd keep her safe."

"She'll be fine. You have to believe that."

"Can you get her handbag? Grab her keys and go to her place. I want you to pack her some clothes. Enough for a while. Then drop the stuff at my place."

Gia smiled. "Is she moving in?"

"Yes." As soon as they found her. "I'm heading to Vander's office."

Vander had bought a warehouse in South Beach to house his business. He'd gutted and renovated it to turn into the Norcross Security offices.

The bottom level was a garage, along with holding rooms and a large gym. The main level consisted of glassed-in offices for his team. The top level with a roof terrace was Vander's living space.

Easton ruthlessly controlled himself as he drove to the Norcross warehouse. He waited for the garage door to open, drove in and parked, then jogged up the stairs.

He made a beeline to Ace's office.

The man's domain was a windowless room covered in computer screens.

Ace Olivera's long, rangy body was sprawled in a chair. He'd been born in Brazil, but raised in the US. The guru of all things tech had his long, dark hair pulled back in a stubby ponytail. He'd spent several years at the NSA before Vander had lured him away.

"Hey, Easton," the man said. "Nothing yet, *amigo*, but I'm working on finding your girl."

Easton paced across the office. "You got them outside the bar?"

"Yeah. They loaded her into a sedan."

Easton knew he was hovering, but he couldn't stop.

Every ping on Ace's computer had him leaning over the man's shoulder.

To his credit, Ace didn't say anything, but it wasn't long before Vander appeared in the doorway.

"Easton, you're slowing Ace down, not helping."

Fuck. He pressed a hand to the back of his neck. He hated this helpless feeling.

For a second, everything blurred, and he heard shouts and echoes in his ears. Knowing that a terrorist attack targeting US troops was imminent, but unable to get the required intel from the captured insurgent. The man had just laughed and laughed. Easton hadn't been able to save them.

"Easton?"

He jerked, and met his brother's gaze.

"Come with me." Vander spun on his heel.

Easton followed Vander upstairs. His brother had a fancy electronic lock on the door, and he pressed his palm against it. It beeped and opened.

The entire floor was open plan, with only Vander's bedroom and bathroom walled off. The place had an industrial vibe, with lots of natural wood and black iron. The sleek, modern kitchen was tucked into the back of the space, and accordion glass doors could be opened up onto the large roof terrace.

Vander didn't have parties up here, or people over often. He guarded his personal space zealously.

Vander crossed the living area and went to a built-in bar. He grabbed a bottle of Scotch, poured two glasses, then turned and handed a glass to Easton.

"Here."

Easton tossed it back and savored the burn.

"So, she's the one, huh?"

Easton looked at Vander. "What?"

"Never seen you like this with a woman."

Easton set the glass down on the coffee table. "Like what?"

"Like you're a rottweiler, and she's your favorite bone."

"I'm not sure that flatters me or Harlow. I want her. Desperately. And I want her safe."

Vander nodded. "Her father's in deep, Easton."

"I suspected as much."

"Could be she's using you for money."

Easton paused, then laughed. "You think I can't spot a user? I can pick them before they open their mouths. Harlow won't fucking take anything from me because I'm her boss." He straightened. "When we get her back, that's going to change. Get her back, Vander."

"I will."

Vander's phone rang.

CHAPTER TEN

She was trying not to freak out.

Harlow's mouth was dry, and she was sitting in an uncomfortable chair in front of a shiny, black, lacquered desk.

There was a man at the door in an ill-fitting suit, with an obvious gun holstered at his side.

She swallowed, her chest so tight it hurt. She had vague memories of the couple in the ladies' room at ONE65, a scratchy-feeling wig on her head, and then just haziness. She'd come to slumped in this fancy office.

"Why am I here?" She'd already asked once, but Mr. Scowly was not a talker.

Again, he didn't respond.

The office had no windows, which was weird. It was a little over-decorated for her taste, with lots of black, and splashes of red, and a lot of weapons displayed on the wall. There were swords, knives, and even a crossbow. It all looked expensive. In a corner was an ornate pedestal that held an old, detailed vase. Maybe Chinese.

Harlow clutched her hands together. Easton would be losing his mind. Her heart bumped in her chest. He'd be looking for her. At least, she hoped he was looking for her.

The office door opened, and she heard a man in the hall murmuring to her scowly guard.

If this was Antoine's doing, she'd be pissed. He promised them forty-eight hours.

Yeah, well, criminals probably don't keep their promises, Harlow.

Through the open door, she heard more distant voices—murmurs, laughter. Like there was a party going on.

The door closed again.

As she sat there in silence, the dread inside her grew.

"Can I get some water please? Whatever drug you guys used to kidnap me made me thirsty."

Mr. Scowly's glower deepened. He moved to a side table, where a carafe of water and several tall glasses sat. He poured her one, stomped over, and handed it to her.

"Thanks." She shot him a glare, then drained the glass.

She'd just set it down, when the door opened.

A thin, stylish woman with salt-and-pepper hair strode in. She wore a sleek black pantsuit with dashes of red details, and a pair of sky-high stilettos. Her hair was cut elfin short, showcasing a long, swan-like neck.

She circled the table and sat. She had whiskey-colored eyes, surrounded by dark eyeliner, and they were like a laser on Harlow.

"So, you're Harlow Carlson." The woman's voice was husky, a smoker's voice.

Well, this wasn't a mistake.

"Yes. And I'm guessing you're Rhoda Pierce."

The woman sat back in her high-backed chair. "Yes, I am."

"Why did you abduct me? If you wanted to talk, there are normal ways to do that. Phone calls, appointments."

"I don't have time for comedy, Ms. Carlson. Your father stole something from me, and I want it back."

A sick feeling washed over Harlow. Rhoda Pierce's gaze was direct, flat, and pretty darn scary.

Harlow dragged in a breath. "I'm sorry, but that has nothing to do with me."

Rhoda cocked her head. "You gave your father money, and you had dinner with Antoine Armand."

Harlow lifted her chin an inch. "Believe me, I didn't want to do either of those things. He threatened my father."

Rhoda smiled—it was sharp and scary. "I'll do more than threaten him. He came to my gaming tables and lost dismally."

God. Harlow's stomach tied into knots. *Damn you, Dad.* That was his plan? Win money back by gambling.

"I'm sorry," she whispered.

"Oh, it's worse than that, Harlow. Can I call you Harlow?"

"Sure." Like she had a choice.

"After losing seventy thousand dollars..."

Harlow tasted bile. Seventy thousand? She was going to kill her father herself.

"...he then stole a dagger from my collection."

Harlow stilled. "What?"

Rhoda opened the laptop on her desk and turned it around. The video on screen showed her father in a suit, shoulders slumped, walking down a wide, red-carpeted hallway. The dramatic art on the walls matched Rhoda's office.

She watched her father run a hand through his hair, lines cutting deep into his cheeks.

Oh, Dad. He looked so dejected.

Then he paused next to a collection of daggers on the wall, just staring at them.

The knives were small, with curved blades, and jeweled hilts.

Then her father snatched one, tucked it into the internal pocket in his jacket, then hurried out of view.

Oh, no.

"The dagger is from the seventeenth century, from Mughal India. It's set with emeralds and rubies, and is worth just over a hundred thousand dollars."

Harlow sucked in sharp breath. "I don't know where he is."

"Would you tell me if you did?"

Harlow matched the woman's raptor-like stare. "Probably not. Look, my friends will be really worried I'm missing."

"I don't care about your friends—"

Suddenly Mr. Scowly's cell phone rang. He answered it quietly, then Harlow heard him curse.

"Kolar?" Rhoda asked.

"Someone took down the guards out front. We need—"

There was a thump outside the office door.

Harlow gripped the arms of her chair, watching as Rhoda frowned.

The door opened and Vander strode in.

Thank God. Harlow felt a rush of relief.

Vander's face was its usual expressionless mask, but he was giving off the vibe that he was truly pissed. He'd changed out of his black suit into more black—black jeans, black T-shirt, and a black leather jacket.

His dark-blue gaze glanced at Harlow, scanned her, then looked back at Rhoda.

"You okay, Harlow?"

"Yes, Vander."

Rhoda stood. "Vander, I had no idea she was yours."

"She's Easton's." Vander stopped in the center of the office, feet spread. "And I'm surprised you didn't, since I called earlier to talk about Carlson."

Rhoda swallowed then swiveled to look at Kolar. "You did?"

Kolar shifted nervously.

"Yeah," Vander continued. "I was displeased to be blown off, and to have to talk with your lackey."

"Kolar—"

"You were busy," the guard bit out. "I dealt with it. I told you I wanted to take on more responsibility."

"You dealt with it?"

The snap in Rhoda's voice made Harlow flinch.

"You had your men snatch a Norcross woman?" Rhoda bit out. "That's dealing with it?"

Harlow was really glad she wasn't Kolar.

"Harlow."

She heard the order in Vander's voice. She shot to her feet and hurried over to him. He touched her cheek briefly, then looked at Rhoda. "She's not a part of this."

"Her father owes me money, and stole a dagger from me. An expensive one."

"Not Harlow's problem."

Rhoda's mouth flattened. "I want Charles Carlson."

Harlow closed her eyes.

"Get in line." Vander took Harlow's arm and pulled her out of Rhoda's slick office.

He led her down the hall and outside. Night had fallen, and as she glanced around, she realized they were at a warehouse in the Embarcadero.

"Thanks," she murmured.

"They didn't hurt you?" He led her over toward a black SUV.

"I'm fine." Except she felt sick to her soul.

"Let's get you home."

EASTON PACED HIS HOME OFFICE. Usually, he found the dark-gray wood paneling soothing, but it wasn't helping today. He'd shed his jacket, and had his sleeves rolled up.

Ace had tracked down Harlow to Rhoda Pierce's warehouse. Easton had wanted to go, but Vander talked him down. Told him that the situation needed a cool head.

And Easton was anything but cool right now.

His phone buzzed and he saw a message from Vander.

Incoming.

Easton jogged down his circular stairs to the bottom floor, then down one side of the sweeping stairs to the front door.

He opened it to find Vander and Harlow on his doorstep. She looked exhausted.

"Easton—"

He yanked her into his arms. She buried her face against his chest and slid her arms around him.

"She's okay," Vander said.

"Thanks, Vander."

His brother lifted his chin. "Her dad owes Pierce. Lost in the games, then stole some dagger. A collectible."

Shit. Carlson had dug himself deeper.

Easton felt tension in Harlow's body. He stroked a hand up her back.

"We'll talk more tomorrow," Vander said. "And my guys will keep looking for Carlson."

"Thank you, Vander." Harlow's words were muffled against Easton's shirt.

"Get some rest, Harlow." Vander met Easton's gaze, and a faint grin crossed his face. "Or try to."

Then Vander turned and jogged down the steps to his black Norcross X6. The SUV's engine gunned, and then it roared away.

"Come on." Easton locked the door and led her inside. She was quiet, maybe slightly still in shock.

He guided her into the elevator, and then they exited on the top floor. He tugged her down the hall, her heels clicking on the wooden floor.

He led her into his bedroom and she blinked. She spared a quick glance at his modern, black iron four-poster bed, before she took two steps toward the open terrace doors.

It was a little cool to be out on the terrace, but Easton had needed it tonight.

"You can't be serious with these views," she breathed.

Easton went down on one knee in front of her, and heard her gasp. Then he helped her out of one high heel, then the other.

He looked up. She was staring at him like she couldn't believe he was real.

He rose, took her hand, and led her onto the terrace.

He'd already liked the house for its size and investment potential, but this terrace had clinched the deal.

Small lanterns flickered, giving off a golden glow. A square hot tub was set off to the right, and a comfy seating area to the left.

She moved to the carved stone railing and leaned out, her eyes closed, and pulled in a deep breath of the night air.

Easton slipped his hands into his pockets and watched her.

Something in him finally settled for the first time in a very long time. He was most often driven to *do*, to *move*, but right now, he was happy to just watch a barefoot Harlow in his house.

Safe. Alive. In his domain.

She stared out to the shadowed Bay. Lights twinkled on the Golden Gate Bridge, and part of San Francisco lay before them, glimmering softly in the night.

"Must be nice to wake up to this," she said.

"It is."

Then she shivered.

He took her hand and led her to the outdoor couch. A blanket was folded over the back and he grabbed it, then draped it around her shoulders.

She sat and he reached for the bottle of cognac and glasses he'd left there earlier.

He poured two glasses and handed her one.

She eyed the amber fluid. "What is this?"

"Cognac."

Her nose wrinkled. "Does it cost a gazillion dollars a bottle?"

"No." He decided not to mention that it was closer to ten thousand.

She set her shoulders back, one hand gripping the blanket, then she tossed the drink down in one quick gulp. She swallowed and set the glass down on the table with a click. Then she sucked in a few breaths. "Yikes."

Easton sipped his. "Feeling better?"

"Not really. Thank you for getting me out. Rhoda Pierce is...scary. Although she's afraid of Vander."

Easton set his own drink down and took her hand. "You shouldn't have been taken at all."

"Is Rome okay?"

"Beating himself up. He takes his job seriously."

"It wasn't his fault."

"I said I'd protect you—"

"It's not your fault either. You've done nothing but help me. My father on the other hand..." She scowled. "I'm so mad at him right now."

Easton was just fucking glad she was safe.

"He gambled and lost *more* money." She threw her arm out, her cheeks flushed. "Then he stole. What was he thinking?"

"He's not. He's afraid, desperate, and fucking up."

She deflated. "What am I going to do?"

"Your father needs to find a solution. Return Pierce's property, and then broker a deal to pay back his debts."

Harlow rubbed her forehead, then looked at him, her gaze running down his arms and lingering on his ink.

"What are you doing with me Easton?" She shook her head. "You should run. Save yourself from this mess. You're lucky that Antoine and Rhoda are wary of the Norcross name, or they'd be looking at you for my dad's debts."

"I'd pay."

She gasped. "No. No way! I'm not taking a cent of your money. *God.*"

Desire ignited in his gut. It'd been a slow simmer for weeks, but now it was a five-alarm blaze.

His need for her was a constant gnaw.

"I don't want to talk about money, or debts, or my dad tonight," she declared.

"You finished?"

She nodded. "My brain just needs to shut down."

"Would you like another drink?"

She obviously detected something in his voice. Her gaze flicked to his face, then dropped to his lips. "No."

Easton turned toward her on the couch, resting his hands on her bare knees.

Her breath hitched.

He slid his hands up to the hem of her dress.

"What would you like to do, Ms. Carlson?"

Her lips parted. "What did you have in mind, Mr. Norcross?"

Fuck. When she called him that, his cock pulsed, hard. He tugged her closer and pulled her onto his lap.

Then he pressed a kiss to the side of her neck and she tilted her head, a faint moan escaping her.

"Why don't I show you?" he murmured.

"Yes, Mr. Norcross," she breathed.

Easton's pulse picked up the pace, his heart thumping. He pulled her face to his and took her mouth.

Her hands drove into his hair. The kiss wasn't gentle, but it turned rougher, close to brutal.

"Fuck," he muttered against her lips.

Heat rolled through him, need a vicious fist in his gut.

"Easton." She shifted against him, her round ass rubbing over his rock-hard cock. "Touch me."

CHAPTER ELEVEN

Harlow didn't want to think or question, she just wanted to feel.

And Easton made her feel so much.

And want more. So much more.

His mouth was on hers, his tongue thrusting deep. The kiss was hot and fierce, and ignited fire in her veins.

She moaned and squirmed on his lap. One of his hands slid under the skirt of her dress, skimming up her inner thigh.

"This is probably a mistake," she panted, then bit his bottom lip. "A sexy, breathtaking mistake."

His fingers teased the edge of her panties.

"*Yes*. I want your hands on me. Touch me, Easton."

"I am," he growled.

"Harder," she begged.

He made a hungry, masculine sound, then his fingers shoved her panties aside, and he found her clit.

Harlow wrenched her mouth free and gasped. He rubbed her clit, and then forcibly pulled her mouth back to his. As he stroked her, she felt her temperature rising. Then she was going up in flames. She circled her hips, moving against his oh-so-clever fingers.

"You're soaked." His finger played with her, before sinking deep.

She opened her eyes, rocking on his hand. "*Easton.*"

She stared blindly at the night sky and wondered if anyone could see them out on the terrace. Probably not, but the thought gave her a little thrill.

He pushed two fingers inside her, stretching her. She cried out, pressing her forehead against his. She held him tight, needing the anchor to keep from flying apart.

"I can feel your sweet pussy clenching on my fingers, Harlow."

His sexy words and deep voice made her belly contract.

"So tight and wet. You'll feel so good when I finally slide my aching cock inside you."

"Easton... Oh, *God.*" She was so close.

He reached behind her and lowered the zipper on her dress. He shoved one shoulder off.

She shivered. The night air was cold, but it was what he was doing to her that earned the reaction.

She was wild for him.

He stroked her nipple through her lace bra. Her nipples were hard little nubs, and she ground down on his hand, just pure sensation now.

"That's it, beautiful." He pulled her up, his mouth closing on one lace-covered breast.

Oh, God. "Yes."

His thumb stroked her clit, his hot mouth sucked on

her nipple. If anyone could see them, they'd see her in her boss' lap, totally undone as he drove her closer to a massive orgasm.

His fingers kept pumping inside her.

"*Easton.*"

"Come for me, Harlow."

She trembled, her hands digging into his shoulders, she was riding a thin edge.

He yanked her closer, his mouth taking hers—a hard, punishing claim.

Harlow's orgasm hit her like a deluge. Her hips moved wildly, and his mouth captured her cries.

She slumped against him, small tremors running through her.

"Fuck, you are so goddamn beautiful, Harlow." He tugged her hair hard and his gaze ran over her face, then he kissed her. It was slower, more deliberate, and left her heart racing.

Then he rose, lifting her like she weighed nothing. She clamped her legs around his lean waist.

His mouth was back on hers. There was nothing gentle about this kiss. It was filled with desperate hunger.

He strode inside.

Harlow kissed him back, wild for him. Eager to feel those strong hands on her again, to hear his masculine groans, and feel the heavy weight of him on her.

She wanted to be possessed by Easton Norcross.

She shimmied against the hard bulge in his trousers. He cursed and dropped her on the bed.

He was silhouetted by the golden glow from the terrace. He didn't look like the handsome civilized businessman now. No, he looked ruthless. A pirate about to claim his spoils.

He leaned over her and gripped her dress. He pulled it off her with quick, impatient yanks.

There was hunger in his gaze as it roamed over her. She lay there in only her black lace bra and panties.

He straightened and unbuttoned his shirt. Harlow's belly contracted. He pulled the fabric off.

Oh, hell. He was perfection. Hard, defined muscles covered in bronze skin. Intricate tattoos crossed his chest, and she was sure each image told a story. Fascinating tribal-like tattoos wound around his arms.

Then his hands were on her. He reached under her and her bra was gone.

"Fuck, you have gorgeous breasts." He cupped one and she arched into him. Each stroke on her skin was an assault on her senses.

Then he gripped her panties. He shocked the hell out of her by ripping them off her.

She gasped. The heat in his gaze left her trembling, the need in her a hot, vicious thing.

He leaned over her, pinning her to the bed. His mouth on hers in a scorching, voracious kiss. She strained against him, loving the feel of that hard body on hers. She fumbled with the waistband of his trousers.

"Off," she demanded.

"Not yet." He bit her neck.

Sensation washed through her.

He moved lower, between her breasts. She arched like a bow.

"Easton—"

Then he nipped her belly. She turned mindless. She wanted him inside her. *Now.*

But he had other ideas.

He shoved her thighs apart. "Need to taste you, Harlow."

Then his mouth was between her legs.

Oh, oh. Her hands clamped in his hair.

He sucked her clit, then licked up along her folds.

"So damn sweet." She felt his warm breath on her sensitive skin. "Knew you would be."

Then his mouth was back on her.

Harlow heard the desperate sounds she made—moans, gasps, cries.

Then her second climax hit her, leaving her gasping for air. "Easton!"

As pleasure flooded her body, she reached for his pants again. She got them open, and finally got his hard cock in her hand.

Oh, boy. It was long, thick and hard.

"Inside me, Easton. That's where I need you."

He left her for a second and she lost his cock. She made a sound of protest, then heard a drawer open and close, followed by the crinkle of foil. Then he moved over her, his face a feral mask of need.

He yanked her legs up, tight against his sides. She locked them against him and grasped his biceps.

Then with a snarl, he buried himself to the hilt inside her with one single thrust.

BRUTAL, obsessive need pounded through Easton.

Harlow was wrapped around both his body and his cock.

Fuck. He gritted his teeth, afraid he might erupt on his first thrust.

He wanted her mindless beneath him. Wanted to watch her splinter apart. Hear her scream his name again.

"I'm the only man fucking you." His voice was deep, guttural.

Her fingers bit into his skin, her cries sweet in his ears.

"Tell me you only want me, Harlow." Fuck, he wasn't usually possessive like this. She drove him crazy. "Tell me you want my cock, my hands, my mouth."

"*Yes*, Easton. Only you."

He pushed back, rising off her, wanting to watch her take him. She lifted her arms above her head, her body on display, and with each thrust, her full breasts jiggled.

He saw her hands clench in the covers. Saw the way she took his cock deep. He growled and slid a hand down her body.

She made a husky mewl of sound. He found her clit and thumbed it.

"So sweet and hot, Harlow."

Her eyes locked with his, her teeth biting on her lip.

"So beautiful." He thrust hard. "Damn, I'm going to come soon."

"Yes," she breathed. "I want to feel you come inside me."

He groaned, and worked that swollen clit. He wanted

her spasming around him when he poured himself inside her.

She gasped. Her body shaking. "Yes, *there*."

He covered her again, his hips driving deep. "Take me, Harlow. All of me."

Her nails raked his back.

With a brutal groan, Easton's climax hit. His vision grayed. He growled her name as tidal waves of pleasure battered him.

When his head cleared, they were both sprawled on his bed, limp as cooked spaghetti.

Easton realized he hadn't closed the terrace doors, and a cool breeze washed over them. He needed to get up and close them, and deal with the condom... As soon as he could feel his legs again.

He looked at the expanse of her smooth, elegant back. She was lying on her side and he stroked her, felt her tremble.

He curled around her and nuzzled her hair. "We're lucky we survived that."

She made a sleepy sound.

Easton smiled. He was feeling pretty fucking content. He kissed her shoulder. Her hair looked like a cloud of spun gold, and he fingered the silky strands.

"You alive?" he asked.

"Still evaluating. Is death by orgasm a thing?"

"I hope not."

He finally mustered enough energy to get off the bed and stride to the doors. He closed them, then headed to the bathroom. When he returned, he found her watching his naked body unabashedly.

"See something you like, Ms. Carlson?"

"I like your body, Mr. Norcross. All hard and bronze and sexy."

He pressed a knee to the bed. "Oh?"

She pulled him down and tumbled him onto his back. Then she straddled him.

Pleased, he cupped her breasts, flicking lazily at her nipples. Her fingers traced his ink across his pecs.

"No one suspects this is under your slick suits. And I've heard you speak French on the phone, all suave and elegant, but you're not. You're tough, protective, and strong." She traced the tattoos on his chest. "When did you get these?"

"Started when I was in the Army. Still add the odd one every now and then. Keeps my mother fretting."

Harlow lowered her head and kissed them.

"Are you hungry?" He fought not to roll her under him.

She licked his flat nipple. "Not for food."

Desire reignited, flames licking at his gut. "I'm hungry." He gripped her hips and yanked her upward.

She let out a little cry.

He pulled her until her thighs straddled his head.

"Grab the headboard, Harlow."

She sucked in a breath, her hands curling around the metal bars.

Easton cupped her ass, then licked along the crease of her inner thigh.

Her body jerked.

His. He pulled her onto his mouth. She was soaked and smelled like heaven.

She tasted even better.

He licked her, and felt her thigh muscles quivering.

"*Easton*. Yes, God, yes." She undulated against his face.

"Like that, baby. Work yourself on my mouth. I'm so hungry for you." He buried his face between her thighs.

She moved on him, grinding against his mouth, making husky, desperate sounds.

"I'm going to lick and suck until you come again, Harlow. Then while you're still coming, I want you to find my cock, put a condom on me, then ride me."

She moaned.

He clenched his fingers on her ass. "You hear me, Harlow?"

"Yes. Yes."

She kept riding his face and he kept working her hard. He sucked that swollen clit, lapped at her sweetness.

His cock was a hard throbbing pain against his abs. He needed her so damn much.

"I could get addicted to this." He sucked her clit between his lips.

Her body convulsed. She threw her head back and screamed, then bucked against him.

So damn beautiful.

Her body still shaking, she scooted back down his body. She found his cock, her smooth hand wrapping around his hardness.

Easton muttered a curse. When she pumped him once, he groaned. He fumbled to find the condoms he'd pulled out earlier. He handed her one.

It was torment to watch her open it, then slide the latex down his cock with single-minded focus. He groaned.

Then she lifted her hips, and lowered herself onto his cock, easing onto him, taking him inch by inch.

She moaned and pressed her hands to his chest.

Shit. Easton locked his muscles, fighting not to move, not to come.

Harlow sank the rest of the way, letting out a long moan, and taking all of him.

Easton gripped her hips. "God, you feel good. Made for me."

"Easton." She started moving. She rode him, gaining speed.

He felt sparks of lightning shoot down his spine. "Yes, like that." His voice sounded like gravel. "You're killing me, baby."

She moaned, moving faster and faster.

She was so hot, the way she took him deep. He felt how wet she was.

"Not going to last." He found her clit and rubbed it.

She rocked wildly, her pussy clamping down on him. Then she splintered apart again.

Her climax triggered his.

Easton gripped her ass, thrusting up. His guttural roar filled the room and he exploded inside her. "Harlow!"

The room blurred, then came back into focus. Harlow was lying limp on top of him. Her sweat-dampened skin stuck to his, her breath puffed against his neck.

He stroked down her back. He was sure his legs wouldn't work this time. "Harlow?"

A small, feminine murmur. She snuggled against him and he realized that she'd fallen asleep.

He grinned at the ceiling, stroking her skin. She'd fallen asleep with his cock still inside her.

Easton liked that. He liked it a lot.

CHAPTER TWELVE

Mmm. Sleep slowly lifted, that warm, drowsy state where everything was good in the world and anything felt possible.

Harlow snuggled into the warm body beside her. God, he smelled good.

Wait.

She cracked one eye open. A naked, fast-asleep Easton came into focus. He was lying on his stomach, one arm bunched under the pillow, and the other one wrapped around her.

Oh, shit.

She sat up. She remembered everything, in perfect detail, of what they'd done to each other during the night.

She'd slept with her boss.

She'd slept with the billionaire who could, and regularly did, have anyone he wanted. And not just slept, had lots of amazing, spectacular sex.

"Harlow, you idiot," she muttered.

She scrambled off the bed and winced. She was very

tender between her legs. Then she looked up through the terrace doors and stopped.

Holy cow. The view was as stunning as she'd imagined. She watched a yacht heading across the Bay, its white sails bright against the dark-blue waters.

Then she turned back and her gaze snagged on Easton.

He was an even better view.

He was sprawled there, still sleeping. But even asleep, he looked powerful and in charge. His bronze skin was a stark contrast to the million-thread-count white sheets.

His back was uncovered, and her greedy gaze traveled over the muscular lines of it. The sheet only covered half of his fabulous ass. She saw red scratches on his skin and blushed. God, she'd left marks on him. Her mouth watered and she took one step back toward the bed.

No.

She swiveled, fighting the urge to escape. She couldn't exactly leave his place. She bit her lip. She was stuck at the scene of the crime.

Shower. She'd take a shower and then decide what to do about the circus her life had become.

When she entered the bathroom, her heart kicked at her ribs. This was *exactly* how she'd renovate a master bathroom. Huge shower with dual heads, gorgeous gray tiles, and a free-standing tub under the window that begged for bubbles.

She stepped into the huge shower stall and slid under the hot water.

Oh, that felt good. She closed her eyes and let her mind go blank.

Only seconds later, she heard the shower door open.

Pulse pounding, she spun.

A gloriously naked Easton stepped inside. Of course, the man didn't look sleepy. No, he was sharp-eyed, hair sexily mussed.

"No." She held up her hands. "I'm taking a shower, then once I'm dressed, I'll work out how to rectify the huge mistake of sleeping with my boss."

Easton kept coming. "You slept with Meredith?"

"Ha ha."

He snaked an arm around her waist and hauled her close. Water rained over them.

"It wasn't a mistake," he said.

"It was. I totally slipped up."

He smiled. "The first time I made you orgasm? Or the second or third time?"

Harlow sniffed. "Don't get—"

"How many times did you scream my name last night? Five? Six? Seven times?"

Harlow cocked her head. "Are you done?"

"Yeah." He lowered his mouth to hers.

She was so weak. She kissed him back.

She found herself pressed up against the tiles by Easton's hard body, panting, and stroking his hard cock.

"Fair warning," he murmured. "You're about to make another mistake."

"Oh, stop talking." She yanked his head down to hers. "Condom?"

He cursed.

She licked her lips. "I know you had your physical the other week." She'd made the appointment for him.

He froze. "I'm in perfect health."

Her pulse was pounding. "So am I, and I have a contraceptive shot."

His fingers flexed on her. "You saying I can take you bare? Nothing between us?"

"If you trust me. I can—"

"Fuck." His body shook and he urged her to wrap her legs around his waist.

She did, and he didn't make her wait. A second later, he slid inside her with a hard thrust.

"*Easton.*"

"There it is."

Then he proceeded to rock her world.

When he finally turned the shower off, her legs were limp, and she clung to him to stay upright.

He led her out of the shower, then wrapped her in a fluffy towel. He pressed a kiss to her nose. "While you get dressed, I'll make us some breakfast."

"You can cook?"

"My mother's Italian-American. She decreed that all her children would know their way around the kitchen."

Harlow paused, savoring the image of Easton working at the stove, not wearing a shirt. *Mmm.*

"Harlow?"

"Right. Um, I don't have any clothes."

"Yes, you do. I asked Gia to get some things from your place. They're in the closet." He stroked her cheek. "I'll meet you downstairs."

Harlow dried off, wrapped herself in her towel, and

headed into his closet. She moaned. It was simply amazing. She touched his shirts and suits, and strode down the long closet. Then she jerked to a halt.

Her clothes were hanging on the other side. She blinked. *All* her clothes. Gia had brought everything Harlow owned.

She also found her skin care and makeup. And her hair dryer.

She wasn't sure if she should thank Easton's sister, or be mad that she'd practically moved Harlow in.

Right. Well, at the moment, she needed to get ready for work. She flicked through her skirts. She needed a pick-me-up today. Harlow selected her favorite Max Mara pencil skirt in blood red. She paired it with a thin, black belt, and a long-sleeved black shirt. Next, she reentered Easton's gorgeous master bathroom and dried her hair. She decided to leave it down for a change. After her makeup was done, she completed the look with a pair of Jimmy Choos with a cute ankle strap.

She headed down the grand staircase, reality poking at her again.

How could she possibly get her dad out of this mess? If her mother found out what was happening, she'd have a breakdown.

Harlow stepped into the living area and kitchen. Easton was standing at the island wearing a navy-blue suit and a blue shirt that brought out his eyes.

Her heart skipped a beat. He was just so *male*. She just stared at him, taking him in.

He sipped his coffee, then looked her way. He

paused, his gaze running over her—from the top of her head, down her body to her shoes, and back to her face.

"That outfit tempts me to convince you to make another mistake before we go to work."

"I look professional," she said.

"Sexy professional." His gaze lingered on her skirt. "It's one thing to imagine what you look like under those skirts while I'm at work, it's another to actually know."

"No sexy thoughts at work."

He made a deep sound. "Impossible. I now also know what sounds you make when you come on my cock."

She gasped.

He skirted the island and poured coffee from a carafe, then pulled a plate out of the oven. It held a perfectly cooked omelet.

He nudged her toward one of the stools at the island and she sat, suddenly overwhelmed. "Thank you."

She couldn't remember the last time someone had cooked her breakfast.

He cupped her face. "You'll get through this, Harlow. I'm right here with you."

She stared into those cobalt-blue eyes. "I'm glad you are."

"You're finally admitting that." He kissed her, taking his time. "Now eat."

She listened to him take a call. He was talking to some banker in Australia. How was she going to make it through the day at the office without giving away the fact that she'd explored every inch of Easton Norcross' body. In great detail. And wanted to do it again.

She gave an internal groan, and then drank her coffee

like it was the elixir of life.

Easton had just finished his call when his phone rang again. He put it on speaker. "Vander."

"Morning." Vander's deep voice. "Harlow there?"

"Yes." She pressed her hands to the island, her pulse dancing.

"We found your father."

She sucked in a breath. "Is he okay?"

"Yeah. I have him here at my office."

She jumped off the stool. "We'll be right there."

"See you soon," Vander said.

Harlow met Easton's gaze. "He's all right." She smiled. "God, I was so worried."

Easton brushed her hair back behind her ear. "Grab your bag and we'll go."

"Wait, what about work? You have meetings this morning—"

"I'll call Gina to reschedule."

Harlow's belly twisted. "I'm causing you so much trouble. I—"

Easton pulled her close. "Do you ever worry about yourself? Or is it just everybody else?"

"Easton—"

He nipped her lips. "This time, I'm taking care of you. You just need to focus on you."

Harlow knew he liked being in charge and taking care of things as much as she did.

But she was realizing that he needed someone to worry about him, too.

BEFORE EASTON HAD EVEN FINISHED PARKING the Aston at the Norcross Security office, Harlow was flying out of the car.

With a curse, he caught her at the stairs leading up to the main floor. He took her elbow.

"You shouldn't run in those heels. You'll break an ankle."

She arched a brow. "You should see what I can do in these shoes."

He smiled.

Harlow rolled her eyes. "Of course, you're thinking naughty things."

He stopped on the stairs and kissed her. "I think naughty things anytime you're close, Harlow Maree. Nothing to do with your shoes."

She gasped. "How do you know my middle name?"

"It's on your employment file. And Vander investigated you, remember?"

She frowned. "Maybe I didn't understand exactly how much Vander was reporting to you."

Easton took her hand and started upward. "Your first boyfriend was Brandon Dalton in high school."

Her mouth dropped open.

"He's an unsuccessful real estate agent now. Divorced twice."

She shot him a look.

"Vander is always very thorough. And what he uncovered is that you're a rare woman, Harlow. One with no secrets." Easton felt that old, familiar darkness rise. "I'd forgotten that people like you exist."

Concern crossed her face. "Easton—"

"What he uncovered is that you're hard-working, you save your money, and you care about your family, a little too much."

Her face softened.

"And you only splurge on clothes and shoes."

"They're an investment." She squeezed his hand. "What you see is what you get with me."

Easton had spent so long uncovering lies and secrets. Ones paid for with blood. Ones that had cost lives. Harlow was like a shining sun in the darkness.

"I hate when you get that look in your eyes."

Her words made him blink. "What?"

"This darkness takes over, and for a second, you aren't here anymore."

He blew out a breath. "Unlike you, I have my secrets." Dirty, dark ones that still stained his soul.

She didn't look away, held his gaze. "I'm here, if you want to share them."

His chest tightened. She didn't push. She didn't fire off questions. "Let's go talk with your dad."

She nodded. They reached the top of the stairs and Harlow looked around. "This warehouse is gorgeous."

Across the space, Vander and Rome were standing talking in front of an office. Harlow and Easton hurried over to join them.

"Harlow." Rome's deep voice was a rumble. "You okay?"

"I'm fine, Rome. Don't even think about beating yourself up. I'm okay."

The big man grunted.

Easton knew Rome wasn't getting over her abduction anytime soon.

Then Harlow made a choked sound. She was looking into the office behind the men.

Charles Carlson sat slumped in a chair.

"Dad?"

Carlson's head snapped up. "Harlow." He shot to his feet.

She raced to her father.

Easton followed. He was staying close. Her father might love her, but he'd put her at risk.

"Princess." Carlson hugged her tightly.

"I've been so worried about you," she said.

Easton caught Vander's gaze and scowled.

"Found him hiding in an office space he'd rented through a secondary company. He was sleeping on the couch."

Easton lifted his chin.

"Dad, Rhoda Pierce had people *kidnap* me."

"*No.*" Carlson's hands flexed on his daughter's arms. "I'm so sorry."

"She said you gambled. Then lost more money, then you stole a dagger of hers."

His chin dropped to his chest. "I can explain—"

"Explain?" Harlow's voice rose. "I'm in danger, Dad. If mom or Scarlett come back, they'll be in danger, too. I've had to have dinner with a criminal, been attacked, and been taken by a really scary lady. How could you explain?"

Carlson slumped. "I'm sorry, Princess."

Easton didn't think it was good enough. The guy

needed to man up. Easton reached out and gripped the back of Harlow's neck. She glanced at him and he hated seeing the pain on her face.

"You're Easton Norcross," Carlson breathed.

He glanced up to see her father staring at him.

"You're dating Easton Norcross?" Carlson asked Harlow.

"He's my boss," she answered.

Carlson glanced between the two of them. "I thought your boss was Meredith Webster."

"I'm temporarily Easton's assistant. Dad, this doesn't matter right now. The knife. Rhoda Pierce wants it back. She's not a lady you cross."

Carlson scraped a hand over his face.

"Dad, where's the knife? You need to return it."

"I can't."

"Dad!"

Easton watched as a bead of sweat rolled down Carlson's temple.

"It's gone."

Easton frowned. Vander came in and leaned against the wall, his arms crossed over his chest.

Carlson looked at him, then Easton.

"Carlson, I'm keeping Harlow safe," Easton said. "You've put her in the path of some bad people. You *will* return the knife."

"I can't." A hoarse whisper. "It's gone."

Harlow stiffened and Easton stepped closer. He pressed his hand to her lower back.

"Explain," he ordered.

Carlson swallowed. "I had it in my car." He ran his

hand across his mouth. "I regretted taking it right away. I stopped to get coffee near Fisherman's Wharf, wondering how to return it without Rhoda knowing."

Of course, the man couldn't just own up to his mistake.

"When I got back to the car, the knife was gone."

"What?" Harlow breathed.

"Nothing was broken. The car was locked. I had the knife wrapped in a handkerchief in the middle console. I have no idea who took it."

"Fuck," Vander said.

"We have to find it," Harlow said.

"We do," Vander agreed. "Otherwise, your dad is fucked."

She gasped.

"Vander." Easton scowled at his brother.

Vander shrugged. "Sorry, Harlow. Don't worry, we'll find it. I'll get Ace working on it, and I'll put out feelers to see if anyone is trying to sell it, or shift the jewels from the hilt."

"Thank you, Vander." Harlow pressed her fingers to her temple.

"Carlson, you need to lay low until we find the knife," Easton said.

Vander nodded. "I have a safe house you can stay at."

Harlow spun. "Easton, it's too much."

"It's fine, Harlow." He rested a hand on her shoulder.

Her father was watching them.

"You help out all your employees, Norcross? And touch them all the time?"

"Dad! Easton has—"

Easton stepped forward. "You mean something to Harlow, and Harlow means something to me. I'm helping you out for *her*, not you. Don't test my patience."

Carlson nodded rapidly, his mouth clicking shut.

"Let's go," Vander said. "SUV's parked out front."

Harlow walked ahead with her dad.

"I'll take him to our Oakland place," Vander said. "Ace'll find the dagger."

"I don't want this to take too long." Easton wanted Harlow safe. They stepped out the front doors.

Vander's lips twitched. "The longer it takes, the longer your gorgeous assistant has to stay with you."

Easton looked at her, and the way her blonde hair glinted in the sunlight. "When this is over, she's staying with me anyway."

Vander raised a brow. "She know that yet?"

"I'm working on it."

His brother smiled. "Damn, I never thought I'd see the day when you finally found the right woman, and she isn't tripping over herself to throw herself at the great Easton Norcross."

"Fuck you."

"No, save that for your blonde bombshell."

A shot rang out.

Easton and Vander tensed.

Another gunshot, and the window of a parked car shattered.

Easton reacted. He took two steps and dived on Harlow.

He took her down to the sidewalk, covering her body with his.

CHAPTER THIRTEEN

Gunshots echoed in Harlow's ears, and a scream stuck in her throat.

Easton lay on top of her—a heavy, solid weight. His cologne filled her senses, the beat of her heart was a roar in her head.

Someone was *shooting* at them.

Oh, God. Oh, God.

Easton wasn't moving. Her heart stopped. Was he hit? God, was he hurt and bleeding?

"Easton—"

"Hold still. Stay down." She felt him shift a little. "Vander?"

"Yeah, I'm on it," Vander growled from nearby.

Where was her dad? Harlow bit her lip, fighting back her fear.

She heard more gunshots close by. She jolted and turned her head. She spotted Vander on the sidewalk, a deadly-looking black pistol in his hand.

Then, the shooting stopped, and Vander sprinted out of view.

"Easton..."

"Just a bit longer, baby. Need to make sure it's safe."

He was literally shielding her with his body. Protecting her. She closed her eyes. People looked at him and just saw a rich billionaire. Probably imagined him as a self-absorbed, rich man who had everything.

They didn't see the hard-working, protective man who'd thrown himself in front of a bullet to protect her.

Something shifted inside her.

He was a man she could lean on. Who wouldn't let her down.

"Clear!" Vander called out.

Easton rose and pulled her up. He kept her close to his front.

"The shooter's gone." A muscle ticked in Vander's jaw.

"Dad?" Harlow scanned the sidewalk. Her pulse tripped. "Where's my father?"

Vander blew out a breath. "I saw him take off."

"No." She shook her head.

Easton hugged her close.

"Judging by the shots, the shooter was aiming for him," Vander noted.

"Oh, no." Harlow clung to Easton.

"He can't run for long," Vander said. "We'll find him again."

"Come on, baby." Easton squeezed the back of her neck. "Let's get to work. Vander will find your father."

"What if the shooter finds him first? Or Rhoda? Or Antoine? One of them is behind this."

"They won't." Easton forced her to look at him. "Your father made this mess. He knows we're here to help. He's just not thinking clearly."

"And he's selfish," Vander muttered. "Putting his daughter on the line."

God. Harlow let out a shaky breath. Her father kept digging himself in deeper.

She let Easton bundle her into his car. By the time they parked at the office, she'd mostly calmed down.

"Okay?" Easton asked, leading her to the elevator.

"No, but I think getting to my desk and keeping busy will help."

He ran his thumb across her lips. "Good girl."

The urge to kiss him was overwhelming. They were alone in the elevator, but it could stop at any second.

"You shouldn't stare at my mouth like that," he said.

"I can't help it," she whispered. "Because now I know exactly what you look like under your fancy suits."

He groaned. "Harlow."

She stepped closer and toyed with a button on his shirt. "And I know the sounds you make when you're deep inside me."

He cursed and yanked her close. He spun her back against the mirrored wall and kissed her.

Oh, yum. She stroked her tongue against his. Right here, right now, it was just the two of them and how they made each other feel.

Then the elevator started to slow and he quickly stepped back.

Harlow pinned what she hoped was a professional look on her face. Crap, she'd need to redo her lipstick.

Two suited men entered.

"Mr. Norcross," one said.

"Morning," Easton replied.

The elevator moved again, the men talked quietly about some upcoming workshop.

Harlow stepped a little closer and in front of Easton. She reached back, fingers grazing his belt buckle. She heard his low hiss.

She let her hand drift lower, her fingers dancing over the hard bulge in his trousers.

His head moved closer, his breath hot on the back of her neck.

"Very naughty, Ms. Carlson." A near soundless whisper. "You're asking for trouble."

She knew she shouldn't do this. They were at work. But when her boss had already blown her mind numerous times, and thrown his body over hers to shield her from bullets, it tended to put some things in perspective.

The elevator slowed again. She felt Easton straighten his jacket across his front.

A woman in a gray suit stepped in with a nod.

The elevator headed upward again. Harlow sensed Easton crouch down. She glanced back and saw he was tying his shoe lace.

Then she felt a light caress on her knee. She controlled her jolt and gasped quietly. Those clever fingers continued up the back of her thigh. They slid through the slit at the back of her skirt.

Harlow bit her lip. His fingers brushed the edge of her panties, and she felt a rush of dampness between her thighs.

The elevator slowed again and his hand withdrew. She missed the touch instantly.

Get it together, Harlow.

The others exited and Easton stepped forward, his suit jacket covering any evidence of his arousal. He held the door open.

"Shall we, Ms. Carlson?"

"Yes. You have a meeting in ten minutes with Albany Capital."

He paused. "Are you all right?"

He was such a good man. "No, but I will be."

When she got to her desk, she was sucked into a vortex of work. Easton went straight into a meeting and Harlow was met by a bunch of messages to return, and a stressed-out Gina to calm down.

Harlow had no time to worry about the fact that she was sleeping with her billionaire boss, or about her father's troubles. She just sent up a silent prayer that her dad was okay.

At lunchtime, she heard Easton on the phone. When she looked in to his office, he was standing at the window, looking mighty fine. She brought his grilled fish and salad in, and set it on his desk. He smiled at her and her belly warmed.

"Okay, Ma. Yes, I'll tell her. Tonight. We'll see you then. Love you."

Harlow stiffened.

"Thanks for lunch," he said.

"Who was that?"

"My mother. Gia's been in her ear, and we're invited to my parents' place for a family dinner tonight."

"Dinner. At your *parents'*." Harlow tried not to hyperventilate.

He arched a brow. "Ma's a fabulous cook. Is there a problem?"

"My father's in debt and breaking laws, and bad guys are shooting at us. You *can't* take me to your parents."

Easton circled the desk. "It'll be fine, Harlow. My parents want to meet you. I told Ma everything."

"Everything?" Harlow squeaked.

"About what's going on, with your dad."

God, Harlow wanted the ground to swallow her. "It's too dangerous."

"I'll be there, as well as Vander, Rhys, and Saxon."

So, a small Norcross Security army. She swallowed. "Fine."

He kissed her nose.

She sprang back and looked at the open door. "Quit that."

His phone on his desk rang and he just smiled at her, looking sexy and far-too-tempting.

Back at her desk, her phone was ringing, too. The next few hours were a whirlwind. She fended off a businessman who was determined to get a meeting with Easton to sell him a million-dollar idea. The guy was persistent and creative. He kept calling from different phone numbers and using different voices.

The office started to thin out as people left for the day.

A moment of calm in the storm had her thinking about the upcoming evening. God, she was having dinner with Easton's parents. They must think he was crazy taking on her mess.

More people left. Easton was still on the phone. The man had no off switch.

When she saw he'd ended the call, she opened his office door.

"Rex Vasquez from Pacifico wants you to call him," she said.

Easton groaned.

"I told him no."

Easton's lips twitched. "Even Mrs. Skilton wouldn't tell him no."

"You've had a long enough day, which included getting shot at." She straightened. "Have you heard from Vander?"

Easton shook his head. "No news."

She nodded, fighting back her disappointment. "We have an hour until we're due at your parents." There, she'd kept her voice pretty steady, not freaked out at all.

"Sorry, I wanted to give us time to go home and freshen up, but that's not going to happen."

Home. Like it was their home. Butterflies lit up in her belly. "I can freshen up here. As long as my outfit is okay."

His gaze heated. "It's more than okay."

"For meeting your mother."

Easton stalked to her, then closed the office door. Then she was in his arms.

Oh, God. The kiss exploded out of control. It felt like

hours and hours since she'd kissed him.

He groaned. "I've watched your ass all day. I've been half hard in every meeting."

She moaned. "We can't do this here."

He backed her up until she bumped against his desk. "Yes, we can. I've thought about this so many fucking times."

"Easton—"

His hand stilled. "You saying no?"

She realized he'd stop. "No." Because dammit, she'd thought about it, too.

He spun her, his hands shaping down her body. "These fucking skirts." He cupped her ass. "Bend over the desk, Ms. Carlson."

Pulse skittering like crazy, she bent over the desk. She was so aware of everything—the hard surface beneath her, Easton's heavy breathing, the slide of her skirt on her skin, her soaked panties.

He slowly peeled her skirt up. "*Harlow*." His hands kneaded her ass, toying with the elastic edge of her panties.

Then he yanked the scrap of lace down her legs.

He sank a hand into her hair, pulling her back enough to kiss her, his pants brushing against her bare ass.

Then one of his hands pressed to her shoulder blades, and the desk was cool under her cheek, while the rest of her was in flames.

His other hand slid between her legs, finding her damp folds.

"Damn, baby, is all this wet for me?" He tugged on

her clit, then thrust a finger inside her. "Have you been wet all day, Ms. Carlson?"

She moaned. "*Yes.*"

"Then time for my naughty assistant to get her punishment."

She heard the clink of his belt and her belly tightened. Anticipation was like lightning in her veins.

She felt the tip of his cock drag through her damp folds. Her palms clutched the desk.

Easton's hands gripped her hips. "Hold tight, baby."

"Easton—"

His hips plunged forward and he buried himself deep inside her.

HARLOW'S husky cries mingled with the pleasure driving Easton.

He bent his knees, then thrust into her again. Their groans mixed.

He needed more. Needed to stamp himself on her.

He picked up speed. She was pinned under him, taking his hard, furious thrusts. He'd never felt this desperate, this possessive.

She whimpered, pushing back against him.

His hot, sexy Harlow.

He leaned over her, his hips slapping against her ass as his cock filled her.

Then her body stiffened, and he felt his own body draw tight.

"Yes, *Easton*," she cried.

Her head tilted, her lips parted and her face clenched with pleasure.

Easton released the last of his control. He thrust harder, felt her inner muscles clenching on his cock.

With a groan, his climax tore through him. His hips bucked, pleasure a hot, heady rush.

Then he slumped over her, tucking his face against her neck.

Jesus, he was wrecked. And he'd never get any work done at this desk again.

He kissed her skin, and she made a contented, humming sound.

"Despite not wanting to move, we'd better get going," he said. "Or we'll be late to my parents."

She stiffened, then elbowed him. "Off. We can't be late!" Her wide, slightly panicked eyes filled her face.

Easton tucked himself back into his pants. "So, something does ruffle the organized Ms. Carlson."

She yanked her skirt down. "My God, we have to get to your parents'. Where are my panties?"

He found them hanging from the arm of the guest chair, and handed them to her.

She made a distressed sound. "Your come is sliding down my thigh." She made a beeline for his private bathroom.

Damn, he wanted to fuck her again. Instead, he tidied up, and when she strode out, she looked as polished as ever, except for her flushed cheeks and swollen lips.

"Ready?" he asked.

"We have to stop at the florist on the way to get your

mom some flowers."

He frowned. "We don't need—"

"No arguments." She held up her palm.

His sister used the same hand move as well. He decided not to argue.

After a detour to the florist, he pulled up at his parents' neat Edwardian in Noe Valley. They were only five minutes late. Vander's BMW bike was parked in the driveway and Rhys' silver Mercedes GTS was at the curb.

Harlow fidgeted in the seat beside him, holding a huge bunch of mixed flowers that he knew his mother would love.

Reaching across the seat, Easton gripped her chin. "They're going to love you."

"Easton, no mother loves the woman her son is sleeping with. I bet she's not liked any of the women you've brought home."

He was silent for second. "I wouldn't know, I've never brought another woman home."

"What?"

Full-blown panic appeared on her face, so he kissed her until she went liquid.

"Oh, you've squashed the flowers."

Shaking his head, Easton got out, then tugged her out of the car.

"Oh, I *love* this house. I love the paint color and contrasting trim. And that door is original." Harlow sighed.

"You like renovating?" he asked, with a small smile.

"It's my little dream. It's nothing."

The front door opened before they reached it.

"Easton." His mother hurried out. Clara Norcross was small and curvy, and kept her dark hair free of grays with regular trips to her hairdresser. "You work too hard."

"I know, Ma."

Then his mother turned to Harlow.

"These are for you." Harlow held the flowers out.

"Thank you, they're beautiful."

"Ma, Harlow. Harlow, my mother, Clara Norcross."

"Call me Clara." Then his mother reached out and pressed a kiss to Harlow's cheek. "You poor thing, Easton told me what's been happening with your father."

"I'm so, so sorry to drag Easton, and Vander, into my mess—"

"*Bah.* Those boys can't be dragged into trouble, they jump into it. They gave me my first gray hair before they were teenagers."

"What gray hair?" Easton asked, deadpan.

His mom swatted his arm.

"And my middle son is very, very good at making trouble."

"I heard that," Vander called out from inside.

"Come." Clara took Harlow's hand. "Let's put these in water and get you a drink."

Harlow shot him a wide-eyed look, then followed his mom inside.

"Harlow!" Gia waylaid them. "How you doing?"

"Fine."

Haven stood right behind Gia. The women disappeared into the kitchen.

Rhys appeared holding two beers. "It's not some

fancy French wine."

"Fuck you." Easton took the bottle.

"You both okay?" Rhys asked. "Heard someone took shots at you this morning."

"We're fine. Harlow bounced back, as she always does."

In the living room, Easton found Vander, Saxon, and his dad. Ethan Norcross had given his sons their tall, muscular bodies, and his rugged face was topped with salt-and-pepper hair.

"Looking forward to meeting your girl, Easton."

"Hi, Dad." He gave his dad's back a slap. Such a solid presence, always supportive. He'd never put his family at risk to keep up appearances. "My girl's had a rough few days."

"Vander said you're helping her out." His father's face hardened. "Her father isn't helping."

Easton felt a flash of anger. "He's in over his head."

Gia, Haven, and Harlow appeared, the three of them holding glasses of wine.

Easton's father lifted a brow. "A blonde bombshell, no wonder you're smitten."

Easton pulled Harlow to his side. "Harlow, this is my father."

She smiled. "Well, now I know why Norcross men are so handsome."

Ethan grinned. "I like her."

Easton's mom bustled out of the kitchen. "Let's eat. Everyone to the table."

Easton slid an arm around Harlow. "Okay?"

She smiled. "Okay."

CHAPTER FOURTEEN

Harlow sipped her wine. She'd found dinner relaxing and fun.

Mrs. Norcross had cooked lasagna, and it had been delicious. Easton and his brothers liked giving each other a hard time in a fun, sibling way, with Gia getting in her fair share of digs as well.

Ethan and Clara Norcross were friendly, supportive, loving parents. As Harlow listened to the conversation, she stared at her red wine. She realized that while she loved her family, they didn't have this type of connection.

Growing up, her father was often busy, or in meetings, and her mother was frequently in bed with a headache. Scarlett was younger than Harlow, and while Harlow adored her sister, they didn't have loads in common.

"Hey." Easton touched Harlow's chin. He had one arm resting along the back of her chair. "Where did you go?"

"Just thinking. You have a great family, Easton."

"Yes, when they aren't driving me crazy." She heard the affection in his voice. Vander called out to him and he turned away.

When she looked up, she found Mrs. Norcross watching her speculatively. Harlow swallowed.

Clara rose, lifting some plates. "Harlow, will you give me a hand in the kitchen?"

Uh-oh. She felt the inevitable interrogation coming on.

Harlow stacked some plates and took them into the bright-white kitchen. It had top-of-the-line appliances, and gorgeous, white-marble countertops.

"Your kitchen is lovely."

Clara smiled. "Easton renovated it for me a few years back."

"He loves you."

"Yes, and he takes good care of those he loves. It's in his blood. When he joined the Army, I wasn't surprised. He wanted to serve his country and help other people."

Harlow nodded.

"But going to war changed him." The older woman's dark eyes turned shadowed. "He rarely talks of it."

"He's told me a little. I see the darkness sometimes."

Clara nodded. "He fights it back, but sometimes he's too hard on himself."

Harlow smiled. "You mean he's a workaholic who can't stop and relax."

"Yes."

They shared a smile of understanding.

"My Easton needs someone who brings him sunshine and joy, but who can handle the dark."

Harlow's belly churned. All she'd brought him was headaches. "I agree. He needs someone like that."

Clara arched a brow. "You talk like that isn't you."

Harlow pulled in a breath, fighting to keep a hold on her emotions. "We both know it isn't. Easton deserves the best, and it isn't me. I'm not bringing him calm and happiness, I'm bringing him stress and problems. I'm not good enough for him."

Easton stalked into the kitchen, his face angry and his gaze on Harlow. "That's bullshit."

She held up her hand. "Easton—"

He grabbed her arms. "I don't want to hear you talk like that about yourself again. You don't think you bring me calm and happiness?"

"No! Because of me you got shot at, and had to beat up two guys, and it's not over yet. You and Vander are spending a fortune to protect me and find my father—"

Easton made an annoyed sound. "I don't care about any of that. You don't think when you make an acerbic comment about how rich I am, or how I work too hard, I don't feel like laughing? You don't think when you smile, I don't feel the warmth?"

Her pulse went crazy. *Oh, God.*

"You don't think when I'm deep inside you, I don't feel happy?"

Harlow's mouth dropped open. His words hit her in her heart, but— "Easton, your mother is standing right there!" Heat flooded her cheeks.

"My mother knows her kids have sex."

Clara laughed softly. "And she has sex, too."

Easton's face froze, then he winced. "Ma, not another

word." He refocused on Harlow and cupped her cheeks. "You don't think when you sleep pressed against me, I don't feel fucking everything?"

"Easton, language," Clara said quietly.

He ignored his mom.

Harlow swallowed, her chest about to burst. "My father—"

"You are not your father. You're not responsible for his actions, or his mess." Easton pressed his forehead to hers. "You're beautiful, smart, hard-working—"

"You should be with someone extraordinary. Some gorgeous woman with four degrees, who speaks French and Italian, who started her own business and turned it into a multimillion-dollar empire with her intelligence, grit, and savvy."

"I don't want your imaginary perfect woman, Harlow, I want you." He nipped her lips. "You see me. You see Easton. You don't see my bank account, or my position, or my influence. You're about as easy to give anything to as hugging a hedgehog."

Harlow sniffed. "Hedgehogs are cute."

His lips quirked. "You're mine now."

She melted against him. She could only put up so much of a fight, and she had no defenses against Easton Norcross.

"And you can always learn French and Italian."

She elbowed him.

"Wonderful." Clara clapped her hands together, her face filled with satisfaction. "Now, time for dessert." She pulled a tray of cannoli out of the fridge.

Harlow met Easton's gaze and he ran his finger down her nose. Then he tugged her back into the dining room.

She ate until her skirt waistband was digging into her skin.

"Time to go home," Easton murmured.

Home. Together.

"Harlow," Gia said. "We're doing drinks tomorrow. It's Saturday, and you need to destress."

"How about we go to Charmaine's?" Haven suggested.

Oh, Harlow had only been to the funky rooftop bar once, and loved it.

Easton leaned forward. "I want Harlow safe until the issues with her father are sorted. No going out."

Thinking of her father made Harlow's contentment from the evening dim.

"Fine," Gia said, undeterred. "Drinks at Easton's bar."

Harlow frowned. "Easton's bar?"

"He has an entire bar room in that big house of his. There's a pool table, and the bar is fully-stocked." Gia reached out and squeezed Harlow's hand. "We'll make our own fun."

"Maybe I have plans," Easton said.

"Now you have better ones," his sister countered.

He shook his head.

Finally, they said their goodbyes.

"I'll call when we have something," Vander said. "Your dad can't have gotten far."

"Thanks, Vander," Harlow said.

Ethan Norcross hugged her, and for a second, she

wanted to hold on to his solid body and absorb as much of his paternal comfort as possible.

"Let my boy take care of you, Harlow. He needs it."

She nodded.

"And take care of him back." Ethan winked.

Clara hugged her too, pressing kisses to both her cheeks. "Everything will be fine, Harlow. You'll see."

In the car, Harlow stared out of the window as they drove back to Pacific Heights. She looked at Easton through the shadowed car. He drove well. It was sexy to watch those long fingers on the wheel.

"What's going on in your head?" he asked, as he pulled into his garage.

"I can't just sit around doing nothing, and letting Vander do all the work. I need to help find my father."

Easton's face hardened. "You aren't traipsing around San Francisco—"

"No," she interrupted him. "I'm not stupid." They headed to the elevator. "I'm going to make a list of dad's friends. He could be staying with one of them, or they could've helped him."

Easton nodded slowly as the elevator ascended. "That's actually a good idea."

She shot him a dry look. "I do have them once in a while."

"I know. The best one you had was when you decided to sleep with your boss."

"I don't remember sleeping with Meredith."

He tugged her closer and nipped her jaw.

"I'm going to make the list tonight, and I'll call

around tomorrow." Harlow felt energized. This was a way to help and take control of the situation.

"Come on." He pulled her down the hall and into a media room. The walls were a dark gray, and the screen was enormous. Huge, black-leather chairs filled the space, and framed, classic-movie pictures were lined up on the walls.

"This is awesome," she said. "Movie nights must be amazing. Big screen. Popcorn."

She saw Easton blink.

She put her hands on her hips. "You've never done a movie night?"

"I don't have time."

"Because you're a workaholic. "

"I sometimes have gaming nights with Saxon and my brothers."

Harlow was totally going to make him do movie nights.

He moved to a small, built-in bar and opened a bottle of wine. He brought her back a glass of deep-ruby-red liquid. She sat in one of the big chairs, snuggling into the leather.

Then she pulled out her phone and started making a list of all her father's friends she could remember. Old work friends, golf buddies, neighbors.

"So, do you want to watch a movie?" Easton asked.

"No," she said. "I want to try one of these games you mentioned."

His dark brows lifted. "Do you game?"

"No, but I'm up for anything." She kicked her shoes off and leaned back.

He eyed her legs. "All right. What game?" He grabbed a controller and the screen lit up.

She studied the options. "How about *Call of Duty*?"

"You want to shoot people?"

"Sure, as long as they aren't real people. Is that okay? It doesn't bring back old memories—?"

"It's fine."

"Okay." She took another controller. "Prepare to have your butt kicked, Norcross."

"YES, *yes*, I'm going to make it!"

Easton glanced at Harlow, enjoying her cries as her fingers stabbed at the Xbox controller.

She was perched on the edge of her chair, no shoes, her skirt hiked up, and totally absorbed in the game.

"Hey, come back here, you coward!" she yelled at the screen.

She bit her tongue, chasing a bad guy on the screen.

Easton was looking at her cute red toenails. He smiled. They'd been playing for almost two hours.

A cut scene hit, and showed a man tied to a chair. Several soldiers moved around him, and an interrogation began.

Easton tensed. He heard the faint rat-a-tat-tat of gunfire. He smelled dust, sweat, and fear.

"Hey." Harlow slid into his lap. She cupped his face, her brow creased.

He blinked and saw that the game was paused, but when he looked back, all he saw was Harlow.

"Are you all right?" she asked.

"Yeah, sorry."

"You have nothing to be sorry about. We can play something else."

"No, I'm okay. I've been fine the last two hours."

"Two hours?" She looked vaguely horrified. "We only started, like, ten minutes ago."

He smiled. "The downside of gaming."

"No kidding." She stroked his cheek. "The interrogation scene? It brought back bad memories?"

He blew out a breath.

As he remained silent, she eyed him. "You don't have to be super-Easton to me all the time. Hell, you've seen me at my very worst."

He sucked in a breath. "Yes, that scene cut a little too close." He grabbed her hand. "I don't suffer from PTSD, but sometimes I have some bad memories, the odd nightmare. But I believed in the work I did, and I don't regret it. Interrogation was my specialty, what I was good at. But in the middle of a battle, it requires that you forget that your enemies are human. You put that aside, and it's only later, you remember they're people. Someone's son, daughter, brother, cousin, father."

"Thank you." She kissed him.

"For what?"

"For sharing, and for doing a hard job so I don't have to, so others don't have to."

She kissed him again. It was slow and lazy. He slid a hand into her hair, slanting his mouth so he could go deeper. He drew in the taste of her.

She pulled back, her face flushed. "My turn to take care of you."

Then she slid off his lap and onto her knees on the floor.

His body locked. "Harlow—"

"Shh, I'm the boss now." With a smile, she undid his belt and lowered his zipper.

Fuck. Every muscle in his body went rigid. The sight of her on her knees in front of him left him weak.

She freed his cock. "Even your cock is beautiful, Easton."

Her husky purr had his cock jumping in her hands. She stroked him, and there was nothing left in his head except pleasure, and the need for more.

Then she licked the head of his cock.

He groaned, pushed back into the chair. She sucked him deep.

Need was a pulse in his gut. He looked down, and felt himself getting harder. Her blonde hair was draped over his legs, her mouth sliding on him.

"Fuck," he growled. "You like sucking my big cock, don't you?"

Her gaze met his, those pretty lips stretched around him. She made a humming sound and he nearly came.

"You like knowing that you push me to the edge." He fisted a hand in that golden hair. "That really, I'm the one on my knees."

She sucked harder, her cheeks hollowing. He cursed and then hauled her up.

"I'm not coming in your pretty mouth tonight. I want to feel your sweet pussy squeezing me when I come."

She moaned, then pushed to her feet. She reached under her skirt and pulled her panties down.

With a growl, he shoved her skirt up to her waist and yanked her to straddle him.

"Yes, yes, yes," she chanted. Her hands gripped his shoulders for leverage.

Easton thrust up as she shoved down.

She cried out.

Seeing stars, he gripped her hips. *Shit*. "Did I hurt you?"

"Not even a little." She moaned. "I love that you're so big."

"Ride me. It's all yours."

One of her hands clenched his hair, gripping hard. She started moving, gliding up and down on his cock.

Easton gritted his teeth. He was on the edge of blowing inside her. "Harder, Harlow."

Instantly, she picked up speed, her breaths coming in hard pants. "I'm so full." Then her hand dropped between their bodies.

His gut clenched. "You rubbing your clit, baby?"

"Yes."

"You are so damn sexy."

She was riding him wildly. Easton gripped her ass, helping pump her up and down on his cock.

"Easton, I'm going to come."

"I'm right with you, baby. I need you. I need to be right here inside you."

She sank down, her head dropping back as she screamed.

Her tight body milked him and the last shred of Easton's control disintegrated. He pounded up into her. "*Fuck.*"

Everything turned white. There was a rush of noise in his ears, then his tortured groan as he violently poured himself inside her.

Inside his Harlow.

When he was conscious enough, he felt her peppering lazy kisses over his face and neck. He pressed his face to her hair, then found her mouth for a long, drugging kiss.

"You don't come like a billionaire," she murmured.

A sharp laugh burst out of him. "You have experience on how billionaires come?"

"Well, no, you're my first."

And her fucking last.

"I just imagined you'd come more like a gentleman." She grinned at him. "Not like a dirty-talking stevedore."

He rose with her in his arms, his cock sliding out of her.

"Easton! I need to clean up."

"I'll clean you up, then this billionaire is going to show you how he's going to go down on you, and make you scream until you're hoarse."

She licked her lips. "Hope you're a billionaire who keeps his promises."

"Oh, I am."

Easton followed through. When he was done, he left her limp, exhausted and fast asleep in the center of his bed.

Damn. He sat and watched her. He wanted to keep her there forever.

He lay down and curled around her. She turned and snuggled deeper into him.

He pulled in the scent of her hair, and for the first time in a long time, his mind easily drifted off to sleep.

He was woken by the peal of his cell phone.

He nabbed it, blinking at the early morning light. "Norcross."

"Easton, it's Hunt."

He sat up. "I'm guessing it's not good, if the police are calling this early."

"You asked me to keep an eye on anything to do with Carlson."

A sleepy-eyed Harlow sat up, watching him warily.

"Yeah," Easton said.

"The Carlson residence was broken into last night."

Shit. "Any sign of Charles Carlson?"

Harlow pressed a fist to the center of her chest. Easton covered her hand with his.

"No," Hunt said. "No one was home."

"Okay, I'll be there soon with Harlow."

"See you there."

Easton slid his hand around the back of Harlow's neck. "Get dressed, baby. Your parents' house was broken into."

She gasped.

"No sign of your father."

She nodded, misery in her eyes.

Easton ground his teeth together. He needed Vander to speed this up and get this situation finished with.

CHAPTER FIFTEEN

They pulled up at her parents' large home in Presidio Heights. It was where Harlow had grown up. Her father had worked a lot, and they'd never lacked for anything. He'd taught them the value of hard work.

Clearly, he'd forgotten that lesson.

There was a police cruiser and another gray sedan at the curb, and she realized the second vehicle was an unmarked police car.

Easton pulled to a stop, then jogged around the Aston and helped her out.

A cold breeze teased her hair that she'd loosely tied back. She hadn't paid much attention when she'd gotten dressed. She'd pulled on some black leggings and a large, oversized cream sweater.

Easton had shocked her by wearing jeans. Dark denim that hugged his ass in a way that made her mouth water, and he'd topped it with a blue sweater the color of his eyes.

A man in a suit broke away from the uniformed officers.

He was cop-hot. Strong face, with a muscular body and a walk that announced he'd once been military. His brown hair was cut short, and she got a glimpse of a holster under his jacket. A badge was clipped to his belt.

"Hi, Easton."

"Hunt."

The men shook hands.

"Harlow Carlson, Detective Hunter Morgan."

"Nice to meet you," Harlow said.

"I wish it was under better circumstances." The detective eyed the two of them. "Sorry for ruining your Saturday morning."

"Was anything taken?" she asked.

Surely if they'd found blood or anything concerning, he would've mentioned it.

"Maybe you could tell me. I tried to contact your parents, but I didn't get an answer on either of their numbers."

"My mom's away at a yoga retreat, and regularly turns her phone off. And my dad's...off on business."

Hunt's green gaze was piercing, and she guessed he wasn't buying that.

"Come on." He jerked his head toward the house.

He led them in the front door. The scent of lemons hit Harlow. It was a cleaning product the housekeeper had used since she was a little girl. Everything looked normal. Her mom liked the Hamptons style—lots of white with touches of blues and wood.

"They got in through the back door to the kitchen," Hunt said.

In the kitchen, broken glass was scattered across the floor.

"They have an alarm," she said.

"Disabled."

Had this been Antoine looking for her dad? Rhoda looking for her dagger?

"The house has been searched, but they were pretty careful, except in the office."

Her father's office was a mess. She gasped, and Easton wrapped an arm around her.

The desk chair was tipped over, things were yanked off shelves, and empty drawers hung open from the desk.

Harlow bit her lip. Behind the desk, the safe set in the wall was open and very empty.

"You know what your dad kept in here?" Hunt asked.

"Some cash, a little jewelry, a few business papers. Nothing hugely valuable." She looked around. "Not worth all this effort."

"You know why someone would break into your father's office, Ms. Carlson?"

"Call me Harlow. And...um..." She wasn't sure how much to tell the detective. Her father was consorting with criminals, had stolen a valuable collectible.

"If we find out anything, we'll let you know," Easton said smoothly.

Hunt sighed, a resigned look on his rugged face. "How much trouble is Carlson in?"

"We'll contact you when we know more."

"Is Vander involved?"

"Vander is involved in a lot of things," Easton replied.

Hunt stared at the ceiling. "Fuck. Sorry, Harlow." The detective pinned Easton with a glare. "This is some fucked-up situation where you keep me in the dark, then pull me in to clean up your mess."

"When a crime has been committed that we need to report, we'll call you. Like we always do."

"You owe me, Norcross."

"I'll buy you a beer."

Hunt snorted. "I want a case of something old, Scottish, and expensive." His gaze turned serious. "Call me if you need me."

Easton nodded. "Thanks, Hunt."

"The uniforms are going to board up the broken window."

"Thank you," Harlow said.

"Let's go." Easton urged her out of the office, and to the front door.

In the car, she twisted her hands together. "We had to lie to a police detective."

"Oh, Hunt was very aware of that. He's used to us... skirting some of the rules."

"You did it to protect my dad."

"Your father isn't a drug kingpin or murderer, Harlow. He got in over his head and he's floundering. This will all be over soon."

Her cell phone rang. *Mom* was on the screen. "Mom?"

"Harlow!" Her mom's voice was almost a screech. "I got a message from the *police*. The house was broken into. Your father isn't answering again."

Harlow pinched the bridge of her nose. "It's fine, Mom. I just left the house, and met with the police."

"Oh, my gosh. What's happening?"

"The window on the back door was broken, but that's it. Everything's fine."

"Where's your father?"

"He's busy with some work deal. You know how he is."

"He works too hard."

Harlow bit her lip. "And he just wants you to relax."

"I do have a Bikram yoga class starting soon."

"Go, balance your chakras."

"I hear that sarcasm, Harlow Maree."

Harlow smiled. Her mom could be funny and sweet when she wasn't being anxious and paranoid. "I like yoga too, Mom, just not as much as you do."

"You're sure everything's fine?"

"Nothing to worry about." Harlow kept her tone as breezy as she could manage. She said goodbye and shoved the phone back into her handbag. Then she let out a long breath.

"You should tell her," Easton said.

"No." Harlow shook her head. "Mom's...delicate. She doesn't deal well with stress. We shield her."

Since she was a child, Harlow knew not to go to her mother with a cut or bruise, or any kind of problem. Her mother would panic and fall apart. Once, when Harlow was eleven, she had broken her arm falling out of a tree. She'd waited an hour until their housekeeper had arrived and told her. Harlow had learned to deal with things herself. And when Scarlett had arrived, after her mother suffering several bad miscarriages, Harlow had helped take care of her baby sister and her mom.

Now, she needed to fix this mess.

She needed to get back to Easton's and call her dad's friends and track him down.

Finally, Easton pulled into his garage and Harlow sprang out of the car.

"I need to start calling—"

He grabbed her ponytail. "First, I'm going to make you brunch."

She had to admit that any time she thought of this sexy man cooking for her, she felt a little tingle right between her legs. "Isn't it too early for brunch?"

"It won't be once I'm finished making it."

She was hungry. "We'd better take the stairs so I can earn it."

He palmed her ass. "As long as you don't do anything to lose these curves."

She smiled at him.

"I'm going to work out while you make your calls," he said.

"Then I really need the stairs."

They walked up the grand staircase and she looked up at the huge, spherical, black-metal light fixture in the center. So grand, but with a modern edge.

"So, what's for brunch?" she asked.

"I'm going to make you croissants."

She stopped and looked back at him. "From scratch?"

He took the last step so they were at eye level. "Yes."

Oh, God, could the man get any more perfect?

Easton smiled. "You should see the look on your face.

Any other woman would be delirious about getting diamonds, but for you it's croissants."

"*Homemade* croissants." She pressed into him and kissed the underside of his jaw. "You've clearly been hanging out with the wrong women."

He caught her chin, his handsome face serious. "Clearly."

Her belly did a slow tumble.

"Come on." He tugged her up the stairs.

"OUR WOMEN ARE SMASHED," Saxon said.

Easton glanced over to where his sister, Haven, and Harlow sat on stools in his bar room. The three of them all clutched martini glasses and were howling with laughter.

Harlow snort-laughed and almost fell off her stool.

Easton smiled. Damn if she didn't look beautiful and cute as hell half drunk. She wore a pretty, flirty, aquamarine dress. Gia and Haven were dressed up, as well.

"You're a goner," Rhys said.

Easton looked back at his brother. Along with Saxon and Vander, they were all on the large sectional, nursing beers.

"Takes one to know one," Vander said.

Rhys looked at Haven and grinned. "Hell, yeah. And I'm happy as hell." He nodded at Easton. "And here's our big bro, watching a gorgeous drunk blonde snorting, which admittedly is cute, like she's a flawless diamond."

"Goner," Saxon agreed.

Vander snorted. "You took forever to admit that you were in love with our sister. At least Easton's moving faster than you."

"And you were ready to knock my teeth out when you found out about me and Gia."

Vander shrugged. "It's a brother's job to intimidate anyone who touches his sister."

Easton listened to Harlow laugh again. "I'm just glad to see her happy and relaxed. Even if it is alcohol-induced." She'd been stressed and sad all day. "She called around to all her dad's friends. No one's seen him, or if they have, they aren't talking. She thinks one guy was lying."

"Name?" Vander demanded. "I'll get Ace or Rome to look into it."

"Gregor Howard."

Vander tapped out a message on his phone.

"I just want her safe," Easton said.

"I've talked with Antoine and Rhoda," Vander said. "Both are pissed, and on the hunt for Carlson. But they also know Harlow's off-limits. Ace has some leads on the dagger."

After they'd sated themselves on breakfast, Easton had worked out in his gym, with her perched on a nearby weight bench, calling all her father's friends. He'd watched as with each call, her shoulders had slumped farther.

He'd then seduced her in the shower, before convincing her to watch a movie. They'd watched the latest Wonder Woman adventure and had a late lunch.

She'd made more calls, and spoken with her mother again, without telling Mrs. Carlson what was going on.

Then Gia and Haven had arrived. Easton had made them cocktails, and then Gia had taken over.

That led them to now, with three tipsy women.

"So, Vander needs a woman, now," Saxon said with a grin.

Vander skewered his best friend with a dark look. "Why?"

"Love, companionship—"

"Hot sex." Rhys winked.

Vander grunted. "I can get hot sex without the rest of it. It all seems like more trouble than it's worth, besides, I don't have the time."

"You just haven't found the right one," Easton said.

The three of them looked at him, but his gaze went to Harlow.

"The one who gets you at a glance, who doesn't let you get away with shit—like lying, or hiding. The one who just has to smile and it lights you up. And when she cries, you want to fucking tear the world apart. The one who sees the stains on your soul, and she still wants you. Just as you are."

The men stared at him, silent.

"Goner," Saxon finally said.

"Fuck, yeah." Vander sipped his beer.

Rhys clinked his Corona against Easton's. "Who's going to be your best man, me or Vander?"

Easton's heart contracted at the thought of marriage, then found its rhythm again. "I'll keep you posted."

"Let's dance!" Gia cried.

"Oh, God," Vander muttered.

Easton put on some music. The women kicked off their heels and claimed a space. They giggled as they danced.

"I'm heading off," Vander said. "I'm going to check out a few things on Carlson."

If anyone could find the man, it was Vander.

"Vander." Harlow appeared and threw her arms around him. "I just want—" she hiccupped "—to thank you for helping me. And looking for my dad. And shooting at bad guys for me."

Saxon and Rhys both chuckled, and Easton just smiled and shook his head.

Vander patted her back. "You're welcome."

"And to tell you I love you. I love *everybody.*" She threw an arm in the air.

Vander stopped her from losing her balance. "You're going to have a wicked hangover tomorrow."

"I'm feeling *way* too good for hangovers. Wow, you sure are pretty. *Gia*, your brother is pretty."

"Which one?" Gia cried.

Harlow blinked. "All of them. Except Vander is a bit scary. Rhys is too hot."

Vander spun her into Easton's arms.

She smiled up at Easton. "Oh, but this one is *juuu-uust* right."

"Come on, Goldilocks," Easton said. "Time for a gallon of water, then bed."

"I really like this one," she whispered.

Easton felt those words deep in his gut.

Saxon and Rhys rounded up their tipsy women. The

trio shared hugs and kisses and several "I love you so much" declarations, until their men dragged them out, laughter and giggling echoing behind them.

"I feel *so* good." Harlow threw both arms out and tilted sideways.

Easton swung her into his arms. "Hold onto that feeling, because you won't tomorrow."

"I love your sister and Haven."

"I'm pretty sure they love you back."

He hitched her up and walked into the elevator and pressed the button.

"I love Saxon, Rhys, and Vander."

"They'll be thrilled."

"And I love martinis!"

"I noticed." With a grunt, he maneuvered her out and down the hall to his bedroom.

Her fingers stroked his cheek and he met her slightly unfocused eyes. "And I'm totally falling in love with you."

Easton found himself speechless. *Fuck.* So many emotions ran through him in a wild tangle.

"It's sort of freaking me out." Her voice lowered. "But *shh*, it's a secret. Don't tell Easton."

"Shit, Harlow, what the hell am I going to do with you?"

She blinked sleepily and snuggled into him. "Keep expecting you to leave. To finally have enough of my mess and get free." Her voice lowered. "To leave me all alone to deal with it."

As everyone else in her life was prone to doing.

"Not gonna happen, sweetheart." He set her on the

bed and she flopped backward. He reached behind her, unzipped her dress, and pulled it off.

When he saw the aquamarine teddy made of silk and lace, he groaned. His cock was hard in an instant. She was so fucking gorgeous, and right now, totally off-limits.

"Wore this for you," she murmured.

"Thanks." She was killing him.

"Easton?" She sat up.

"Yeah?"

"I think I'm going to puke."

Shit. "Come on, baby." He lifted her again. "I've got you."

CHAPTER SIXTEEN

Harlow leaned back in the warm, bubbly water, trying not to think of anything.

She tried to enjoy the nighttime view of San Francisco and the bay. She was sitting in Easton's kickass hot tub on his terrace.

It wasn't some cheap tub. No, it was actually built into the terrace and lined with gorgeous blue tiles.

Suddenly, he strode out onto the terrace and she sank lower in the heavenly water. Gia hadn't packed all of Harlow's clothes, after all. Harlow didn't have any swimwear here, so she was naked.

She watched Easton stride toward her. God, he was gorgeous. He was in another pair of jeans today—these ones well-worn. They fit him like a dream, and he wore a loose, button-up shirt untucked, in a soft gray.

She sank even lower in the water. She was still feeling totally embarrassed that she'd drunk way too much the night before. She couldn't remember the last time she'd done that.

There was a clicking sound as Easton set a glass of something down on the edge of the hot tub.

"What's that?" she asked. "It had better not be alcoholic." Her stomach protested at the thought.

He sat on the edge of the tub. "Sparkling water with a squeeze of lemon."

Harlow eyed him in the darkness and took a sip. "I'm so sorry for getting drunk last night."

She'd woken up in agony. Her head had been trying to split itself open, and Easton had poured water and aspirin into her, then let her sleep until lunchtime. Then he'd bullied her out of bed and made her eat something.

She'd spent Sunday afternoon curled on his couch, calling more of her dad's friends, and calling some a second time. She was certain his good golf buddy, Gregor, was covering for him.

While she'd done that, Easton had done some work.

"You have nothing to be sorry for," he said. "Last night was supposed to be a chance for you to have fun, relax."

A damp strand of her hair had escaped the messy bun she'd piled on top of her head. She stuck it back up. "Being around someone that drunk is no fun."

His lips twitched. "You're a cute drunk."

"Those two words do not go together, Easton."

"You have a really cute snort laugh."

With a moan, she sank deeper in the water.

"And you're a sexy dancer," he continued.

"You aren't helping." She grimaced. "What else did I do?"

"You declared your undying love for everybody."

Oh, no.

"You even hugged Vander."

She closed her eyes. "I'm never drinking again."

Easton laughed, a low, sexy chuckle.

"You didn't mention the fact that I vomited in your toilet in your beautiful bathroom." Embarrassment was alive in her belly. "Thankfully, I only have hazy memories of that."

"I held back your hair."

With a massive groan, she dunked her head under the water.

Easton pulled her up, towing her to the side so their faces were inches apart.

"Harlow, you needed last night to let loose. I didn't mind taking care of you. I liked it."

"You liked me puking on you?"

"You didn't puke *on* me. Your aim was great, so you didn't get any on me."

She'd puked in front of her sexy, handsome billionaire boss turned lover. *Ugh.*

He stroked her nose. "You know what I liked?"

"What?" she whispered.

"That you, a strong, organized woman who keeps tight control on everything, trusted me enough to let your hair down. Trusted me to look after you."

God. Her heart squeezed. She had a shining moment of clarity and realized that she was falling in love with him.

This was a *disaster*.

Easton Norcross didn't keep women. He'd been linked to tons of beautiful, accomplished women. Eventually, her time would be up, and he'd totally and utterly break her heart.

"Come out of the tub. I'm going to feed you."

Well, for now, he was hers. She was holding onto him for as long as she had him.

"I should call a few more people. I want to try Gregor again. He's not answering my calls now."

Easton held out a towel. She rose quickly and he wrapped it around her.

"No calls."

"Easton—"

"We're having a light dinner, then early to bed."

She huffed out a breath. "I'm not a little girl."

"Oh, I'm well aware of that." His hand curved around her hip and he pressed a kiss to her forehead. "Later, in bed, I'm going to do some very adult things to you."

Everything inside her quivered. "My father—"

"There is nothing we can do tonight, baby. I gave Gregor's name to Vander. He'll find out if the man is hiding your father, or knows where he is." Easton urged her inside.

Out of the warm water, the cold air assaulted her wet skin.

"Dinner, bed, followed by slow, lazy sex, then sleep."

She spun to face him. "Are you even real?"

"Standing right here, baby."

She went up on her toes and kissed him.

Easton was a man of his word. He followed through with his light dinner of shrimp linguine with a white wine sauce that was delicious. In bed, he covered her with that hard body and proceeded to make love to her. Slow, deliberate, sexy—he rocked her world and they'd come together.

She'd slept tangled up in his arms.

Now it was Monday, and she was at her desk at Norcross Inc. Her hangover was thankfully a bad memory. She was trying not to be freaked out by the fact that they'd gotten ready for work together this morning like an old married couple. They'd showered together—which had included quick, thorough sex against the tiles. He'd cooked breakfast while she'd made the coffee. She'd made sure he didn't forget a file that he needed for a meeting, and he'd given his firm opinion on what shoes she should wear with her slimline black pants and white shirt.

She shook her head and focused on her computer. Easton was already on a video call to New York with Zane Roth. They were working on a joint deal together.

Harlow plowed through a load work. Easton told her that Vander had some good leads and would check in later.

"Harlow Maree!"

The female voice shouted across the office and made Harlow's head whip up. She saw other people staring.

A petite woman was descending on her.

Her sister.

They were night and day. Scarlett had been conceived via IVF, using a donor egg. She had ruler-straight, black hair, some Asian ancestry, and their father's blue-green eyes like Harlow.

While Harlow was tall and blonde, Scarlett was small and dark-haired.

Harlow rose. "Scarlett, this is my workplace. You can't come in here and yell."

"I can when you've been *lying* to me, and helping to cover up Dad's fuck-ups."

"*Scarlett.*" Harlow grabbed her sister's arm. "Keep it *down*."

"So, were you ever going to tell me that Dad is in debt to his eyeballs, and dragged you into his disaster? Like always, he'd expect you to fix everything."

"I wanted to keep you safe—"

"I'm *not* a child. Is it true some goons tried to kidnap you?"

"How do you know about this?"

"I called Dad and made him spill his guts."

"Wait, he answered his phone?"

"Don't deflect, fib, or tell me not to worry my pretty little head, Harlow."

"What's going on?"

Easton's deep voice came from behind Harlow. He rested a hand on her shoulder.

Scarlett's eyes went wide, her mouth dropping open.

"Easton, this is my sister, Scarlett. Scarlett, my boss, Easton Norcross."

Her sister's gaze dropped to Easton's hand, her eyes narrowing. "You have a hot, famous billionaire boss? I thought you worked for Meredith?"

Harlow sighed. "This is a temporary assignment."

"And now you're sleeping with him?" Scarlett whisper-yelled.

"Scarlett, this is my workplace!"

"You want to talk about professional workplace behavior right now, when it's very clear there is something going on between you and Mr. Tall, Dark, Handsome, and Insanely Wealthy?"

Harlow grabbed her sister's arm and dragged her into Easton's office.

He followed and closed the door behind them.

"Scarlett spoke with Dad," Harlow told him.

"Ah," Easton said. "I told you, you should've told her."

Harlow shot him a look. "No one likes a know-it-all."

He smiled.

Scarlett blinked. "Oh, well, I totally get it, Harlow."

Harlow sighed. "He cooks, too."

Her sister got a dreamy look on her face.

Harlow cleared her throat. "We need to talk about Dad—"

The door opened and Vander strode in. "Hey."

Easton lifted a hand.

"Morning," Harlow said. "Uh, sorry about proclaiming my undying love for you the other night."

Vander's lips twitched. "You were cute."

Her sister made a sound. "Are you collecting hot guys, Harlow? And you somehow failed to mention this to me?"

She shot her sister a look. "Scarlett, this is Vander Norcross, Easton's brother. Vander, my sister, Scarlett."

Vander nodded.

Scarlett dropped into a chair, a hand to her chest. "Hi."

Then Vander's face hardened. "I have bad news."

Harlow stiffened. She couldn't breathe. Easton slid an arm around her.

"Things are heating up. I haven't found your father, but Rhoda is done being patient. That also means that Antoine has stepped up his game to find your father. If we don't find him first..."

Scarlett gasped.

Harlow closed her eyes and leaned into Easton. *Oh, God.*

EASTON SAT HARLOW IN A CHAIR. She looked shaky, but her chin lifted. Facing her problems head on.

Scarlett looked pale and pissed.

"Rhoda knows we're looking for Carlson and the dagger, but she has a reputation to keep," Vander said.

Easton nodded. "If she comes across soft, others who owe her money will step out of line."

Vander lifted his chin. "She's already had a couple of people pushing the boundaries."

"God, I'm going to kill Dad." Scarlett's voice was shaky.

"Rhoda wants your father, dead or alive," Vander said.

With a cry, the sisters grabbed each other, hugging each other tight.

"And Antoine doesn't want to lose out here. He's put more men on the street to find your father, too."

"Fuck." Easton gripped Harlow's shoulder. "It'll be a war."

Harlow reached up and grabbed his hand tightly.

"And that means Carlson's family could be targets," Vander said. "A way to draw him out. They know Harlow's off-limits, but they could get desperate."

"What about mom?" Harlow said. "And Scarlett?"

"I sent Rome out to watch your mom," Vander said.

"Thank you, Vander," she said shakily.

Easton and Vander shared a look. Easton nodded his thanks.

"And Scarlett?" Harlow hugged her sister.

Easton crouched in front of the pair. They didn't look alike, but they had the same eyes, and the exact same look of worry on their faces.

"I'm sending Scarlett to Gia. Saxon's house has good security, and they have spare rooms."

"Gia is Easton's sister," Harlow told Scarlett. "She's great."

Scarlett swallowed. "I'm sorry. I rushed in here thinking just about me. You always try to protect me."

"It's my job as your big sister, Lettie."

Scarlett squeezed Harlow's hand. "I'm all grown up, Low. You don't have to be the one shouldering everything all the time. But I never dreamed that Dad was in this much trouble."

Harlow nodded and bit her lip.

Scarlett met Easton's gaze, assessing for a second, before she looked back at Harlow. "I'm glad you have people helping you."

"We're going to keep you safe," Easton said. "And Harlow is staying with me."

"Really?" Scarlett drawled.

Harlow elbowed her sister. "I need you to stay safe. Let Easton and Vander find Dad."

"As long as you're safe, too."

The sisters hugged each other.

"I'll call Gia and Saxon," Vander said. "Give them a heads-up. I can take Scarlett over to their place." He glanced at Harlow's sister. "Only problem is that I'm on my bike."

"Bike?" Scarlett breathed. "Like a motorbike?"

A faint smile crossed Vander's lips. "Yeah."

Scarlett jumped up. "Take me, I'm all yours."

"He's too old and dangerous for you," Harlow said. "Be good."

"You have a hot guy already, so don't be greedy." She winked at Vander. "Let a girl dream a little."

Vander shook his head and opened the door. "Let's go."

After they left, Easton pulled Harlow into his arms. "It's going to be okay."

"It doesn't feel like it."

Easton nuzzled her hair. When she tilted her head back, he took her mouth.

She made a hungry sound, and wound her arms around his neck, then kissed him back.

"Mr. Norcross, I have the report—oh. *Oh.*"

Harlow jerked back like she'd been electrocuted. Easton held on to her, and looked over at a wide-eyed Gina.

The woman stared at them for a second before her gaze zipped around the room like it didn't know where to land.

"Thanks, Gina," he said calmly. "Leave the report on my desk."

The woman did as requested, and hurried out.

"Harlow—"

"Oh God, this will be all over the office in the next hour." She squeezed her eyes closed. "Gina is lovely, but she has no filter."

"So? I was never planning to keep our relationship hidden, like a dirty little secret."

"It's different for men. You'll be the big man tapping his assistant, all sly grins and admiration. I'll be the one sleeping her way to the top, and people will start to wonder if I'm actually any good at my job. And then I'll have to dodge sleezy passes from assholes who think I'm an easy lay."

Black anger roared through him. He tugged her up so her face was inches from his. "If *anyone* says, or does, anything inappropriate, you tell me."

"You can't fight my battles, Easton. Especially once this situation is over, Mrs. Skilton returns as your assistant, and I'm out of your life—"

He growled. He wanted to shake her. "You planning to scrape me off already?"

Her eyes widened. "What?" She shook her head. "I know you...you don't keep women around."

Fuck, this pissed him off. "I think you're keeping a wall up between us, Harlow. You're too scared to trust me. You're determined to take care of everything yourself, and not share with anyone."

She pulled away. "With everything going on, I'm doing my best, Easton."

"Let me in, Harlow." Frustration made his voice sharp.

She stared at him, swallowed. "I have. As much as I can."

"Actually lean on me," he said.

"Easton—"

His phone rang.

She straightened. "That's your next video call with Horizon Tech."

"I don't give a fuck."

She headed for the door. "We'll...talk later."

"Running away, sweetheart?"

She lifted her chin. "I'll be right outside."

He watched her go, then slammed his palm down on the desk.

He was fucking falling in love with Harlow Carlson, yet she felt like water in his hands. He couldn't get a good grip.

And he was afraid that once she was safe, she'd disappear.

He reached for the phone.

Well, there was one thing he was good at, it was closing a deal. He'd get her where he wanted her.

Where he needed her.

The rest of the day was a blur of work. Harlow made an effort to avoid him. His lunch appeared on his desk while he was in the restroom. And she only brought reports in when he was busy talking on calls.

Every time he went to her desk, she had to take a call, or pop over to talk with a colleague.

Late in the afternoon, Vander called. "Got a lead on Carlson. Gregor Howard has been helping him out."

"Bring him in, Vander."

"Yeah. I have to dodge Armand and Pierce's goons while I'm doing it. Those two have made it a contest to bring Carlson in first."

Shit. "Scarlett?"

"She and Gia are as thick as thieves. Scarlett has announced that she may never move out of Saxon's gorgeous house, that Saxon is mighty fine, and if we have a hot guy for her, she's ready and willing." Vander's voice was dry and amused.

Easton's lips twitched. "Okay."

"How's Harlow holding up?"

Easton squeezed on the phone harder with his fingers. "On the surface she's acting fine, but she's stressed and scared."

"You'll get her through this."

"If she ever truly lets me in. She thinks that when this is over, I'll be done with her."

Vander was silent for a moment. "Well, she has no evidence to make her believe otherwise. You've dated, but you've never kept a woman long."

"Because none of them were her."

"She know that?"

"I moved her into my place, I'm helping her every way I can, I introduced her to Dad and Ma—"

"Easton, I think it takes more than that. You have to tell her what she means to you."

"How the hell did you get good at giving relationship advice?"

"I'm a private investigator. I watch, I gather intel...all so I can avoid this particular trap."

Easton laughed. "The tougher they are, the harder they crash and burn."

Vander grunted. "Not me."

Easton hoped his brother met someone who cracked through that tough shell of his. Someone who gave him hell, because Vander thrived on a challenge, but who gave him peace, as well. If anyone had seen and done too much, it was Vander.

"Thanks, Vander. Let me know as soon as you find Carlson."

"Will do, bro."

Easton glanced out the window and saw the sun was setting. It was time to go home. He realized he'd usually stay at least another hour, but he was excited to go home with Harlow.

He grabbed his jacket and strode out of his office.

She was sitting at her desk, looking so fucking beautiful.

"Let's go home."

She spun. "Keep your voice down. People might think you mean together."

He looked at the ceiling. "I do mean together." He did understand her concerns, even if he didn't like them. But he wasn't hiding how he felt for her for long. "Fine. Can I give you a ride home, Harlow?"

"Sure." She packed her gear and grabbed her handbag.

In the elevator, she stood with two feet between them.

The doors closed.

"Vander has a lead on your father."

She released a breath. "That's good."

Easton wanted to reach for her but curled his fingers into his palms. "Let's get home. You need a glass of wine, and I'm going to make risotto."

She turned toward him. "You're angry with me. About not wanting people to know that we're...that I'm..."

"Living with me? Sleeping with me? Having sex with me?" *Mine.*

She nodded.

"I do understand not wanting people gossiping about you, Harlow. And I'm actually aware that I'm the man in charge, and that gives me a lot of power. I just...hate that you want to hide it."

Her face changed, then she moved to him and wrapped her arms around him. "Let's go home."

He smiled. Just having her close helped. "Can I kiss you?"

"Yes," she murmured.

He kissed her until they reached the parking garage. He helped her into the Aston, and soon, he was pulling out onto the street.

They hadn't gone far when he stiffened. "You buckled in?"

She frowned. "Of course, why?"

He glanced in the rearview mirror. "We're being followed."

She stiffened. "What do we do?"

"We lose them. Hang on." He accelerated and yanked the wheel.

Harlow cried out, and the tires screeched. The Aston Martin shot down a side street.

Behind them, a dark SUV sped up, cutting through traffic and setting horns honking.

Easton thrust his foot on the accelerator.

CHAPTER SEVENTEEN

Harlow pressed her palm flat to the door as Easton threw the car into another hard turn.

Her throat tightened, a scream struggling to break free.

Easton's face was hard and focused. He weaved them around another car.

"No one is crazy enough to come after you," she cried.

"Someone's crazy, or desperate."

She looked back through the rear window. The big, black SUV roared closer.

Her pulse skittered. This was all her fault. She should never have dragged Easton into this. He could crash his gazillion-dollar car, he could get hurt, or worse.

Her chest locked. The thought of Easton hurt was inconceivable.

The car ahead of them slowed, its brake lights glowing red in the darkness.

Easton slammed on his brakes. She looked back, and saw the SUV bearing down on them.

"Easton!"

"Hang on." He jerked the wheel. They swerved onto the wrong side of the road.

Harlow gasped. The headlights of an oncoming car blinded her.

Then Easton whipped them around the slow car and back into their lane. Horns blared behind them.

She looked back and saw that the SUV was stuck and she grinned, but a second later, it forced the car in front of it to the side of the road. The SUV sped toward them.

"They're still coming!" Then she saw a man lean out of the SUV passenger-side window, with something in his hand. "Oh my God, they have a gun!"

"Get down," Easton growled.

She ducked down and then heard bullets ping off the car.

"Oh, my God, oh, my God." She slid lower in the seat.

Easton swerved and turned down another street. She saw him stab at the dash.

"Yeah." Vander's deep voice came through the speakers.

"Got a black SUV shooting at us," Easton said.

Vander cursed. "We'll track you. I'm coming. Saxon and Rhys aren't far away, either. Hang on."

Easton turned again.

Harlow looked out the window and gasped. "Easton, cable car!"

He gunned it, speeding through the intersection, just in front of the cable car.

They raced down the hill.

Her heart was hammering like a drum. She looked back and couldn't see the SUV anymore.

She let out a shaky breath.

Suddenly, another SUV shot out a side street ahead of them.

"Look out!"

He slammed on the brakes and swerved. The Aston cut across the street and slammed into a parked car.

Harlow screamed. Metal crunched and glass shattered. There was a loud thump and she was violently thrown forward, face hitting the airbag.

Then suddenly, everything was still. Her ears were ringing, and her chest hurt where the belt had dug in. She blinked, trying to clear her head. She shoved the airbag out of her way.

"Easton?" She swallowed and turned her head.

He was slumped forward, not moving.

"Easton." Oh God, blood was running down the side of his head. The windshield was smashed, and bits of glass glinted in his black hair.

"Please, be okay." Frantically, she unclipped her belt and reached for him. Her hands were shaking. "God, Easton."

He had blood over half his face. She touched his cheek and he moaned. Relief shot through her. He was alive.

"Easton—"

Her door was yanked open. Gasping, she spun in her seat.

A man reached in, gripped her arm, and dragged her out.

"Let me go!"

He was a big guy, stone-faced, with a bald head and a thick beard. He yanked her away from the car. Fear was slick and oily inside her, and she tried to pull away from him.

With a grunt, the man smacked her in the side of her head.

She saw stars and staggered. *Jesus.* She fought to think through the pain.

Then anger hit her. Easton was hurt. These assholes had chased them and made them crash. And they'd *shot* at them.

With a cry, she kicked the man in the leg.

He cursed.

Harlow kicked again, this time aiming between his legs.

She got lucky, with perfect aim, and she felt something squish. *Ew.*

The man made a strangled sound and bent over.

Harlow backed up. The man straightened and pulled a gun from under his jacket.

She froze. *Oh, shit.* Her heartbeat was a roar in her head.

"You're coming with me, even if I have to put a bullet in you," he growled.

"Who the hell are you?" she cried.

"Shut up."

Car tires screeched nearby. She heard shouts.

Gunshots echoed through the night.

With a cry, Harlow ducked. The man threatening her shouted and clutched his chest. He crashed to the ground.

She spun.

And saw Antoine's creepy cousin, Hugo, walking toward her, gun in hand and a smirk on his face.

Fuck. She took a step back.

Hugo fired.

The bullet whizzed past her. Her chest was too tight for her to scream.

"You're mine now, pretty bird."

"Back off, asshole," a deep, male voice said.

Easton.

She turned her head. He stood on the other side of the Aston, gun in his hand, and aimed right across the roof at Hugo.

He looked terrible, with blood covering the side of his head, but he seemed steady.

"Put the gun down," Easton said.

"Fuck you, Norcross. She's coming with me."

Easton fired.

Hugo ducked and swiveled. Then he lifted his gun, aiming at Easton.

"No!" Without thinking, Harlow leaped at Hugo. The gun fired.

Everything moved like molasses. Pain seared across her arm.

"Harlow!" Easton roared.

She fell backward and hit the ground. She blinked and everything came back into focus.

She heard more gunshots. Saw people running.

Then she heard the roar of a motorcycle and saw the sleek, black bike screech in. Rhys Norcross leaped off, gun in hand.

Then Saxon and Vander sprinted into view.

Easton dropped down beside her.

"Dammit, Harlow. What the fuck were you thinking?" He pulled her coat open.

Red blood blossomed all over her white shirt, and bile rose in her throat. "That I didn't want him to shoot you. That I had to protect you."

Easton froze, staring at her for a beat.

Then his hands tore at her shirt. "Hold on. I've got you. You hold on, Harlow."

EASTON FOUGHT BACK the panic making his heart hammer against his ribs.

He tore open Harlow's shirt, conscious of Vander barking orders at the others and securing the scene.

When Easton had seen Harlow jerk and go down...

Fear tasted really bad. He was so damn terrified. He'd been in too many firefights to count with the Rangers. He'd seen so many good soldiers die from bullet wounds, bodies ripped to shreds.

He remembered trying to save a new Ranger who'd been shot in a nasty firefight in Iraq. Simon had been young, idealistic, and he'd died in Easton's arms.

Watching Harlow fall...

He got her shirt open and saw her wound. The air shuddered out of him.

"Is it...?" She swallowed. "God, how bad is it?"

"It's—"

"Tell me the truth, Easton." She grabbed his hand, squeezing her eyes closed.

"It barely nicked you." The relief made his head swim.

Her eyes popped open. "What do you mean?"

Vander appeared out of the darkness, his face tight. "She okay?" He looked down, and his body relaxed. "Barely nicked her."

Harlow sat up. "I went down. I'm bleeding everywhere. It can't be a nick."

"Baby—" Easton fought back a smile at the indignation on her face.

"It also hurts. A lot."

Vander made a noise suspiciously like a snort.

Easton pulled her close, and pressed her coat against her arm to staunch the blood flow.

"The bullet grazed your arm."

"That counts as shot, right?" she said.

"Sure." He was just damn glad she was alive. He held her tighter. "You never, *ever* jump at a man holding a gun again."

"I couldn't let him shoot you."

Fuck. He'd been shot at a lot, even taken a bullet twice, not that he'd ever tell her, but what Harlow had done for him... It undid him.

"You see a gun, you run in the opposite direction."

He tipped her face up and kissed her. "Or I'll spank your ass red."

She gasped, and damn if she didn't squirm a little.

Then she cupped the side of his face. "You're bleeding."

"Broken glass from the crash. "

"You're all right?"

"Yeah."

"My arm really does hurt," she murmured.

"I know. I'll get you to the hospital. You might need stitches."

"*No*, I don't want to go to the hospital. It's just a nick."

Now it was just a nick?

She glanced around. "I just want to go home. Be safe."

"Baby, you need to see a doctor—"

"I hate hospitals, Easton." She gripped him. "I *hate* them."

He saw the fear in her eyes.

"Baby?"

"My mom had several bad miscarriages. We spent a lot of time there. And my grandmother died in the hospital. I just don't like them."

He tugged her closer.

"At the hospital...everything's out of your control," she whispered.

"Okay, baby. It'll be all right."

"Hunt incoming," Vander said.

Easton watched as the unmarked police car pulled

up. Hunt slid out, and strode toward them. He was in jeans and a black shirt with his badge on his belt.

He eyed the wrecked Aston, then looked at the men Rhys was standing over. One of them was bleeding from a gunshot wound.

"You guys okay?" Hunt asked.

"I got shot," Harlow said.

Hunt's face hardened, his green gaze going to where Easton held the coat on her arm.

Easton ran his tongue around his teeth. "Nicked."

"A *bad* nick," she added.

"Hence why we need to go the hospital."

"No." She leaned into him. "You have a big first aid kit at home. Please." She kissed his jaw.

Shit. He was a goner.

"I'll call Ryder," Hunt said. "He isn't working tonight and he's in the city. He can be here quickly."

Ryder Morgan was Hunt's brother, who was a paramedic, and also donated his time at a free clinic in the Tenderloin.

Ryder had also been an Air Force combat medic, not to mention, Vander used him for off-the-books treatments, if any Norcross guys got banged up, and didn't, or couldn't, go to the hospital.

Easton nodded. "Thanks."

Hunt made the call. Several police cruisers screeched to a halt. Hunt directed the uniforms to deal with crowd and traffic control.

"Guys over there likely belong to Rhoda Pierce." Vander nodded at the kneeling men. "And Hugo Durant was here."

"Antoine Armand's nasty piece of work cousin?" Hunt asked.

Harlow shuddered. "He's the one who shot me. He tried to shoot Easton."

A muscle ticked in Hunt's jaw. "Now I need to know what the fuck is going on."

"Talk to Vander," Easton said. "I need to take care of Harlow." He lifted her and carried her toward a Norcross SUV. Saxon appeared and tossed a set of keys at Easton.

"Scarlett?" Harlow called out.

"She's safe," Saxon said. "How about you worry about you right now, sweetheart?"

She nodded at Saxon and then turned her head, her gaze catching on the ruined Aston. "Oh, Easton, your car."

"It's just a car."

"A really expensive car."

He opened the passenger door of the X6 and set her down.

"I can replace it." He cupped her cheek. Damn, his hand was a bit unsteady. "I can't replace you."

"I'm okay, Easton."

"I hope you've learned your lesson about attacking men with guns."

Her gaze met his, strong and steady. "I'd do it again."

He felt those words deep in his gut. "Harlow—"

"I heard someone got hit and needs patching up," a deep, gritty voice said.

Easton glanced back over his shoulder and then heard Harlow gasp.

The man standing there looked like a darker, edgier

version of Hunt. He had a long, rangy body, a lot of scruff across his hard jaw, and light-brown hair in need of a cut. He had the same green eyes as his brother. He was in black jeans, with a tight, black Henley, and a battered, tan-leather jacket. He was holding a large, black bag in one hand.

"I got shot," Harlow said.

The newcomer raised a brow.

"Nicked," Easton said.

"It's bleeding, a lot," Harlow said. "And it hurts, a lot."

The man's lips twitched. "You find yourself a little wildcat, Norcross?"

"Yep," Easton replied.

Harlow sniffed. "My name is Harlow."

"And I'm Morgan. Ryder Morgan." Ryder set the bag down, and Easton stepped aside to let him treat Harlow.

"Wow, you look like Hunt, but different." She cocked her head. "You look like Hunt decided to go undercover, or turned to the other side of the law."

Ryder's lips twitched. "You are a sassy one."

Easton crossed his arms. "She has no problem telling people what she thinks. Even her boss."

Ryder raised a dark brow. "You work for him?"

"Temporarily."

"I want to know, does he ever sleep?"

Her cheeks pinkened. "Yes."

Ryder laughed. "Well, Harlow, I can assure you that I pay all my taxes, and I'm a law-abiding citizen."

Easton snorted.

Ryder grinned and snapped on some gloves. "Hey,

skirting around in the gray doesn't make me a criminal." He reached for Harlow's arm. "Let's see what we've got." He looked at her shoulder, pulling her shirt down to bare her bicep. "Nick."

Harlow rolled her eyes.

"It's pretty bad as far as nicks go." Ryder was still grinning. "It might need a couple of stitches."

He started cleaning the wound and Harlow winced. Easton grabbed her hand.

"Didn't you duck fast enough, Harlow?" Ryder asked.

"She didn't duck," Easton said. "She ran *at* the guy with the gun."

Ryder shook his head, putting some ointment on the crease. "Why would you do something that stupid?"

"He was going to shoot Easton."

Ryder's hands stilled. "You jumped a gunman to protect Norcross? You do know he's a former Ranger, right?"

"I don't care if he's Iron Man. He was in danger and hurt. That's all I saw."

Shit. Easton's throat was tight. He squeezed her hand and their gazes met.

"Goner," Ryder murmured under his breath. "Okay, Harlow. I'm going to numb the area, then give you a few stitches. I promise you my best work."

She dragged in a deep breath. "Okay." She squeezed Easton's fingers harder. "Don't let go."

"Never."

CHAPTER EIGHTEEN

Easton was quiet as they drove the Norcross SUV back to his place. She felt a weird vibe radiating off him.

She now had a bandage on her arm and was the proud owner of two stitches.

"You okay?" she asked.

He didn't look her way, just gave one curt nod. Ryder had given him a quick once-over as well, and proclaimed him fine, with the exception of a few small cuts on his forehead. He'd cleaned up a little, but there were still blood smears on his temple. That dark vibe seemed to swirl around him, getting denser.

Once he parked inside his garage, Harlow felt some of the tension drain out of her. She felt safe here. Easton was still quiet as they headed up in the elevator.

He turned on the lights and they walked into the kitchen. Harlow dumped her bag on the island. Her bloodstained coat was long gone, and she looked down at her white shirt. It was ruined. It looked like something from a horror movie set.

She turned, and saw Easton just standing there, staring at her.

"Easton?"

He pressed a hand to the back of his neck. "I said I'd keep you safe, and you got shot."

"Nicked. You know I'm okay."

"We were in a high-speed car chase, you got shot—"

"None of which is your fault." It was like a light bulb going off in her head. All this dark brooding was guilt. "It's Antoine's and Rhoda's fault, with a side helping of blame for my father."

She strode to Easton. He stared at the blood on her shirt.

"I need to send you away," he said. "Somewhere safe."

"*No*. I'm not leaving. I'm not the main target here. Really, I almost got you killed."

"What?" His brows drew together.

"I dragged you into this. Your car is wrecked. You've been shot at, you had to shoot at people. You should run, Easton. Far and fast."

"Hell, no."

She pressed her hands to his chest. "Then I guess we're stuck with each other."

"Which is lucky, since you love me."

Harlow's lungs stopped. A roar started in her head. "What did you say? Why would you think that?" Man, was that high and squeaky voice hers?

"You told me the other night. When you were drunk."

Oh, God. She wanted the floor to swallow her whole. "Oh. Well, drunk people say...things."

"You telling me that it isn't true?" Emotions swirled in his deep blue eyes like smoke.

She looked to the side. *Hell.* He wanted to crack her open, strip her bare.

Easton gripped her chin and forced her to meet his gaze.

"I hope it's true," he said quietly, "because I'm in love with you."

Harlow's world stopped. Her mouth dropped open and she couldn't breathe, couldn't think. She tried to talk, but no words came out.

"Oh, God," she gasped finally.

He pulled her flush to his chest. "I love you, Harlow Carlson."

"How is this even possible?" she whispered.

"Because we're perfect for each other. Because in such a short time, you've become my everything."

She felt a prick of tears, emotion alive in her chest.

"And seeing Hugo shoot at you, seeing you fall and not knowing—" His voice cracked.

She cupped his cheeks. "I'm okay. We're both okay."

"I've seen a lot of people get shot who weren't okay."

Oh, Easton. He carried such weight.

One of his hands slid into her hair. "You have to be okay."

"I'm right here, Easton." She took his hand and placed it flat against her chest. "Feel my heart beating."

Fire ignited in his eyes. His hand curled around her breast. He pulled her up on her toes and kissed her. The kiss was hard, raw. There was no finesse, his tongue thrusting into her mouth. She moaned.

One of his strong arms snaked around her, then she found herself whirled and lifted.

Harlow gasped. He carried her to the dining room table and set her down on the edge. Then his mouth was on hers—hard, demanding. So good, but with an edge. A desperate, greedy edge.

He reached down and undid her pants. He dragged them down her legs, taking her panties with them. Next, he pulled away her ruined shirt. Jaw tight, he balled it up and threw it away. Her bra followed.

She sat there naked, his gaze burning into her.

"Easton."

Intensity pumped off him. He pushed her flat on her back. His gaze locked on the white bandage on her arm. Then he bent over her and kissed it.

Oh, boy. She quivered.

His mouth traveled lower, then he tugged her nipple into his mouth.

She arched into him, her hands sliding into his hair.

"I shouldn't touch you. You're hurt."

"It's just a nick," she panted.

"I should take care of you—"

She tugged his hair until that intense blue gaze met hers. "You are. I'm not made of glass. You need this. I need this. Take what you need, Easton."

With a groan, his mouth took hers again. Harlow

kissed him with everything she had, taking, giving, wanting more.

She felt his hand between them at his belt. Then his knuckles slid between her thighs. He stroked her, sliding through her wet folds, then his hand was gone and she felt the head of his cock.

Yes. With a jerk of his hips, he thrust deep, filling her.

"Easton!" She wrapped her arms and legs around him.

He drove into her, finding a hard, unforgiving rhythm. "Take me, Harlow."

"*Yes*. You feel perfect inside me."

"Made for me. So tight. *Fuck*."

He slammed into her and she held him tighter. She heard the table scrape on the floor.

"Easton, I—" There was no time to finish. Pleasure hit her in a hot rush. With a sharp cry, she reared up and bit his neck.

He growled, his hips bucking faster, then he lodged his cock deep and groaned through his own release.

They stayed there on the table, both panting. It took a while, but finally their breathing slowed.

Harlow ran a hand down his back.

"Is your arm okay?" he asked.

"What arm?"

When he pulled her up to sit, she smiled.

That earned her the faintest tip of his lips. "You're okay."

"I told you that." She licked her lips. "You're really in love with me?"

He would never realize that it was the hardest question she'd ever asked.

"Yes, Harlow Carlson. I, Easton Norcross, am in love with you."

Her chest filled with warmth, then she blinked. "Oh no, when people ask about when we both shared our "I love yous" it can't be when we were naked on the dining room table."

He smiled and she was glad to see it. The darkness was sliding away.

"Well, you're naked," he said.

True. He was still mostly dressed.

"And really, the first time you told me that you love me was when you were drunk."

She wrinkled her nose. "Shut up."

His phone vibrated and he pulled it out. "There's someone at the front door."

"Who?"

"Ace." He tilted the phone to show an image of Ace at the front door on the security camera.

She frowned. "Why?"

"Get dressed, baby." Easton helped her off the table. "I'm heading out with Vander. Ace is going to stay with you."

She straightened. "Heading out? Why?"

Darkness licked his eyes again. He shrugged off his shirt and wrapped it around her. "Durant shot you. He hunted you. I won't let that stand."

"Easton—" Fear was like snakes in her belly.

"Go up and shower, get ready for bed. I'll let Ace in, and then get ready to go."

She grabbed his arm. "Promise me you won't get hurt." She reached up and stroked the cuts at his temple. "That you'll come back to me."

"I'll be here when you wake up, baby."

He kissed her, and it was soft with something she'd never felt before. God, was this what love felt like?

"Now, go and change," he said. "I have no desire for Ace to see you naked in only my shirt."

"You come back safely, Easton."

He lifted her hand and kissed her fingers. "I promise."

WHEN EASTON LET himself into the house, the sun was just starting to rise over the city.

He'd spent the night out with Vander. There'd been no sign of Hugo Durant, or Charles Carlson.

They'd pressed Armand pretty hard, but the man had claimed he'd cut Durant loose.

"I would never hurt Harlow, Norcross." Antoine shook his head. "Hugo crossed the line."

Easton had hated the guy even saying her name. Only the knowledge that she was safe, and tucked up in his own bed, had stopped him punching Armand.

But he had used his interrogation skills. They'd followed Durant's trail, and Easton had questioned some of his "friends." As he headed up the stairs, and he curled his hand into a fist, his newly torn knuckles stung.

He found Ace in the formal living area, laptop open, kicked back in an armchair.

"Hey," Easton said.

"Hey." Ace straightened. "Any luck?"

Easton shook his head. "Durant is a cockroach." He'd slithered into a dark hole somewhere.

"He seems pretty fixated on Harlow."

Easton's lips flattened. "He's not going to get near her."

"Sick fucks like him don't give up easily."

"Armand's cut him loose."

"Makes him even more volatile."

Easton felt his gut tighten. "Thanks for looking out for her."

"Easy job. She's sweet, funny. She was wired when you left, made me some coffee. She was worried about you. Then she crashed."

"She still asleep?"

Ace nodded, then rose. "I'll get going."

"Any sign of Carlson?"

"Narrowed down some options. We're getting closer, I can feel it. We'll bring him in soon."

Easton scraped a hand through his hair. He'd need caffeine to get through today. "I want this over, and Harlow safe."

Ace slapped his back. "Hang in there, *amigo*."

Easton let Ace out, then headed upstairs.

When he entered his bedroom, he didn't even look at the view. His gaze went straight to the woman sprawled in the center of his bed. She'd half kicked off the covers. She was on her stomach, one long leg hitched up. That drew her pajama shorts up, giving him a beautiful view of her panty-covered ass.

He swallowed a groan and sat on the edge of the bed. He reached out and stroked her thigh.

She made a cute sound and rolled over. Then she peered at him out of sleepy eyes.

"Hi," she murmured.

"Hi. You got some sleep?" *Damn.* He looked at the bandage on her arm and his gut went tight. Last night could've been much worse.

He could have lost her.

She rose up on an elbow, her blonde hair in a tangle. "I did. You didn't."

"There's a pot of coffee with my name on it somewhere."

She sat up, and stroked his stubbled jaw. "Any luck finding creepy Hugo?"

Easton shook his head. "He can't run forever." Easton slid a hand under her tank top, and cupped her breast. He thumbed her nipple. "Time to shower and get ready for work."

She licked her lips, her nipple beading. "Right. You have some important meetings today. And your charity director wants to talk to you today about the Veterans Picnic, and she wants a big masquerade charity ball this year. So brace."

"Harlow, you aren't coming into the office today."

She blinked, her sleepiness gone. "What?"

"It's too dangerous. I want you protected—"

"I'm *not* staying here doing nothing. I'll go crazy."

He cupped her shoulders. "I know. I'm taking you to the Norcross Security office. You'll be safe there. I'm sure Vander can find something for you to do."

She sighed. "When will this end?"

He slid his thumb along her cheekbone. "Soon, baby. Hang in there."

He hugged her and she held on tight.

They showered together, and ate breakfast. Exhaustion was an old companion that Easton had learned to deal with in the Rangers. But he was a little out of practice. He sucked back a second cup of coffee, then locked the fatigue down.

Harlow rushed in wearing jeans. Dark ones that hugged her body. She'd tucked them into knee-high, brown boots and she was wearing a gray sweater with a draping neckline. She looked gorgeous.

"I have something for you," he told her.

She raised a brow. "What?"

He held open a small box and saw her go still.

Harlow stared at the sapphire-and-diamond earrings. "No."

"Yes. It's just a little gift."

"I can tell that they're expensive."

Shit, he wasn't going to tell her about the matching necklace yet.

"I want you to wear something of mine."

"Easton—"

"Please. Seeing you get shot last night—"

"Nicked!"

He cupped her cheek. "Please?"

She sighed. "Oh, fine." She snatched the box.

"You are so fucking hard to give things to."

Her face softened and she lifted one earring. "They're beautiful, Easton. Thank you."

They drove to the Norcross Security office in the X6. He pulled into the garage beside a row of other SUVs.

"Will you borrow this SUV until you get a new Aston?" she asked.

"No. I have a driver coming to pick me up. And I have another car, remember? The R8."

"Oh, right." She waved a hand. "You billionaires always have a spare sports car lying around."

As they headed for the stairs, he swatted her ass. "I hear that sarcasm, Ms. Carlson."

She grinned.

He was happy to see her smiling. And he really liked seeing those pretty sapphires on her ears.

They walked into the main office. It was busy today, with several people sitting in offices, or walking through the central open space.

Harlow raised a brow. "Who are all these people?"

"Vander subcontracts on larger cases, and he has a few extra employees for specialized jobs. Like surveillance and security."

Saxon strode out of an office and spotted them. "Hi. Harlow, how are you doing?"

"Okay."

The man reached out and gave her a quick hug. "You gave us a scare."

"Well, as I've been told numerous times, it was only a nick. How's my sister? She hasn't driven you crazy yet?"

Saxon grinned, lighting up his handsome face. "She must save that for you."

Vander appeared. "I hear I have an extra employee today."

"You paying me?" Harlow asked. "Maybe you could lure me away from my current boss. He's a workaholic dragon—"

Easton tugged her so she collided with his chest and then kissed her. It took two seconds to have her melting against him. "Be good."

She nodded. "Be safe. Don't freak poor Gina out. She's terrified of you."

He kissed her again, then he met Vander's gaze over her head. His brother nodded, getting Easton's message to keep Harlow safe.

"Watch out," Easton warned his brother. "She'll have your office organized and alphabetized, if you aren't careful."

Harlow poked her tongue out. Easton felt the urge to kiss her again, and decided why the hell not? He left her breathless.

"Go make some millions," she said.

"I'll pick you up this afternoon. Remember, be good."

"Go." She shooed him out.

Easton strode out to meet his driver. He hated leaving her, and made himself drag in a deep breath. It was time to focus on work, but for the first time, he was finding that impossible.

CHAPTER NINETEEN

Harlow opened the small file room and shuddered. "You can't be serious with this?"

Vander shrugged one broad shoulder. "Most of our files are electronic. Ace has those organized."

But this small file room was overflowing with files, reports, and towering piles of paper.

Harlow pushed up her sleeves. "I'm going to get this organized."

"Have at it. Stay inside."

She saluted him.

Vander winced, swiveled, and strode off to his office at the end of the floor. It was the only one with walls. The rest of the space was divided by glass walls. She glanced around and spotted Rhys kicked back in the desk chair in one of the offices. He was focused on the large computer screen in front of him, phone pressed to his ear. God, these Norcross brothers sure were eye candy.

Harlow turned back to the file room and decided to

get to work. It would keep her busy, and keep her mind off things.

It took a few hours, not counting a quick lunch break, but she was finally done. She stood back and blew a strand of hair out of her face. Her arm was throbbing, but the end result was a neatly organized file room.

Rhys walked past and stopped. He raised a brow. "We'll never find anything."

She snorted. "Do you ever come in here?"

He grinned—and it was a sexy one. "Hell, no."

Harlow rolled her eyes. She strolled through the main area, considering heading toward the coffee machine, when her phone pinged. She saw it was a call from Easton. "Hi."

"How are you doing?" he asked.

"Fine. I just reorganized Vander's file room."

"He has a file room?"

She laughed. "A now-organized one. How's work?"

"Busy. I like it better when you're here. I think I made Gina cry."

"Easton!"

"Hang on—" she heard a muffled voice talking to him "—I have to go. Meeting."

"Okay." She paused, wondering if she should say this. "Um, love you."

He was silent for a beat. "I love you, too."

She ended the call and grinned to herself. Despite the craziness and worry, she was in love with a hot, sexy man. A protective man, who could cook. Oh, and also happened to be a billionaire.

She pressed her hands to her hips. Now, she needed

something to do. Something that wasn't reorganizing the rest of the Norcross Security office. She wanted to help find her dad and get this stressful situation sorted before someone else got hurt.

She strode down the row of offices. She peeked through one doorway and found a medical room, which was surprisingly organized. Then she stopped at another door.

There were no windows in this one, and the walls were covered in flat screens. Ace was sitting in the center at a desk, sipping a large travel mug of coffee.

"Wow, this looks like mission control at NASA," she said.

Ace flicked two fingers at her. "Nope. And I was NSA, not NASA."

He was looking outrageously handsome today. He wore a checked shirt with his sleeves rolled up. His dark hair was in a short ponytail, and she wondered what it looked like when it was down.

"You doing all right?" he asked.

"Fine. Anxious and worried, but my gunshot wound is fine."

Ace grinned at her.

"Fine, my nick. Did you get some sleep?"

"I grabbed a few hours, then came in. I'm used to it from my NSA years."

"So, you weren't a Ranger, or one of these uber-secret Ghost Ops guys?"

Ace shook his head. "Nope, but I spent many an all-nighter in the office when we had important missions."

She nodded and studied the screens. A lot of them showed traffic cameras or CCTV footage.

"What are you doing?"

"Searching for your father, and this boy." Ace tapped a keyboard and an image of a boy popped up. He looked like he was eleven or twelve, with dark hair, brown eyes, and a belligerent look on his face. He had worn clothes and a red baseball cap.

"Who's that?"

"Daniel Brewer. He stole the dagger out of your father's car."

She gasped. "A *kid* has the dagger?" *Jeez.*

"I tapped into CCTV near Fisherman's Wharf. He likes to pick pockets there, and break into cars. He's been laying low. Probably deciding how to sell the knife. He tried a couple of pawnshops, but the owners ran him off."

"And Dad?" She searched the screens for any signs of her father.

"I've narrowed it down to some properties owned by his mate, Gregor Howard."

"I *knew* Gregor was lying to me."

"He was staying in a rental property owned by Gregor. Vander searched it, but your father had already left. Vander questioned Gregor, and he said that he gave your dad access to several places. He'll turn up soon."

She swallowed. "What if Antoine or Rhoda find him first?"

Ace didn't reply.

Harlow shook her head. "It's damn hard being angry and loving someone at the same time."

"I know."

The understanding in his voice had her turning her head.

Ace sighed. "When I was younger, my kid brother tried drugs for the first time, and OD'd."

"Oh, Ace." She touched his hand.

His jaw worked. "He's alive, but he suffered brain damage. The Rodrigo I knew, my best friend, he's gone. He's in a home. I see him every week, and we all go there for birthdays and Christmas."

"I'm so sorry."

"I'm still angry at him. We always talked about how bad drugs were, and not to get involved with them. He'll never stop being my brother and I'll never stop loving him." Ace stared at his screens, lost in his own pain.

Harlow bit her lip and decided to change the subject. "Any word on my mother?"

"She's fine. Rome said she does a lot of yoga, and drinks a lot of green smoothies."

Harlow smiled. "Sounds like Mom. Wait, Rome's watching her, so is he attending the yoga retreat?" Her brain tried to imagine big, bad Rome in a downward dog, and failed.

Ace snorted. "I highly doubt it."

She stared at the screens. "Now what?"

"We wait."

Ugh. She dropped into the chair and idly swiveled it.

Ace watched her and shook his head. "You're bad at this."

"I prefer to do, to get things done."

"Chill, *querida*."

"Easy for you to say."

"Imagine that pretty dagger in your hand."

"You charming a lady with your dagger, Latin Lover?"

The female voice made Harlow swivel. A smiling young woman stood in the doorway. She was tall, long, and lean, in black jeans and a blue shirt.

She was gorgeous, with gleaming, dark-bronze skin, and black hair cut super-short and shaped against her head. She had a long, graceful neck, large, dark eyes, and lips that Harlow would kill for. She wasn't exactly beautiful, but she was striking.

"Ah, *gatinha*, give me some credit," Ace drawled.

The woman sauntered in and perched on the edge of the desk. She crossed her long legs. "I don't know, give you some tequila, and your endearments get very raunchy."

"I'm Brazilian. It's in my blood." Ace nodded his head at Harlow. "Harlow, this is Magdalena Lopez. She's like the little sister none of us ever wanted." He reached out and patted Magdalena's thigh.

The woman wasn't looking at Ace, so Harlow was pretty sure he missed the flash in her eyes. It was clear Magdalena didn't appreciate the little-sister comment, but she hid it well.

"It's Maggie. People who call me Magdalena die in their sleep. Painfully." Maggie broke into some rapid-fire Spanish.

Ace fired back, the language a little different, and the accent slightly more guttural.

Harlow assumed it was Portuguese. "You understand each other?"

"Close enough," Maggie said.

"What's *gatinha* mean?" Harlow asked.

Maggie rolled her eyes.

"It means kitty." Ace grinned. "Because this one has a thing for birds. She's our rotor head."

"Beats being a computer nerd," Maggie shot back.

Ace sure as hell didn't look like a computer nerd, and didn't seem worried by the jibe.

"Rotor head?" Harlow prompted.

"Helicopter pilot," Maggie said. "When I'm not running my drone and helicopter photography business, I fly the Norcross boys where they need to go."

Norcross boys? Harlow tried to imagine how Vander felt about being called a boy by a woman younger than him.

"Why are you here today, *gatinha*?" Ace asked.

"I needed to see Vander about maintenance for the Sikorsky. I'm on my way out." Maggie smiled at Harlow. "Don't let him charm you into seeing his dagger. He isn't choosy who he shows it to."

Ace cursed in Portuguese and Harlow smiled. "We were talking about an actual dagger. A stolen one."

"And Harlow belongs to Easton," Ace added.

Harlow scowled. "I don't *belong* to him. I'm not an object."

Ace held his hands up. "Figure of speech, *querida*."

"Easton. Hmm, good for you," Maggie drawled. "He is one long, cool drink of water."

Ace's brow creased. "He's too old for you."

"I'm twenty-six, Ace, not sixteen." Maggie jumped

off the table. "Well, good luck with the dagger. I've got to go." She waggled her eyebrows. "I have a date."

"A date?" Ace frowned. "With who?"

"A big, buff guy I met at the gym. He's a personal trainer."

Ace snorted. "What do you know about him? What's his name? I can look him up—"

"Bye, Ace. Nice to meet you, Harlow." Maggie ducked out.

Ace scowled, and to Harlow, it looked like he was watching Maggie's ass as she left.

Hmm, maybe not so sisterly after all.

They sat there quietly and Ace started tapping on the keyboard. She looked at the screens and then a second later, she spotted something.

"Ace, that's the kid. Daniel Brewer!"

Ace leaned forward and zoomed the camera in. "No ball cap."

"So? You said he works the streets, so he'd be smart and good at avoiding attention."

The boy wasn't looking directly at the camera.

"How can you be sure it's him?" Ace asked.

"The way he hunches his shoulders is the same. And he's got on the same battered running shoes."

Then the boy turned, and they had a clear view of his face. It was Daniel.

Ace cursed. "Saxon," he bellowed.

A second later Saxon appeared in the doorway. "You shouted?"

"We've got Daniel Brewer at Fisherman's Wharf."

Saxon stiffened and peered at the screen. "You sure?"

"Look," Harlow cried. "In his pocket."

There was a long, white object, sticking out of Daniel's pocket.

"What do you think, Saxon?" Ace asked.

Saxon frowned. "Could be a knife."

"I'm sure that's the dagger," Harlow interjected. "And I'll bet that's my father's handkerchief it's wrapped in."

"Okay, I'm on it." Saxon headed for the door.

Harlow leaped to her feet. This would help get Rhoda off her father's back. "Wait, I'm coming."

Saxon stared at her for a beat. "No."

He left Ace's computer room and jogged through the office.

Harlow ran to follow his long strides. She tailed him down to the garage. He slid into the Norcross SUV and she quickly jumped into the passenger seat.

"Harlow, you need to stay here. Safe."

"Daniel Brewer is just a kid. And you're a hot badass who can keep me safe."

He stared at her again.

She sighed. "I need to help, Saxon. Everyone is doing so much, and I'm a born fixer. It's killing me to just wait."

Saxon released a breath. "I'd better not regret this."

She smiled. "You won't."

CHAPTER TWENTY

Harlow tapped her finger against the door, eager to get to Fisherman's Wharf. She hoped they could find Daniel Brewer. The place was always packed with tourists.

Saxon pulled out of the parking garage, then called Vander to let them know. "Got Harlow with me. She wanted to come."

"What?"

Harlow winced. Vander's unhappy vibe came through the line, loud and clear.

"I *have* to do this, Vander. I can't just keep organizing your office. I need to help."

"Fine." A long-suffering note in his voice. "Bring her back safe."

Saxon drove to Fisherman's Wharf and found a parking spot. They strolled along the restaurants and shops, and she fought the urge to hurry.

"Relax." Saxon grabbed her hand. He pulled her

close, like they were a couple out for a stroll. "Try not to look like you're on a mission."

Harlow took a few deep breaths.

"Good," Saxon said. "You don't want to scare the kid off."

Saxon's phone pinged. "Message from Ace. Brewer's at Pier 39."

She nodded. They walked down to the crowded pier. The popular tourist attraction and shopping area was busy. Lots of tourists were heading to see the sea lions.

"There." Saxon pulled her close. "Don't turn too quickly."

She spotted the kid by a shop window. A group of tourists walked past, laughing. She watched as the boy ducked out and picked their pockets.

"Wow, he's good."

Saxon grunted.

Together, they strolled closer. She sensed Daniel move in behind them.

Saxon spun, and pushed the boy up against a railing.

"Hey!"

"It's okay." Harlow held her hands out. "We just want to talk."

"And we want the knife you stole," Saxon growled.

The kid bristled. "I didn't steal nothin'."

Harlow stepped closer, a smile pinned to her face. "Settle down."

"Who are you?" Suspicion creased his forehead.

"I'm the daughter of the man you stole the knife from. It was already stolen. Now my dad and I are in trouble."

Saxon started scowling. "He doesn't need the details."

"I've got this." She looked back at Daniel. "Can we talk?" She waved at a sub shop nearby. "We could grab something to eat."

Something flared in the boy's eyes. "I could eat. Especially with a hot babe like you."

She frowned at him. "What are you, like—" she figured boys were much like men, so she added a few years to her estimate of his age "—thirteen?"

He puffed his chest up. "Eleven."

"Too young to be calling women babes."

He grinned at her.

Shaking her head, she looked at Saxon. "You're buying, since I ran out without my purse."

Saxon raised a brow and shook his head. He held the door open and they moved into the restaurant, and found a table.

Daniel sat across from them and fidgeted, eyeing them warily.

A server bounced to a stop beside the table. "I'm Becky. What can I get you?"

"I'll have a meatball sub," Daniel said. "And fries. Chocolate shake. Large. And two cookies."

Harlow raised her eyebrows.

"Coffee. Black," Saxon said.

"Nothing for me," Harlow said.

"You sure, Blondie?" Daniel asked. "Chicken sub looks good."

She opened her mouth, then closed it. The boy looked too thin. "I'll have the chicken sub. Extra cheese."

The boy nodded approvingly.

"Drink?" Becky asked.

"You probably want a soda," Daniel said.

Saxon muttered under his breath.

"I'll have a soda," Harlow said. "Mountain Dew. Extra-large."

Becky bounced away.

"Give us the dagger," Saxon said.

Daniel's chin jutted at them.

Harlow pressed a hand to Saxon's arm. "Daniel, like I said, I'm in trouble."

The boy fiddled with some sugar packets from the bowl on the table. "Sucks to be in trouble."

"It sure does. It all started with my dad." She launched into her tale of woe. Their food arrived, and Daniel started mowing through his at an alarming rate while he listened.

"Armand." The boy shook his head. "Bad news."

"Tell me about it."

"Sucks that you had to have dinner with him." The boy eyed Saxon. "Bet your man was pissed."

"He was. Oh, Saxon's not my man. He works with my...man's brother." It felt so weird to call Easton her man.

Daniel grunted and sipped some shake.

She finished the story. "So, I really need the dagger."

"That's some story, Blondie." The boy eyed her untouched sub. "You going to eat that?"

She pushed it toward him and watched him tear into it.

"You can't unload the dagger," she said. "I know you tried."

His brown eyes narrowed.

"We'll pay you," she said.

Saxon made an unhappy noise.

"A thousand dollars," she said.

Saxon choked.

"It's worth more than that," Daniel said.

"Sure, but you'll never sell it. It belongs to Rhoda Pierce."

"Fuck." His nose wrinkled.

"You shouldn't curse, Daniel." She shoved her soda at him.

He eyed her and took the cup. "Two thousand."

"Done. Saxon will pay you."

Saxon cursed under his breath.

She smiled at him. "You shouldn't curse, either."

"I want my money first," Daniel said.

Saxon pulled his wallet out. "I don't carry two G around with me. I've got five hundred." He slapped a wad of cash on the table. "Consider it a down payment."

"Wow." Harlow never had cash. "Who carries cash around like that?"

"Me. When I have to pay informants, or bribe young extortionists."

Daniel leaned forward, and the money disappeared.

"The knife," Harlow said. "Then we'll go and get the rest of your money."

The boy pulled a wrapped object out of his pocket, and set it on the table.

Her heart tripped. Her father's initials were embroidered on the handkerchief. This was one step toward fixing the chaos in her life.

She flipped open the cloth and saw the jewels in the knife's hilt gleam. There were scratch marks on it, so she guessed Daniel must have tried to pry them free.

"Does your mom know you're out picking pockets?" she asked.

His chin jutted again. "She's dead."

Her chest squeezed. "Your father?"

"Never knew him. Just have a step. He's an asshole, and *no one* can make me go back to him."

The ugly look in Daniel's eyes made Harlow feel sick. She wanted to hug him.

After Saxon paid for their meal, they left the shop, the dagger tucked into the inside pocket of Saxon's jacket. They stopped at a bank, and Saxon paid the boy the rest of his money.

"Thanks, Daniel. Wait." She turned to Saxon. "Do you have a pen and paper?"

He pulled out a pen and an old receipt.

She scribbled on it. "Daniel, this is my number. And the number of my...man. You need anything, you call us. Anything at all."

The boy's stony look said he'd never call, but he took the paper and pocketed it. "Stay safe, Blondie."

"Wait," Saxon said.

Daniel froze.

"He took your watch," Saxon said dryly.

Harlow gasped. Her silver watch was gone. "Daniel!" Damn, the kid was good.

With a rueful shrug, he handed it back.

Then in a blink, he disappeared into the crowd.

Harlow felt a sharp pain under her heart. "I hate leaving him alone."

"You can't save everyone, Harlow." Saxon touched her arm. "Let's get back to the office."

HARLOW LOOKED at Ace's screens.

Surveillance work was boring with a capital *B*. Ace was tapping on his keyboard, running some sort of search.

Saxon had locked the dagger in the office safe, and told her that Vander would organize a meeting with Rhoda Pierce. The plan was to return to dagger and ask her for some time to pay back her dad's debt.

Then Saxon had dumped Harlow back with Ace. She was pretty sure he was still mad about the two thousand dollars.

She tapped her nails on the desk and glanced at the screens. One feed came from directly outside the Norcross Security office. A man hurrying down the sidewalk caught her eye.

Wait, she knew that walk.

"Oh my God, that's my dad." She shot to her feet.

Suddenly, a car screeched to a stop in the street. Harlow stiffened.

The windows opened, and a pair of gun barrels appeared.

"Dad!"

They opened fire. Her dad jerked and fell.

"No!" There were no thoughts in Harlow's head, just a wave of pure panic.

She raced for the door and heard Ace shouting. He grabbed her arm, but she slipped free, and sprinted through the office toward the front doors.

She heard more shouting behind her, but she had to get to her father.

He was shot. He was hurt.

She'd just made it through the front door when someone tackled her, and she hit the ground with a heavy weight on top of her.

"Don't move."

Vander's voice.

People ran out of the Norcross office. There was more gunfire, then the sound of a car speeding away.

Dad. Oh, *God.* "My dad."

"Stay down until it's safe," Vander growled.

"Clear." Rhys' voice.

Vander leaped off her and pulled her to her feet. "Ace, stay with her."

Ace wrapped an arm around her waist. Frantically, she peered ahead. Her father was sprawled on the pavement.

"Dad." She pushed against Ace's arm, but he was strong and held her in place.

"Just wait, *querida.*"

Vander and Rhys knelt by her father. Then Rhys rose, cell phone pressed to his ear.

"Ace." Her voice trembled.

"Hold on."

She bit her lip, tears burning her eyes. Then, with a rough jolt, she broke free and ran.

Ace's Portuguese curses echoed behind her.

Vander saw her coming and intercepted her. He caught her against his hard body.

"Vander." She met his dark gaze. "Let me help him."

Vander stared at her for a beat, then nodded.

They crouched beside her father. Together, they rolled him over, and bile rose in her throat. There was so much blood.

"Put pressure on his wounds," Vander ordered.

Vander pulled her dad's jacket off. She wadded it up and pressed it over the horrible wounds in his chest.

Harlow fought back tears. His blood was warm on her hands. "Hang on, Dad. It's going to be okay."

"Ambulance is on the way," Rhys said.

Vander touched Harlow's arm. "We're going to get him to the hospital, Harlow."

She nodded. "He's going to be okay, right?"

Vander's mouth flattened, and a sob caught in her throat.

"I'll call Easton," Vander said quietly. "Tell him to meet us at Saint Francis."

She nodded, tears spilling down her cheeks.

Then Vander gripped the back of her neck and squeezed.

She sniffed, holding on by a thread. She couldn't lose it.

"Damn glad my brother found a woman with beauty, smarts, and strength," Vander said.

She bit her lip and nodded.

It wasn't long before she heard the wail of sirens. She kept the pressure on, and then heard the paramedics talking to Vander, and the rattle of a gurney.

"Move back, Harlow," Vander said.

She swallowed. "I can't." She felt frozen, ice sliding through her veins. She was worried that if she let go, she'd lose her dad.

Vander gripped her shoulders. "Let go, babe. Let them help him."

She lifted her hands off her father. The paramedics moved in, working fast, and Vander pulled her against his chest.

"I don't want to fall apart," she said.

"Then just hold on."

"I'll get blood on your shirt."

"Won't be the first time I've had blood on me." He stroked a hand down her back. "Come on. Let's get to the hospital."

CHAPTER TWENTY-ONE

Easton stormed through the doors of the hospital waiting room. He spotted Rhys in a chair, hands dangling between his legs.

"Rhys."

His brother looked up. "Carlson's in surgery. Took two bullets to the chest."

Fuck. "Harlow?"

Rhys nodded his head toward the door. Easton covered the ground quickly and shoved it open.

Vander leaned against the wall, his arms crossed. Harlow was at a sink, scrubbing her hands.

They were covered in blood. Her gray sweater was streaked with it.

Easton's internal organs tried to rearrange themselves. He already knew it wasn't hers, but the sight of her like this was something he didn't like. At all.

Vander pushed away from the wall, squeezed Easton's shoulder, then left.

"Harlow."

Her head whipped up, meeting his gaze in the mirror above the sink. Her eyes were wide, her face pale.

He wrapped his arms around her from behind.

She leaned into him and made a hiccupping sound. "Easton, there was so much blood."

"He's in surgery, baby. He's fighting."

"I can't get the blood off."

"Here." He moved to the side and slid her hands under the water again. Soon, the water washed clear.

He pulled her sweater off, leaving her in a pretty, silver-gray bra. He grabbed a cloth off a stack of them beside the sink, and wiped away any remaining streaks of blood off her skin.

Her wounded eyes met his. "Thank you."

"I'm here, Harlow. Lean all you want."

Her chest hitched. "I'm afraid that if I do, I'll fall apart."

"So, fall apart. I'll catch the pieces."

She bit her lip, her voice a whisper. "I'm really afraid that I'll do that, and then you'll disappear."

He pulled her to him, holding her hard, and pressed his cheek to her hair. "I'm not going anywhere."

She gripped him. "I'm so afraid he'll die. I've been so mad at him..."

"You've got to have hope, baby. And he knows you love him."

Easton felt fresh tears soak his shirt. He stroked her back until he felt her drag in a shaky breath.

"Here." He lifted the sweater he'd brought with him.

"My spare sweater I keep at work."

"Vander warned me you might need it."

She pulled on the pink, scoop-neck sweater. "Thank you."

He took her hand and pulled her into the waiting room. Rhys was sprawled in a different chair. Vander was standing by the window.

"Any news?" Harlow asked.

Vander shook his head.

Easton towed Harlow to a chair. She clutched his hand like a lifeline.

The doors opened and Saxon strode in, his suit jacket flaring. He lifted his chin.

Vander strode to meet him. "You meet with Pierce?"

Saxon nodded. "But we were too late. It was Pierce's people who shot Carlson."

She squeezed Easton's fingers.

"It's done now," Saxon said. "Pierce said her quarrel with Carlson is done. As long as she has no trouble with Norcross, she's happy to get her seventy grand whenever Carlson can pay."

"One down, one to go," Vander said.

"Antoine," Harlow whispered.

Easton scowled. They still had to come to some sort of agreement with Armand. And even if he had cut Hugo loose, the man had gone underground and was likely still carrying a grudge. Easton was worried about what the man might do.

"Gia's bringing Scarlett over," Saxon said.

Moments later, the doors flung open and Scarlett raced in, Gia a step behind her. Ace trailed the women.

"Harlow!" Scarlett made a beeline for her sister.

Harlow leaped up, and the sisters engulfed each other and started crying.

Gia moved to Saxon and pressed a kiss to his lips. Then her gaze met Easton's. "Any word?"

"He's in surgery."

Gia nodded. "I'll get everyone some bad coffee."

An hour later, Easton could see that Harlow and Scarlett were barely holding it together. There was still no update on Charles Carlson. When the waiting room door opened again, he glanced up to see Rome holding it open. A slender blonde entered.

She was an older, slimmer version of Harlow.

Harlow blinked. "Mom?"

"My girls."

The woman hurried over and hugged her daughters. "Is he…? Is there any news?"

Harlow slid an arm around her mother. "Not yet. But no news is good news. Why don't you sit down?"

"No." Eleanor Carlson straightened. "I know I haven't always been the strongest, most organized person. And maybe not the most perfect mother. I know I've leaned on you too much, Harlow, but I'm not sitting down."

Mrs. Carlson lifted her chin, a move Easton had seen Harlow do too many times to count. And despite her bravado, he saw the woman's hands were clutching her handbag. She was nervous, but not backing down.

"Mr. Nash told me that your father got himself in trouble."

Harlow shot Rome a narrow look.

Mrs. Carlson touched Harlow's hand. "He didn't

give me all the details, but I want them, Harlow. I'm not hiding or burying my head in the sand. And I'm not letting your father and you take care of everything for me. Look where that's got us. Your father shot—" The woman's voice cracked.

"Okay, Mom." Harlow hugged her. "Let's sit down and I'll start at the beginning."

Easton stepped up behind Harlow and squeezed her shoulder.

Eleanor Carlson looked up at him, and blinked. "Who are you?" Her voice was breathy.

"I'm Easton Norcross."

The woman's eyes widened. "The billionaire?"

"Easton is my boss," Harlow said.

"I thought your boss was a woman called Meredith?"

"I was temporarily reassigned to Easton."

Easton felt the urge to shake her. He hated that she was hiding their relationship.

He dragged in a deep breath. His feelings weren't important right now, not while Charles Carlson's life hung in the balance.

"Easton and his family—" Harlow waved at the others "—have been keeping me safe. All of us."

Her mother's mouth dropped open.

"And I'm staying with Easton." Harlow's gaze met his. "And I'm...in love with him."

His fingers flexed on her shoulder.

"Oh." Mrs. Carlson swallowed. "And how do you feel about my daughter, Mr. Norcross?"

"Mom!"

"I've met handsome, rich men before, Harlow. They

take what they want, then discard it when they're done." The woman's gaze met his head on. Behind him, Easton heard Saxon and his brothers chuckling quietly.

Eleanor Carlson was clearly finding her spine.

"I want to know your intentions toward my daughter."

Harlow groaned.

Scarlett snickered. "Mom, did that yoga retreat include some sassiness lessons?"

"Mrs. Carlson, I'm in love with your daughter," Easton said.

Harlow's face softened, and she smiled.

"And I plan to marry her."

Harlow choked. "What?"

Eleanor smiled. "Well, that's very good to hear."

Harlow shook her head. "I... I..."

"Not right now." He cupped Harlow's jaw. "But eventually."

Harlow started breathing fast. "I...need a second."

"She's going to hyperventilate," Scarlett said.

Easton smiled. "Nothing like knocking the ever-efficient Ms. Carlson off balance."

Harlow rallied enough to elbow him. "I guess that means that one day, I'm going to have your babies."

He froze, his mind going blank. Babies? Then his brain filled with an image of Harlow, her belly swollen with their child.

"Ha, got you back," she said.

He shook his head. "Tell your mother what's been going on with your father."

When he looked up, he saw Scarlett smiling at him.

He wandered over to join Saxon, Rome, and his brothers. Saxon slapped his arm. "Welcome to the gang."

Vander looked at the ceiling and Rome shook his head.

"The whipped gang," Rome muttered.

"The regular sex with a gorgeous woman who lights up your soul gang," Rhys corrected.

Easton watched mother and daughters. Harlow used her hands as she talked.

Finally, Eleanor Carlson jumped to her feet, her hands balled into fists. "I'm going to *kill* him."

"I have no idea exactly how much he owes Antoine, but it's a lot," Harlow said.

Mrs. Carlson pressed her fingers to her temples.

Suddenly, the door opened, and an older female doctor in blue scrubs stepped out.

"Charles Carlson's family?"

Harlow whirled. "That's us."

With arms around each other, the women stood in front of the doctor. Easton stood right behind Harlow, pressing his hand to her back.

"My name is Dr. Navarro," the doctor said. "He made it through surgery."

"Thank God," Mrs. Carlson breathed.

"He'll have a challenging recovery ahead, but nothing vital was damaged. He's very lucky."

Harlow and Scarlett sobbed.

"Can we see him?" Mrs. Carlson asked.

"He's in recovery and still unconscious. Mrs. Carlson, you can pop back for a short visit. I suggest everyone else come back tomorrow when he's awake."

"Thank you, Dr. Navarro," Harlow said.

Rome jerked his chin. "I'll stay with Mrs. Carlson."

Easton nodded. "Mrs. Carlson, you're welcome to stay the night with us."

"Please call me Eleanor, Easton. And no. I'm staying here."

Easton ran a hand over Harlow's hair. She turned to him and he pulled her close.

SINCE EASTON HADN'T SLEPT the night before, it didn't surprise Harlow that she woke first the next morning.

Warmth spread through her. She got to watch him sleeping.

Her father was alive, and the knife had been returned. Her mom and her sister were safe. Right now, Harlow could just breathe, and enjoy watching her man sleep.

She was on her belly, and he was on his side, facing her, with one muscled arm a delicious, heavy weight across her lower back.

God, he was so handsome.

Not sleek and pretty. No, he was ruggedly handsome. Even in sleep, he didn't look boyish. The sharp blade of his nose, his high cheekbones, and ink-black lashes resting on his cheeks. There was so much to take in. Stubble covered his jaw, and his Italian heritage was stamped all over him.

With a happy sigh, she nestled into the pillow and

watched him. Finally, she got to see him totally relaxed. She already knew that he was bad at switching off, too busy trying to outrun the darkness of his past. She smiled. She'd help him with that. Help him learn to relax.

This amazing man was in love with her. She reached up and traced his full bottom lip. He shifted a little, his arm tightening on her.

She moved closer and ghosted her lips over his, then let her hands stroke down his pecs.

As her fingers stroked his stomach, his eyes opened.

"Good morning, Mr. Norcross," she whispered. She slipped her hand inside his boxers. She wrapped her fingers around his hardening cock.

"It's a very good morning, Ms. Carlson." His voice was rumbly with sleep.

His mouth took hers and she kissed him back, all the while stroking his cock. It hardened under her touch.

Mmm-mmm.

Easton muttered a curse. His hand pulled her closer, then it shifted and slid inside the loose leg of her shorts.

Harlow gasped.

He touched her clit, toying with it before sliding a finger deep inside her.

She moaned, and stroked his cock faster. They tormented each other, Harlow riding his hand while he thrust his hard cock into her fist.

She was coming apart at the seams, a big orgasm brewing. She *needed* him inside her. Connected to her.

She sat up and pushed him flat on his back. She straddled him and quickly shoved her pajama shorts off.

He shoved his boxers down and she positioned his cock then sank down.

"*Harlow.*" His deep voice was strangled.

She leaned forward, planting her hands on his chest. She moaned. "I love you inside me."

"So damn tight and sweet." He cupped her ass. "Move."

She did. She rode him hard and fast. She really wanted to watch him come.

His hand went between her thighs, and found her clit again. Their gazes locked.

"Love you, Harlow."

She broke. With a cry, her body was engulfed with pleasure.

A second later, Easton arched, his head pushing back into the pillow. "*Fuck.*"

His hips jerked up and she felt him coming inside her.

Harlow collapsed on his chest. She knew her tangled hair was everywhere, but she didn't have enough energy to move.

Easton wrapped his arms around her and she focused on getting her breathing under control.

"A very nice way to wake up," he murmured.

She smiled against his pec.

"You going to move?"

"Maybe." She didn't want to.

"You going to fall asleep again?" His voice was laced with amusement.

"Maybe."

He slapped her butt. "You have to get up, baby. We need to shower and get to the hospital."

She raised her head. "And you need to get to the office."

He shook his head, a lock of his dark hair falling across his forehead. "I'm not going to work. I emailed Gina last night. I'm taking the day off."

Harlow gasped. As far as she knew, Easton had never taken a day off. "How many days off have you taken, last-minute?"

He cocked his head. "Does it matter?"

"Yes."

"None."

She fisted her hands in the black silk of his hair and kissed him.

"As much as I want to roll you under me and stay in bed all day," he said, "we need to get to the hospital."

She nodded.

When they entered the hospital, Harlow's stomach twisted with nerves. What if something bad had happened? What if her father had taken a turn for the worst?

Easton pressed a hand to her lower back. "They would've called if there was a problem."

"Get out of my head," she said.

They rode the elevator to her father's ward. The smell of the hospital seeped into her senses, setting her on edge.

Yesterday, she'd been too worried and panicked to think about being in the hospital. Now that she was here, she felt eight years old again, her mother bleeding, screaming.

"Hey." Easton turned her to face him.

"Hospitals." She licked her lips. "I hate them."

He kissed her. Deep, with lots of tongue, until she was clinging to him and her panties were damp.

"Okay, now?" He had a faint smile on his face.

"Hmm, you're a good, if cocky distraction. I might need distracting again later."

He threaded their hands together. "Deal."

After a quick stop at the nurses' station, they reached her father's room. Rome was leaning against the wall outside, cradling a takeout coffee cup.

"Hey, Rome," Easton said.

The big man nodded. "Harlow, your mom's inside."

Harlow smiled. "Thanks for watching out for her." She reached the doorway and saw her mother in a chair beside the bed. Her father was propped up. He was pale, but awake.

"Mom? Dad?"

Charles Carlson's head whipped up. "Princess." He shook his head slowly. "I'm so sorry. It's not enough, I know—"

Harlow hurried to him, and kissed his cheek and grabbed his hand. "I was *so* worried about you."

"I brought this down on all of us. You bore the worst of it."

"I haven't been alone. I've had help."

Her father nodded and met Easton's gaze. "I'm grateful, Norcross."

"Dad, Easton's brother Vander found the dagger. He returned it to Rhoda Pierce."

Her father shuddered. "Thank God."

The door opened and Scarlett stormed in.

"Scarlett," her dad said.

"Dad, I am so angry at you—" Scarlett sucked back tears. "And I'm damn glad you're okay." She rushed to the bed and gently hugged him.

"Dad, we need to talk about Antoine," Harlow said.

Her father pulled in a shuddering breath. "When I get out of here, I'll take care of everything."

Harlow's stomach turned over. She'd heard this story before.

"No." She shook her head. "Dad, you've tried to fix this. You got shot, you got me shot—"

"You got shot?" her mother cried.

Her father's jaw dropped. "What?"

"Nicked. I'm fine." She looked hard at her dad. "If I've learned anything during all of this—" she glanced at Easton "—it's that you can't always do everything alone. Sometimes you need help."

Her sister straightened. "We're *all* going to help sort this out. I'm going to take out some student loans. I can pay for my own college degree."

Their father's mouth dropped open. "Sweetie—"

"No, Dad." Scarlett held up a hand. "I'm doing it."

Then their mom stepped forward. "I can cut back. No more spa retreats."

"Ella—"

"No, Charles." Her mother lifted her hand. "And I'm canceling our cruise."

Her father's chin dropped.

"And...we're selling the house," their mom declared.

Harlow gasped and her dad's head shot up.

"No," he breathed.

"Rock on, Mom." Scarlett grinned.

"It's our family home—" their dad started.

"The girls are grown. It's just you and me rattling around in that big place. It's time to downsize."

Harlow had never seen her mother so take-charge.

Her father swallowed. "It will go long way to pay the debt...but not all of it."

Harlow's stomach dropped. "How much, Dad?"

Her father swallowed.

"Charles," her mom snapped.

"Three and a half million."

Oh. God. Harlow couldn't breathe.

Her mom dropped into the chair.

Scarlett shook her head. "Wow, Dad, when you screw up, you go big."

Easton cleared his throat. "I'll pay the remainder—"

Harlow swiveled. "Absolutely *not*."

Her dad shook his head.

Easton gripped Harlow's shoulders. "Listen. A loan. We'll sort out a repayment schedule."

Harlow's father lifted his head, hope on his face.

Swallowing, Harlow shook her head. Everyone came to Easton looking for money, looking to take from him. She wasn't going to do the same thing.

"Baby, I love you," he said. "I want you safe and happy. This is a small thing for me. Let me do this."

"I'll pay you back, Norcross," Charles said.

Harlow nibbled her lip.

Easton ran a finger down her nose. "What do you say, Ms. Carlson? You going to lean on me?"

She was still torn, but she didn't want to see her family in danger anymore, or Easton getting shot at. "Okay, Mr. Norcross."

He smiled. "Good." He dropped a kiss to her lips. "I'll call Vander. Get him to set up a meet with Armand." Easton frowned. "The man took a shine to Harlow, and his crazy cousin is fixated on her."

"Hugo?" Charles scowled.

"He's probably long gone by now," Harlow said. "Let's just focus on getting a deal sorted with Antoine."

Scarlett threw her hands in the air. "Then we can have a party to celebrate. Dad's alive, and this whole mess is just about over, and Harlow is in love with a billionaire."

Easton smiled. "I have a well-stocked bar at home. I'll call Mrs. Richardson to organize food."

"Who's Mrs. Richardson?" Harlow asked.

"My housekeeper. "

"You have a housekeeper?"

"Yes. I don't clean my house myself."

Of course, he didn't. "I've never seen her."

"She comes in during the day. Oversees the cleaning crew, and stocks the fridge with food."

"Must be nice to be rich."

"Baby, just saying, you're mine now, so you're rich, too."

"Oh, God."

Behind Harlow, Scarlett laughed.

CHAPTER TWENTY-TWO

Harlow paced Easton's living area.

Everyone else was chatting. Her mom and Gia sat on the couch, deep in conversation. Men's voices were a deep rumble from the kitchen.

Pop.

She looked over, and saw that her sister had just popped the cork from a champagne bottle.

"Oh, my God," Scarlett cried. "I love *Moët & Chandon*."

"My favorite," Gia called out. "Pour me a glass."

Haven sat on the stool, Rhys beside her. Ace and Saxon were talking, beers in hand.

But Harlow was too nervous.

She couldn't believe that this was all going to be over any second now. Although until Vander and Easton returned from talking with Antoine, it wouldn't really be over. They were due back any minute.

And then she'd have to move back to her place.

Her stomach turned to knots. Easton had moved her

in to keep her safe, and now she was safe. Everything had happened between them so fast.

She had to go home, and then... Her throat tightened. What if after all the excitement, he wasn't really in love with her?

Stop it, Harlow.

She focused on the fact that her father was safe. Antoine would agree to the deal, wouldn't he?

She heard the doorbell ring.

"I'll get it," Scarlett yelled, champagne flute in hand.

"It's Rome," Ace said, looking at his phone.

Moments later, Rome joined them. Saxon tossed a beer at the man.

Harlow kept pacing. Finally, she heard the elevator.

She raced out, circling the stairwell. She met Easton's gaze.

He smiled. "It's over. Armand accepted the deal. Your father's clear, and you're safe."

It was like a weight lifted off her. She jumped on him and he caught her.

Harlow kissed him. And when she lifted her head, she saw Vander smiling at them.

"You do smile," she said.

"Sometimes." Unfortunately, it disappeared. "The only dampener on the good news is that Durant is in the wind."

Her gut clenched.

Easton's hands tightened on her. "Armand cut him loose, and the last he heard, Hugo is planning to go back to France."

Her gut loosened. "So, he's gone. You know what, I

think I need some champagne. My sister is already working her way through the bottle."

Easton patted her ass. "I have a wine cellar, remember?"

She smiled. "Thank you. Both of you. I... Things would've turned out very differently without your help."

Easton squeezed her and Vander inclined his head.

"All you have left to do is help me move back to my apartment tomorrow."

Easton froze. "What?"

"I'm outta here." Vander vanished like a ghost.

"I'm safe now." Nerves were alive and kicking inside her. She smoothed her hand over his shoulder. "I can't just stay here."

His dark brows drew together. "Why not?"

His angry tone rattled her. "Why not? Because people date for a period of time, then move in after careful consideration—"

"Is that in a fucking rulebook somewhere?"

"Easton. Everything happened at light speed. It's been crazy. I want to know that what's between us is real." She'd do anything to protect it, even if she didn't like it.

His scowl deepened and he set her on her feet. "You don't think our love is real?"

She bit her lip. "You're twisting my words—"

"I love you, and I want you in my fucking bed every night. I want—"

"Hey, guys." Scarlett appeared, Gia behind her.

"It's a party," Gia said. "Time to celebrate."

Harlow found herself dragged back into the living

room. Her gut still felt curdled, and she hated fighting with Easton like this. She desperately wanted to sort things out. She was crazy in love with him. She wanted to be with him.

She just didn't want to do anything that would jeopardize it. If they rushed things before they'd built a solid foundation, things could crumble.

She met his unhappy gaze across the room. He looked away, sipping a beer and talking with Vander.

After the party, once it was just the two of them, they'd talk. She'd seduce him out of his bad mood.

Food was spread out on the island, and she grabbed some cheese and crackers. She talked with her mom, who was so relieved that things were resolved.

It took a little while to realize that her sister was missing. Harlow frowned. When had Scarlett disappeared?

Harlow stepped out of the living area, and gripped the railing by the stairs. "Scarlett?"

She checked the powder room. No sign of her sister.

Then Harlow's phone pinged.

It was a text.

She opened it and ice slid through her veins. It was a picture of Hugo, smiling in a deranged way.

I have your pretty sister.

Front door. Now.

Tell any Norcross fucker, and I'll slit her throat instantly.

Harlow couldn't breathe. *No. No. No.*

She looked back toward the party, could hear everyone laughing and talking.

If she told Easton—

Dammit, she couldn't risk her baby sister.

But Harlow had no illusions. If she went to Hugo, he'd hurt her.

Think, Harlow.

She raced into Easton's office, and found a piece of paper and a pen. She scrawled a note.

Trying to act calm, she wandered back into the party. She opened the refrigerator, and popped the note inside, by the beers. The men were almost ready for fresh ones. They'd find the note shortly.

She'd go out, then stall Hugo until help arrived.

Not a great plan, but it was the best she could do on short notice.

She looked back. Easton was turned away from her. She drank in his handsome profile, her heart pounding so loud she was sure that he'd hear it.

Then she turned and quickly jogged down the stairs. She had no shoes on, but there was no time to go and find any.

She opened the front door.

Instantly, hands grabbed her and yanked her out of the house. Hugo pulled her roughly down the front steps.

"Where's Scarlett?" There was no sign of her sister.

Hugo grinned and pointed upward.

In a floor-to-ceiling window above, Harlow had the perfect view of her sister asleep in a huge armchair.

Oh, no. Harlow felt like a hand squeezed her lungs.

"She's inside, but now you're not." He knocked her phone out of her hand. It hit the sidewalk and he stomped on it.

Shit. Harlow jerked back. "Fuck off, Hugo."

Without warning, he slammed his fist into her face.

She cried out. The pain was horrible, nausea slamming into her. Her eyes watered.

He punched her again and everything went foggy.

Moments later, she groggily opened her eyes. She found herself in the back of an SUV.

Her pulse rocketed. *Oh, fuck.* Her shit plan had failed. Fear tasted like pond scum in her throat.

Her wrists were tied together and her face throbbed. "This isn't going to work, Hugo."

He took a corner fast, the tires screeching.

"Easton and his brothers will tear the city apart to find me." *Please, Easton. Find me.*

Hugo laughed. "*Non.* They won't. They'll run around in circles, but you won't be in the city."

The SUV braked, rocking hard. She looked out the window.

A row of yachts. They were at the San Francisco Marina.

Hugo got out, then opened her door. He dragged her out of the car. Her mouth was dry, her face hurt, and she stumbled.

He dragged her toward the walkway leading to the boats.

Harlow dragged her feet, trying to slow him down.

Suddenly, he jerked her up, his face inches from hers. She smelled onions on his breath.

"You want me to hit you again?"

"No."

"I'd like it." He smirked.

She saw in his eyes that he would enjoy it. He was sick.

He stroked his fingers down her neck. "We are going to have so much fun together, Harlow."

Her lungs locked.

Then he spun, and kept dragging her. They reached a sleek, white motorboat, named *Knot-a-Care.*

He threw her in, and she hit the floor.

Hugo untied the ropes mooring the boat, tossed them free, then strode past her to the controls. Then he gunned the engine, and the boat moved.

Oh, no. Screw this. She was diving off. She'd take her chances in the water.

She scurried to the side.

He grabbed her, a wiry arm pulling her against him.

"Oh no, little bird. My life is a fucked up mess, and it's all your fault. You have to pay."

Yeah, right. Harlow rolled her eyes. Just like a loser to blame someone else for their problems.

"I want a little revenge." Hugo's hand cupped her breast. He squeezed it cruelly.

Him touching her like that made her skin crawl.

"We're going across the Bay. We'll be far, far away from Norcross, and we can have a good time." He pinched her nipple.

Harlow bit her tongue. She wouldn't give him the satisfaction of hearing her cry out.

"You'll scream for me Harlow. I promise."

EASTON SIPPED HIS BEER, not really listening to the story Ace was sharing.

Harlow wanted to move out. His fingers squeezed on his beer bottle. She wanted to give them *time*. He didn't need time. He loved her. She loved him. She was his.

End of story.

He took another sip. She'd just been through a pressure cooker. He lowered the beer bottle. *Hell*. He had no right to make demands of her right now. They needed to talk things through.

He scanned the space for her. There was no sign of her, although she'd been in the kitchen a moment ago.

"Fuck." Vander's deep voice. His brother was standing at the open fridge.

Easton stiffened.

His brother turned, a note in his hand.

Easton strode over and snatched it. It was in Harlow's handwriting.

Hugo has Scarlett

Front door.

Hurry.

Fuck. Easton's heart stopped.

"Hey." Scarlett wandered in. "What did I miss?"

He lunged for her. "Where have you been?"

"I fell asleep on a chair in your living area. I didn't get much sleep last night." She sobered. "What's wrong?"

"Hugo has Harlow." Easton raced for the stairs.

He heard Vander, Rhys, and the others right behind him.

The front door was ajar, and he sprinted outside. His gut clenched. "No sign of her."

"Here." Rhys crouched.

A broken cell phone lay on the pavement.

Easton took it. "It's Harlow's. *Fuck*!"

"Come on." Vander jogged back inside.

They sprinted upstairs. "My office," Easton ordered.

"Ace," Vander called.

"Already on it." The tech man appeared, laptop in hand. He set it on Easton's desk.

Saxon, Rhys, and Rome stood with them.

"Where's Harlow?" Scarlett demanded.

"Gia, keep Harlow's mother and sister in the kitchen," Easton said.

His sister hesitated.

"Please. We need to find Harlow and bring her home."

With a nod, Gia herded the women back to the kitchen.

Ace pulled up Easton's security cameras.

Easton watched on screen as Harlow headed for the door.

"She thought he had her sister. Of course, she'd go out there." Easton turned her phone over in his hand, stabbing at the cracked buttons. Suddenly, it flared to life. He read the message. "The fucker threatened Scarlett if Harlow told us."

On-screen, he watched her open the door. Hugo grabbed her, then punched her.

"He's a dead man," Easton growled.

Hugo carried Harlow to a vehicle, which was partly in view on the street.

"Dark-green, Jeep Grand Cherokee," Vander said.

"I've got a partial plate," Ace clipped. "Searching, but with only a partial it might take a while."

"I'll call Hunt." Vander pulled out his cell phone.

Easton stood there, trying to get air into his lungs. Hugo was a sociopath. He had Harlow. He'd hurt her.

"Pulling up all CCTV and traffic cams in the area," Ace said.

On Ace's screen, Easton saw several smaller screens of footage. But this was like searching for a needle in a fucking haystack.

"Hold it together, bro," Rhys said.

There was understanding in Rhys' voice. Haven had been taken, and Rhys and the others had rescued her, but Rhys had struggled to deal with the terror until they had.

"Hunt's got the vehicle details." Vander lifted a hand. "It was reported stolen in Chinatown. Full plate is—" Vander called it out.

"Got it!" Ace said. "North of here. Crossing Lombard Street."

Where the fuck was Hugo taking her? "Do you think he's heading for the Golden Gate Bridge?"

"Maybe," Ace said.

Easton pressed his hands to the back of his neck. "If that bastard hurts her—"

Vander met his gaze. "We'll get her back."

"You get her to wear a tracker?" Saxon asked.

Easton shook his head. "Took me forever to get her just to accept the earrings, but not a necklace yet." He should have forced the issue. "We *have* to find her."

Then Easton's cell phone rang. He yanked it out but didn't recognize the number. He was going to ignore it, but what if Harlow had gotten free? What if she was calling him?

"What?" he barked.

There was silence. "This Blondie's man?" a young voice asked.

"Blondie?" Easton frowned. "Who is this?"

Saxon spun and waved his hand. "The kid. Brewer."

"Blondie?" Easton said. "You mean Harlow?"

"Yeah," the boy replied. "I'm out at San Francisco Marina. Jeep pulled up and Hugo Durant pulled Blondie out of the vehicle. She didn't look happy, and Durant is bad news. She gave me your number."

Easton's pulse skyrocketed. "Thanks, kid. You see where they went?"

"Yeah. On a boat called *Knot-a-Care*. With a K. Stupid name for a boat. They're pulling out now."

Shit. "Okay. You did the right thing. We'll get her." Easton looked to the others. "They're on a yacht called the *Knot-a-Care*. San Francisco Marina."

"Let's go." Vander nodded. "Ace, call Maggie."

"On it."

"Find a helipad where she can pick us up. Rome, find a boat. Follow on the water."

Rome nodded and vanished.

Vander met Easton's gaze. "You should stay here."

"Fuck that. You know I can do this."

"It's not your skills I'm worried about."

"She's mine. I'm bringing her home."

"Got a gun?"

With a nod, he moved to a cabinet behind his desk. The door swung open to reveal his gun safe. He touched his palm to the biometric lock, and pulled out his Glock 19.

Ace straightened. "Maggie will pick you just south of the Palace of Fine Arts, at the Letterman Digital Arts Center Recycled Water Pond. She also has a drone in the air. She's redirected controls to me. I'm rerouting it over the bay."

"Good. I'll get Gia to keep an eye on Mrs. Carlson and Scarlett." Vander shifted. "Let's roll."

Easton sat in the passenger seat of the X6, as Vander drove them to meet the helo. As the SUV screeched to a halt, he heard the familiar *thump-thump* of rotors.

A black Sikorsky swept in over the familiar shape of the rotunda at the Palace of Fine Arts to hover above the grass near the pond. Easton followed Vander, Rhys and Saxon behind him, as they jogged toward the helicopter.

As they leaped aboard, Easton was hit with a flashback to his Ranger missions. Except this mission was the most important one of all.

He pulled in a breath and realized his head was clear. Harlow was his focus.

Maggie was in the pilot seat, headset on. She waved and pointed. "Vests and earpieces."

Under the seat, Easton spotted a box of bulletproof vests and sleek earpieces so they could communicate.

Vander grabbed a vest and earpiece, then dropped into the seat beside Maggie.

As Easton pulled his vest on and fastened the Velcro, the helo lifted off. Moments later, they were flying out over the Bay. He slipped his earpiece in.

Vander leaned back. "Ace has the boat on drone camera. Two minutes to intercept."

Easton's jaw was rock solid as he stared out the side of the helicopter. Alcatraz Island came into view.

Then he spotted a white dot against the royal blue of the water. It got larger, and the boat took shape.

Vander slid into the back.

"Hugo will know we're coming, so expect a hostile welcome. Maggie will get into position, we'll drop ropes, and rappel down."

It was risky as fuck. They weren't fully decked out. It was a small boat. And it was certain that Hugo would be armed. He could hurt Harlow.

Vander gripped Easton's shoulder. "We'll get her."

He nodded.

They got closer and now he saw Hugo at the controls of the boat. Where was Harlow?

Then Easton spotted her on the deck, her wrists tied together.

She looked up.

At the same time, Hugo pulled a handgun.

Not going to stop us, asshole. Easton gripped the edge of the door. Time to get his woman back.

CHAPTER TWENTY-THREE

The noise of the helicopter overhead was loud.

Harlow saw Maggie in the cockpit, face focused as she swung the helicopter around.

Then Harlow saw Easton.

Her heart leaped into her throat. *He'd come for her.* Like she'd known he would. He stood in the doorway, the wind whipping his hair around his face.

Hugo moved, and when she glanced at him, she saw him pull a gun.

No!

He fired. The helicopter jerked. She saw Hugo grinning, swiveling to aim right at Easton.

No fucking way. Time slowed down, her muscles bunching. She had a split second to remember that she'd promised Easton that she wouldn't throw herself at armed men. A flash of bright orange beside her caught her eye.

There was a large life vest under the bench. She grabbed it with her bound hands, and leaped up.

She smacked the life vest into Hugo's head. He shouted, and the gun flew out of his hand.

She heard it hit something with a clatter. She swung again.

Hugo roared and grabbed at her.

They spun, the life vest trapped between them. Then they lost balance and fell.

Hugo fell first and Harlow crashed on top of him. She heard him grunt.

"You asshole." She slapped at his head.

"You bitch." He tried to buck her off, but she squeezed her thighs harder. He reared up and grabbed a handful of her hair, his face contorted.

Behind him, she saw ropes fly out of the side of the helicopter.

But Easton didn't wait for a rope. He leaped out.

She sucked in a sharp breath, watching him fall.

He landed beside them on the deck and rammed the barrel of his gun against Hugo's temple.

"Let her go."

Easton's furious words made Hugo freeze.

Vander stepped into view. "Do what he said, asshole."

Vander's icy tone sent shivers through Harlow. Damn, the man was scary.

Terror rippled across Hugo's face and his hand in her hair loosened. Suddenly, she was yanked off him, and into Easton's arms.

"Face down, Durant," Vander barked.

She heard grunts, but all she could see was Easton. His face was dark, his jaw tight.

"You got my note," she said.

"*Fuck.*" He pulled her face against his chest, his arms tight around her.

She gripped his vest awkwardly with her bound hands. "I knew you'd come."

He pulled back, his hands either side of her head. "You're *not* moving out."

"Easton—"

"No. No fucked-up shit about time and space. You sleep in *my* bed, and you stay with me."

"Okay."

He paused. "Okay?"

"Yes, Easton. I'll stay. I love you."

He yanked her close. His kiss was hard and punishing.

When they came up for air, she saw the helicopter still hovering above. Maggie grinned and waved, then the aircraft whirled away.

"Fuck!" Rhys yelled.

Harlow looked over and saw Hugo break free of Rhys' hold. From near the boat controls, Vander cursed.

Hugo charged right at Harlow, face twisted with rage.

Easton spun fast. He landed a vicious punch to Hugo's face.

The man's head snapped back.

"How's that feel, asshole?" Easton punched him again. Hugo almost tipped sideways. "That's how you hit her out in front of my place. You're a coward, terrorizing women and people weaker than you."

Oh, her man was a badass. She saw the Ranger front and center right now.

Hugo snarled. "Bitches and whores. They deserve what they get!"

Harlow grimaced. *What a waste of space.*

Easton hit him again and Hugo staggered back.

Vander stepped forward and landed a hard front kick to Hugo's gut.

He hit the edge of the boat, flipped, and then crashed into the water.

"That should cool him off," Vander said.

Hugo thrashed around in the water, spewing a stream of angry-sounding French.

A laugh escaped from Harlow, and she gripped onto Easton. She spotted a speedboat racing toward them, Rome at the wheel.

"Should we get Hugo?" she said.

"Rome will fish him out," Vander said.

Easton untied her hands, then slid his into her hair. "Are you all right?"

She nodded. "I'm right where I feel safest."

Emotion moved through his eyes.

"You're my hero, Easton Norcross."

He smiled, his gaze moving over her face like he was trying to memorize it.

"How did you find me?" she asked.

"It's all thanks to your friend, Daniel Brewer."

She gasped. "Seriously?"

"He saw Hugo drag you out of the Jeep at the marina. He called me."

"Easton, we have to help him. He's all alone, on the

streets. His mom died, and I think his stepdad hurt him—"

"Okay, okay." Easton pressed a hand over her mouth. "You just can't help but worry about everybody else."

She pushed his hand away. "Get used to it, because from now on, you're the number one person I'm going to worry about." She leaned closer. "The darkness can't have you, Easton, because you're mine."

He rubbed a thumb over her lips.

Rome brought the speedboat alongside their boat. Rhys climbed over, and together, they hauled Hugo out of the water.

Saxon took the controls of their boat and got the engine started.

They headed back to the marina, Harlow sitting pressed against Easton, the wind in her hair.

When they pulled into the marina, the lights of a police cruiser were flashing, and Hunt, in a suit, standing with his hands on his hips, was waiting for them.

Rome and Rhys marched Hugo up the ramp. He was twisting and screeching. Hunt took him, and shoved him toward the cruiser.

Harlow spotted a small form in the crowd that had gathered. She squeezed Easton's arm.

"Look." She raised her voice. "Daniel!"

The boy froze, and she could see him contemplating running.

He moved a shoulder. "Blondie, glad you're okay."

"Thanks to you." She desperately wanted to hug him, but instead, she held out her hand.

He eyed it suspiciously, then gingerly shook it.

The boy's gaze went past her, widened. "You're Easton Norcross."

Easton wrapped an arm around Harlow. "Thanks for the call, kid."

Daniel looked at Harlow. "Wait. Your man is Easton Norcross?"

"Yes."

"Nice." Then he goggled. "You're *Vander Norcross*." He breathed it the same way he might greet a movie star.

Vander raised a brow. "Yeah."

"You're like...awesome and a badass."

Vander looked amused. "Thanks for the assist in saving Harlow."

Daniel looked like he grew two inches taller. "No problem."

"Harlow!"

Harlow looked up and saw her mom and Scarlett pushing through the crowd.

She broke free of Easton and ran to them. "I'm okay."

They hugged, and her mom started crying. In one long rush, Harlow told them what happened.

"This is the young man who told Easton where you were?" Her mother eyed Daniel.

"Yes," Harlow answered.

"Young man." Eleanor reached out and hugged Daniel to her. "Thank you."

Daniel's face froze and he watched Harlow's mom like she was a ticking time bomb.

"Are you hungry?" her mom asked.

The boy lifted a shoulder. "I could eat."

"Then come with me." She grabbed his hand and led him away. Scarlett followed, shaking her head.

Harlow smiled.

"Should we go home, Ms. Carlson?" Easton asked.

"That sounds wonderful, Mr. Norcross." God, home. *Their home.* Love filled her.

EASTON FINISHED HIS CALL. Outside his office, he heard Harlow talking on the phone.

Rising, he reached the office door and leaned against the jamb. She was sitting at her desk. Her golden hair was in a neat twist, and she wore a black shirt with a deep *V* that gave him a nice view of her cleavage. He couldn't see it, but he knew she was wearing a fitted, tan skirt that had driven him crazy that morning when she'd first appeared wearing it.

He could just make out the faint bruising on her face under her makeup. It had been a week and a half since Hugo had been locked up.

"No, thank you, Mr. Kingston. Yes, I'm looking forward to seeing you when you come for your meeting with Mr. Norcross." She laughed. "You are such a charmer."

Lucky that Kingston was almost eighty, or Easton wouldn't be happy.

"Bye, now." She touched the phone. "Mr. Norcross' office." She huffed out a breath. "Mr. Nelson, I know that's you, even when you use a different voice. Mr. Norcross isn't a bank or a charity. Just because he's worked hard and is successful, he's not here as a shortcut on *your* journey. Now, goodbye." She ended the call.

Easton's heart warmed. He walked up behind her and leaned down until his lips brushed her ear.

"I really want to kiss you right now."

She shivered. "We're at work, remember?"

Always so proper. "Then I might need you to stay late for some private dictation."

She turned her head. "Whatever you need, Mr. Norcross."

"Fuck, I'm hard."

She smiled.

That. He'd give up all his millions to see that smile every day.

"Delivery for Harlow Carlson."

They both looked up. A deliveryman was obscured by an enormous bunch of red roses.

Harlow stood. "Wow. I'm Harlow." She glanced at Easton and raised a brow.

He scowled. "Not me." But tomorrow, he was ordering her flowers. Not roses. Harlow deserved something beautiful, exotic, and unique.

She pulled the card out while Easton signed for the arrangement and tipped the deliveryman.

A funny look crossed her face. "They're from Antoine."

Easton cursed.

A smile played along her lips. "Apologizing for everything, and Hugo."

"Did he mention luring your father into debt? Or his criminal activities? Or blackmailing you?"

She tugged Easton into his office and closed the door. "I'll donate the flowers to a hospital, or something." She smoothed her hands up his shirt. "Does that make you feel better?"

Easton grunted.

She kissed him, nibbling on his bottom lip. "I'm sure when you send me flowers, they'll be much more impressive."

Easton reached into his pocket and pulled out a long box. "I can do better than flowers." He flicked open the lid.

The huge, teardrop sapphire was surrounded by diamonds, hanging on the delicate chain. It matched the earrings he'd given her.

Her mouth opened.

"Say yes," he said. "I want to see this against your skin."

"How much did it cost?"

"It doesn't matter." God, it was hard to give her anything.

She sighed. "You're going to do things like this a lot, aren't you?"

He decided now wasn't the time to tell her that he'd purchased a row of old Victorian houses, hoping she'd like to renovate one of them. Or all of them.

He'd tell her later.

"If you help me learn to relax, I'll help you learn how to graciously accept a gift."

She turned, offering him her neck. "Yes, but your gifts have exorbitant price tags."

He slid the gem around and fastened the chain. As he'd known, it looked beautiful against her skin.

"Gorgeous." He spun her and kissed her.

Mmm, he'd never get enough of his lovely Ms. Carlson. He nudged her toward his desk.

"No." She groaned and looked at her watch. "We have to meet everyone at Sotto Mare for dinner. Our parents are meeting for the first time." She kissed him, then kissed him again and groaned. "We can't be late."

Damn. He was tempted to push that skirt up and set her on his desk anyway, dinner be damned.

But his mother wouldn't let him live it down.

They packed up, and Easton drove them to the Italian-style, seafood restaurant. When they arrived, his family was already there with Scarlett.

Harlow hugged her sister. Easton greeted his parents, nodded at his brothers. Saxon was there as well, Gia and Haven sipping cocktails on stools nearby. Rome, Ace, and Maggie arrived. Harlow's best friend, Christie, and her husband were there, too. They'd had them over for dinner a few days before.

"Maggie, martini?" Gia asked.

"Hell, no. Beer for me."

"Woman can drink us all under the table," Ace grumbled.

The pilot winked and headed for the bar.

"I see you convinced Harlow to wear the necklace," Saxon said.

Easton watched as Harlow laughed with Haven and her sister. "Yes."

"Bet you didn't tell her about the GPS tracker embedded in it." Saxon grinned.

"Not yet."

"Happy?" Vander swirled his drink.

"Hell, yeah. She's officially moved in. She's subletting her apartment until her lease is up." Easton smiled. He'd never felt more content than he did now. Happy for a future with Harlow in it.

He saw her turn and smile at him, before her gaze shifted past him.

Easton glanced back and saw Eleanor leading Charles slowly across the restaurant. A young boy walked with them.

"Where's the food?" Daniel asked.

Harlow held out a plate of oysters and cracked crab. The boy wrinkled his nose, then shrugged. He took an oyster, then took a second one.

He was wearing new jeans and a shirt, his hair brushed neatly.

Mrs. Carlson had been busy. She'd pulled lots of strings, and become a temporary foster parent for the boy.

"Easton." Charles nodded.

The man was still pale, but doing well. His wife was bullying him into rest and rehab.

"Charles."

"Harlow, that necklace is *stunning*." Eleanor kissed her daughter's cheek.

"Thanks, Mom. Dad, how are you feeling?" Harlow hugged him.

"Like I got shot."

"Sit." She helped him into a chair. "Now, I want you to meet Easton's parents."

Introductions were made. Easton's mom and Harlow's gushed.

"The Realtor came by today," Eleanor told everyone. "We're having an open house this weekend. He's already had a lot of solid interest."

"Good crib," Daniel mumbled around a mouthful of crab. "Should get a good price."

Easton smothered a smile, and saw Saxon roll his eyes.

"Vander," Daniel said. "I wanted to talk to you. About coming to work for you."

To his credit, Vander kept a straight face. "Finish school, kid. Then we'll talk."

The boy's chest puffed up. "Deal."

Vander's cell phone rang. "I've got to take this." He pressed the phone to his ear and stepped away.

Harlow pressed into Easton. She sighed.

"Good?" he asked.

She nodded. "Look."

Their mothers were talking, his mother's hands waving as she talked.

"You realize that they're probably planning our wedding," he said.

"*I'll* be planning our wedding."

"Will you?" He tilted his head. "You proposing?"

"No." She leaned in. "I expect my hot, billionaire boyfriend to propose in style."

He smiled. "Noted."

Vander reappeared. "Rome, got a new job for you."

Rome lowered his beer. "When?"

"In two days, Princess Sofia of Caldova is arriving. You're her new bodyguard."

"My God, I've seen her in magazines," Harlow exclaimed. "She's gorgeous. The perfect princess. Slender, elegant, strawberry-blonde hair. Cheekbones I'd sell my soul for."

Rome's face went blank. "Great."

He didn't sound very enthused.

Vander raised a brow. "Rome's met her. He was her bodyguard in New York a few months ago."

"Oh, wow," Harlow said. "Does she live up to her nickname? The Ice Princess? They say she's haughty, proper, and has been linked to a bunch of princes and dukes all over Europe. She's been engaged three times."

Rome sucked back some beer. "She's very...royal."

Easton narrowed his gaze. There was something in Rome's eyes... It made Easton wonder just what Princess Sofia was like.

"Rome and the Princess." Harlow clapped her hands together. "I can't wait to see this."

"Live it up," Rome rumbled.

Eventually, their group moved to the table. Everyone was eating, talking, and laughing.

Easton smiled, his chest feeling full. There was no darkness here.

Harlow leaned into him. "What are you thinking?"

"That I'm fucking happy." He gripped her jaw. "That everything I did was worth it because I earned you as my reward."

"Easton." Emotion was alive in her eyes. "I love you,

just as you are, with everything you've done, and everything you'll ever do."

"I know. I love you, too."

She leaned closer, and he felt one of her hands slide under the table, and down his abs. His body responded and he gritted his teeth. *Hell.*

"So, how long until we can go home, Mr. Norcross?"

An image of her flashed in his head. Of her on their bed, naked except for that sapphire nestled between her breasts.

"Whenever you want, Ms. Carlson. I'll give you everything you want. Always."

"I only need your love."

And she'd have it, every minute of every day.

I hope you enjoyed Easton and Harlow's story!

There are more Norcross stories on the way. Stay tuned for **THE BODYGUARD** starring Rome Nash, coming next month on the 27th of April.

If you'd like more action-packed romance check out the

covert allies of Norcross Security, **Team 52**, and read on for a preview of the first Team 52 book, ***Mission: Her Protection***.

Don't miss out! For updates about new releases, free books, and other fun stuff, sign up for my VIP mailing list and get your *free box set* containing three action-packed romances.

Visit here to get started: www.annahackett.com

Would you like a FREE BOX SET of my books?

PREVIEW - MISSION: HER PROTECTION

It was a beautiful day—ten below zero, and ice as far as the eye could see.

Dr. Rowan Schafer tugged at the fur-lined hood of her arctic parka, and stared across the unforgiving landscape of Ellesmere Island, the northernmost island in Canada. The Arctic Circle lay about fifteen hundred miles to the south, and large portions of the island were covered with glaciers and ice.

Rowan breathed in the fresh, frigid air. There was nowhere else she wanted to be.

Hefting her small pickaxe, she stepped closer to the wall of glacial ice in front of her. The retreating Gilman Glacier was proving a fascinating location. Her multi-disciplinary team of hydrologists, glaciologists, geophysicists, botanists, and climate scientists were more than happy to brave the cold for the chance to carry out their varied research projects. She began to chip away at the ice once more, searching for any interesting samples.

"Rowan."

She spun and saw one of the members of her team headed her way. Dr. Isabel Silva's parka was red like the rest of the team's, but she wore a woolen hat in a shocking shade of pink over her black hair. Originally from Brazil, Rowan knew the paleobotanist disliked the cold.

"What's the latest, Isabel?" Rowan asked.

"The sled on the snowmobile is almost full of samples." The woman waved her hand in the air, like she always did when she was talking. "You should have seen the moss and lichen samples I pulled. There were loads of them in area 3-41. I can't *wait* to get started on the tests." She shivered. "And be out of this blasted cold."

Rowan suppressed a smile. *Scientists.* She had her own degrees in hydrology and biology, with a minor in paleontology that had shocked her very academic parents. But on this expedition, she was here as leader to keep her team of fourteen fed, clothed, and alive.

"Okay, well, you and Dr. Fournier can run the samples back to base, and then come back to collect me and Dr. Jensen."

Isabel broke into a smile. "You know Lars has a crush on you."

Dr. Lars Jensen was a brilliant, young geophysicist. And yes, Rowan hadn't missed his not-so-subtle attempts to ask her out.

"I'm not here looking for dates."

"But he's kind of cute." Isabel grinned and winked. "In a nerdy kind of way."

Rowan's mouth firmed. Lars was also several years younger than her and, while sweet, didn't interest her in that way. Besides, she'd had enough of people trying to set her up. Her mother was always trying to push various *appropriate* men on Rowan—men with the right credentials, the right degrees, and the right tenured positions. Neither of her parents cared about love or passion; they just cared about how many dissertations and doctorates people collected. Their daughter included.

She dragged in a breath. That was why she'd applied for this expedition—for a chance to get away, a chance for some adventure. "Finish with the samples, Isabel, then—"

Shouts from farther down the glacier had both women spinning. The two other scientists, their red coats bright against the white ice, were waving their arms.

"Wonder what they've found?" Rowan started down the ice.

Isabel followed. "Probably the remains of a mammoth or a mastodon. The weirdest things turn these guys on."

Careful not to move too fast on the slippery surface, Rowan and Isabel reached the men.

"Dr. Schafer, you have to see this." Lars' blue eyes were bright, his nose red from the cold.

She crouched beside Dr. Marc Fournier. "What have you got?"

The older hydrologist scratched carefully at the ice with his pickaxe. "I have no idea." His voice lilted with his French accent.

Rowan studied the discovery. Suspended in the ice, the circular object was about the size of her palm. It was dull-gray in color, and just the edge of it was protruding through the ice, thanks to the warming temperatures that were causing the glacier to retreat.

She touched the end of it with her gloved hand. It was firm, but smooth. "It's not wood, or plant life."

"Maybe stone?" Marc tapped it gently with the axe and it made a metallic echo.

Rowan blinked. "It can't be metal."

"The ice here is about five thousand years old," Lars breathed.

Rowan stood. "Let's get it out."

With her arms crossed, she watched the scientists carefully work the ice away from the object. She knew that several thousand years ago, the fjords of the Hazen Plateau were populated by the mysterious and not-well understood Pre-Dorset and Dorset cultures. They'd made their homes in the Arctic, hunted and used simple tools. The Dorset disappeared when the Thule—ancestors to the Inuit—arrived, much later. Even the Viking Norse had once had communities on Ellesmere and neighboring Greenland.

Most of those former settlements had been near the coast. Scanning the ice around them, she thought it unlikely that there would have been settlements up here.

And certainly not settlements that worked metal. The early people who'd made their home on Ellesmere hunted sea mammals like seals or land mammals like caribou.

Still, she was a scientist, and she knew better than to make assumptions without first gathering all the facts. Her drill team, who were farther up on the ice, were extracting ice core samples. Their studies were showing that roughly five thousand years ago, temperatures here were warmer than they were today. That meant the ice and glaciers on the island would have retreated then as well, and perhaps people had made their homes farther north than previously thought.

Marc pulled the object free with careful movements. It was still coated in a thin layer of ice.

"Are those markings?" Isabel breathed.

They sure looked like it. Rowan studied the scratches carved into the surface of the object. They looked like they could be some sort of writing or glyphs, but if that was the case, they were like nothing she'd ever seen before.

Lars frowned. "I don't know. They could just be natural scoring, or erosion grooves."

Rowan pushed a few errant strands of her dark-red hair off her face. "Since none of us are archeologists, we're going to need an expert to take a look at it."

"It's probably five thousand years old," Isabel added. "If it is man-made, with writing on it, it'll blow all accepted historical theories out of the water."

"Let's not get ahead of ourselves," Rowan said calmly. "It needs to be examined first. It could be natural."

"Or alien," Lars added.

As one, they swiveled to look at the younger man.

He shrugged, his cheeks turning red. "Just saying. Odds are that we aren't alone in this universe. If—"

"Enough." Rowan straightened, knowing once Lars got started on a subject, it was hard to get him to stop. "Pack it up, get it back to base, and store it with the rest of the samples. I'll make some calls." It killed her to put it aside, but this mystery object wasn't their top priority. They had frozen plant and seed samples, and ice samples, that they needed to get back to their research labs.

Every curious instinct inside Rowan was singing, wanting to solve the mystery. God, if she had discovered something that threw accepted ancient history theories out, her parents would be horrified. She'd always been interested in archeology, but her parents had almost had heart attacks when she'd told them. They'd quietly organized other opportunities for her, and before she knew it, she'd been studying hydrology and biology. She'd managed to sneak in her paleontology studies where she could.

Dr. Arthur Caswell and Dr. Kathleen Schafer expected nothing but perfection from their sole progeny. Even after their bloodless divorce, they'd still expected Rowan to do exactly as they wanted.

Rowan had long-ago realized that nothing she ever did would please her parents for long. She blew out a breath. It had taken a painful childhood spent trying to win their love and affection—and failing miserably—to realize that. They were just too absorbed in their own work and lives.

Pull up your big-girl panties, Rowan. She'd never been abused and had been given a great education. She had work she enjoyed, interesting colleagues, and a lot to be thankful for.

Rowan watched her team pack the last of their samples onto the sled. She glanced to the southern horizon, peering at the bank of clouds in the distance. Ellesmere didn't get a lot of precipitation, which meant not a lot of snow, but plenty of ice. Still, it looked like bad weather was brewing and she wanted everyone safely back at camp.

"Okay, everyone, enough for today. Let's head back to base for hot chocolate and coffee."

Isabel rolled her eyes. "You and your chocolate."

Rowan made no apologies for her addiction, or the fact that half her bag for the trip here had been filled with her stash of high-quality chocolate—milk, dark, powdered, and her prized couverture chocolate.

"I want a nip of something warmer," Lars said.

No one complained about leaving. Working out on the ice was bitterly cold, even in September, with the last blush of summer behind them.

Rowan climbed on a snowmobile and quickly grabbed her hand-held radio. "Hazen Team Two, this is Hazen Team One. We are headed back to Hazen Base, confirm."

A few seconds later, the radio crackled. "Acknowledged, Hazen One. We see the clouds, Rowan. We're leaving the drill site now."

Dr. Samuel Malu was as steady and dependable as the sunrise.

"See you there," she answered.

Marc climbed onto the second snowmobile, Lars riding behind him. Rowan waited for Isabel to climb on before firing up the engine. They both pulled their goggles on.

It wasn't a long trip back to base, and soon the camp appeared ahead. Seven large, temporary, polar domes made of high-tech, insulated materials were linked together by short, covered tunnels to make the multi-structure dome camp. The domes housed their living quarters, kitchen and rec room, labs, and one that held Rowan's office, the communications room, and storage. The high-tech insulation made the domes easy to heat, and they were relatively easy to construct and move. The structures had been erected to last through the seven-month expedition.

The two snowmobiles roared close to the largest dome and pulled to a stop.

"Okay, all the samples and specimens to the labs," Rowan directed, holding open the door that led inside. She watched as Lars carefully picked up a tray and headed inside. Isabel and Marc followed with more trays.

Rowan stepped inside and savored the heat that hit her. The small kitchen was on the far side of the rec room, and the center of the dome was crowded with tables, chairs, and sofas.

She unzipped and shrugged off her coat and hung it beside the other red jackets lined up by the door. Next, she stepped out of her big boots and slipped into the canvas shoes she wore inside.

A sudden commotion from the adjoining tunnel had Rowan frowning. *What now?*

A young woman burst from the tunnel. She was dressed in normal clothes, her blonde hair pulled up in a tight ponytail. Emily Wood, their intern, was a student from the University of British Columbia in Vancouver. She got to do all the not-so-glamorous jobs, like logging and labelling the samples, which meant the scientists could focus on their research.

"Rowan, you have to come now!"

"Emily? What's wrong?" Concerned, Rowan gripped the woman's shoulder. She was practically vibrating. "Are you hurt?"

Emily shook her head. "You have to come to Lab Dome 1." She grabbed Rowan's hand and dragged her into the tunnel. "It's *unbelievable.*"

Rowan followed. "Tell me what—"

"No. You need to see it with your own eyes."

Seconds later, they stepped into the lab dome. The temperature was pleasant and Rowan was already feeling hot. She needed to strip off her sweater before she started sweating. She spotted Isabel, and another botanist, Dr. Amara Taylor, staring at the main workbench.

"Okay, what's the big issue?" Rowan stepped forward.

Emily tugged her closer. "Look!" She waved a hand with a flourish.

A number of various petri dishes and sample holders sat on the workbench. Emily had been cataloguing all the seeds and frozen plant life they'd pulled out of the glacier.

"These are some of the samples we collected on our first day here." She pointed at the end of the workbench. "Some I completely thawed and had stored for Dr. Taylor to start analyzing."

Amara lifted her dark eyes to Rowan. The botanist was a little older than Rowan, with dark-brown skin, and long, dark hair swept up in a bun. "These plants are five thousand years old."

Rowan frowned and leaned forward. Then she gasped. "Oh my God."

The plants were sprouting new, green shoots.

"They've come back to life." Emily's voice was breathless.

THE CLINK of silverware and excited conversations filled the rec dome. Rowan stabbed at a clump of meat in her stew, eyeing it with a grimace. She loved food, but hated the stuff that accompanied them on expeditions. She grabbed her mug—sweet, rich hot chocolate. She'd made it from her stash with the perfect amount of cocoa. The best hot chocolate needed no less than sixty percent cocoa but no more than eighty.

Across from her, Lars and Isabel weren't even looking at their food or drink.

"Five thousand years old!" Isabel shook her head, her dark hair falling past her shoulders. "Those plants are millennia old, and they've come back to life."

"Amazing," Lars said. "A few years back, a team working south of here on the Teardrop Glacier at Sverdrup Pass brought moss back to life...but it was only four hundred years old."

Isabel and Lars high-fived each other.

Rowan ate some more of her stew. "Russian scientists regenerated seeds found in a squirrel burrow in the Siberian permafrost."

"Pfft," Lars said. "Ours is still cooler."

"They got the plant to flower and it was fertile," Rowan continued, mildly. "The seeds were thirty-two thousand years old."

Isabel pulled a face and Lars looked disappointed.

"And I think they are working on reviving forty-thousand-year-old nematode worms now."

Her team members both pouted.

Rowan smiled and shook her head. "But five-thousand-year-old plant life is nothing to sneeze at, and the Russian flowers required a lot of human intervention to coax them back to life."

Lars perked up. "All we did was thaw and water ours."

Rowan kept eating, listening to the flow of conversation. The others were wondering what other ancient plant life they might find in the glacial ice.

"What if we find a frozen mammoth?" Lars suggested.

"No, a frozen glacier man," Isabel said.

"Like the Ötzi man," Rowan said. "He was over five thousand years old, and found in the Alps. On the border between Italy and Austria."

Amara arrived, setting her tray down. "Glaciers are retreating all over the planet. I had a colleague who uncovered several Roman artifacts from a glacier in the Swiss Alps."

Isabel sat back in her chair. "Maybe we'll find the fountain of youth? Maybe something in these plants we're uncovering could defy aging, or cure cancer."

Rowan raised an eyebrow and smothered a smile. She was as excited as the others about the regeneration of the plants. But her mind turned to the now-forgotten mystery object they'd plucked from the ice. She'd taken some photos of it and its markings. She was itching to take a look at them again.

"I'm going to take another look at the metal object we found," Lars said, stuffing some stew in his mouth.

"Going to check for any messages from aliens?" Isabel teased.

Lars screwed up his nose, then he glanced at Rowan. "Want to join me?"

She was so tempted, but she had a bunch of work piled on her desk. Most important being the supply lists for their next supply drop. She'd send her photos off to an archeologist friend at Harvard, and then spend the rest of her evening banging through her To-Do list.

"I can't tonight. Duty calls." She pushed her chair back and lifted her tray. "I'm going to eat dessert in my office and do some work."

"You mean eat that delicious chocolate of yours that you guard like a hawk," Isabel said.

Rowan smiled. "I promise to make something yummy tomorrow."

"Your brownies," Lars said.

"Chocolate-covered pralines," Isabel said, almost on top of Lars.

Rowan shook her head. Her chocolate creations were gaining a reputation. "I'll surprise you. If anyone needs me, you know where to find me."

"Bye, Rowan."

"Catch you later."

She set the tray on the side table and scraped off her plates. They had a roster for cooking and cleaning duty, and thankfully it wasn't her night. She ignored the dried-out looking chocolate chip cookies, anticipating the block of milk chocolate in her desk drawer. Yep, she had a weakness for chocolate in any form. Chocolate was the most important food group.

As she headed through the tunnels to the smaller dome that housed her office, she listened to the wind howling outside. It sounded like the storm had arrived. She sent up a silent thanks that her entire team was safe and sound in the camp. Since she was the expedition leader, she got her own office, rather than having to share space with the other scientists in the labs.

In her cramped office, she flicked on her lamp and sat down behind her desk. She opened the drawer, pulled out her chocolate, smelled it, and snapped off a piece. She put it in her mouth and savored the flavor.

The best chocolate was a sensory experience. From how it looked—no cloudy old chocolate, please—to how it smelled and tasted. Right now, she enjoyed the intense flavors on her tongue and the smooth, velvety feel. Her mother had never let her have chocolate or other "unhealthy" foods growing up. Rowan had been forced to sneak her chocolate. She remembered her childhood friend, the intense boy from next door who'd always snuck her candy bars when she'd been outside hiding from her parents.

Shaking her head, Rowan reached over and plugged in her portable speaker. Soon she had some blood-pumping rock music filling her space. She smiled, nodding her head to the beat. Her love of rock-and-roll was another thing she'd kept well-hidden from her parents as a teenager. Her mother loved Bach, and her father preferred silence. Rowan had hidden all her albums growing up, and snuck out to concerts while pretending to be on study dates.

Opening her laptop, she scanned her email. Her stomach clenched. Nothing from her parents. She shook her head. Her mother had emailed once...to ask again when Rowan would be finished with her ill-advised jaunt to the Arctic. Her father hadn't even bothered to check she'd arrived safely.

Old news, Rowan. Shaking off old heartache, she uploaded the photos she'd taken to her computer. She took a second to study the photos of her mystery object again.

"What are you?" she murmured.

The carvings on the object could be natural scratches. She zoomed in. It really looked like some sort of writing to her, but if the object was over five thousand years old, then it wasn't likely. She knew the Pre-Dorset and Dorset peoples had been known to carve soapstone and driftwood, but this artifact would have been at the early point of Pre-Dorset history. Hell, it predated cuneiform—the earliest form of writing—which was barely getting going in Sumer when this thing had ended up in the ice.

She searched on her computer and pulled up some images of Sumerian cuneiform. She set the images side by side and studied them, tapped a finger idly against her lip. Some similarities...maybe. She flicked to the next image, chin in hand. She wanted to run a few tests on the object, see exactly what it was made of.

Not your project, Rowan. Instead, she attached the pictures to an email to send to her archeologist friend.

God, she hoped her parents never discovered she was here, pondering ancient markings on an unidentified object. They'd be horrified. Rowan pinched the bridge of her nose. She was a grown woman of thirty-two. Why did she still feel this driving need for her parents' approval?

With a sigh, she rubbed a fist over her chest, then clicked send on the email. Wishing her family was normal was a lost cause. She'd learned that long ago, hiding out in her treehouse with the boy from next door—who'd had a bad homelife as well.

She sank back in her chair and eyed the pile of paperwork on her desk. *Right, work to do.* This was the reason she was in the middle of the Arctic.

Rowan lost herself in her tasks. She took notes, updated inventory sheets, and approved requests.

A vague, unsettling noise echoed through the tunnel. Her music was still pumping, and she lifted her head and frowned, straining to hear.

She turned off her music and stiffened. Were those screams?

She bolted upright. The screams got louder, interspersed with the crash of furniture and breaking glass.

Team 52

Mission: Her Protection
Mission: Her Rescue
Mission: Her Security
Mission: Her Defense
Mission: Her Safety
Mission: Her Freedom
Mission: Her Shield
Also Available as Audiobooks!

PREVIEW: TEAM 52 AND THS

Want to learn more about the mysterious, covert *Team 52*? Check out the first book in the series, *Mission: Her Protection.*

When Rowan's Arctic research team pulls a strange object out of the ice in Northern

Canada, things start to go wrong...very, very wrong. Rescued by a covert, black ops team, she finds herself in the powerful arms of a man with scary gold eyes. A man who vows to do everything and anything to protect her...

Dr. Rowan Schafer has learned it's best to do things herself and not depend on anyone else. Her cold, academic parents taught her that lesson. She loves the challenge of running a research base, until the day her scientists discover the object in a retreating glacier. Under attack, Rowan finds herself fighting to survive... until the mysterious Team 52 arrives.

Former special forces Marine Lachlan Hunter's military career ended in blood and screams, until he was recruited to lead a special team. A team tasked with a top-secret mission—to secure and safeguard pieces of powerful ancient technology. Married to his job, he's done too much and seen too much to risk inflicting his demons on a woman. But when his team arrives in the Arctic, he uncovers both an unexplained artifact, and a young girl from his past, now all grown up. A woman who ignites emotions inside him like never before.

But as Team 52 heads back to their base in Nevada, other hostile forces are after the artifact. Rowan finds herself under attack, and as the bullets fly, Lachlan vows to protect her at all costs. But in the face of danger like they've never seen before, will it be enough to keep her alive.

Team 52
Mission: Her Protection
Mission: Her Rescue
Mission: Her Security
Mission: Her Defense
Mission: Her Safety
Mission: Her Freedom
Mission: Her Shield
Also Available as Audiobooks!

Want to learn more about *Treasure Hunter Security*? Check out the first book in the series, *Undiscovered*, Declan Ward's action-packed story.

One former Navy SEAL. One dedicated archeologist. One secret map to a fabulous lost oasis.

Finding undiscovered treasures is always daring, dangerous, and deadly. Perfect for the men of Treasure Hunter Security. Former Navy SEAL Declan Ward is haunted by the demons of his past and throws everything he has into his security business—Treasure Hunter Security. Dangerous archeological digs – no problem. Daring expeditions – sure thing. Museum security for invaluable exhibits – easy. But on a simple dig in the Egyptian desert, he collides with a stubborn, smart archeologist, Dr. Layne Rush, and together they get swept into a deadly treasure hunt for a mythical lost oasis. When an evil from his past reappears, Declan vows to do anything to protect Layne.

Dr. Layne Rush is dedicated to building a successful career—a promise to the parents she lost far too young. But when her dig is plagued by strange accidents, targeted by a lethal black market antiquities ring, and artifacts are stolen, she is forced to turn to Treasure Hunter Security, and to the tough, sexy, and too-used-to-giving-orders Declan. Soon her organized dig morphs into a wild treasure hunt across the desert dunes.

Danger is hunting them every step of the way, and Layne and Declan must find a way to work together...to not only find the treasure but to survive.

Treasure Hunter Security

Undiscovered

Uncharted

Unexplored

Unfathomed

THE SPECIALIST

Untraveled
Unmapped
Unidentified
Undetected
Also Available as Audiobooks!

ALSO BY ANNA HACKETT

Norcross Security

The Investigator

The Troubleshooter

Team 52

Mission: Her Protection

Mission: Her Rescue

Mission: Her Security

Mission: Her Defense

Mission: Her Safety

Mission: Her Freedom

Mission: Her Shield

Mission: Her Justice

Also Available as Audiobooks!

Treasure Hunter Security

Undiscovered

Uncharted

Unexplored

Unfathomed

Untraveled

Unmapped

Unidentified

Undetected

Also Available as Audiobooks!

Eon Warriors

Edge of Eon

Touch of Eon

Heart of Eon

Kiss of Eon

Mark of Eon

Claim of Eon

Storm of Eon

Soul of Eon

Also Available as Audiobooks!

Galactic Gladiators: House of Rone

Sentinel

Defender

Centurion

Paladin

Guard

Weapons Master

Also Available as Audiobooks!

Galactic Gladiators

Gladiator

Warrior

Hero

Protector

Champion

Barbarian

Beast

Rogue

Guardian

Cyborg

Imperator

Hunter

Also Available as Audiobooks!

Hell Squad

Marcus

Cruz

Gabe

Reed

Roth

Noah

Shaw

Holmes

Niko

Finn

Theron

Hemi

Ash

Levi

Manu

Griff

Dom

Survivors

Tane

Also Available as Audiobooks!

The Anomaly Series

Time Thief

Mind Raider

Soul Stealer

Salvation

Anomaly Series Box Set

The Phoenix Adventures

Among Galactic Ruins

At Star's End

In the Devil's Nebula

On a Rogue Planet

Beneath a Trojan Moon

Beyond Galaxy's Edge

On a Cyborg Planet

Return to Dark Earth

On a Barbarian World

Lost in Barbarian Space

Through Uncharted Space

Crashed on an Ice World

Perma Series

Winter Fusion

A Galactic Holiday

Warriors of the Wind

Tempest

Storm & Seduction

Fury & Darkness

Standalone Titles

Savage Dragon

Hunter's Surrender

One Night with the Wolf

For more information visit www.annahackett.com

ABOUT THE AUTHOR

I'm a USA Today bestselling romance author who's passionate about ***fast-paced, emotion-filled*** contemporary and science fiction romance. I love writing about people overcoming unbeatable odds and achieving seemingly impossible goals. I like to believe it's possible for all of us to do the same.

I live in Australia with my own personal hero and two very busy, always-on-the-move sons.

For release dates, behind-the-scenes info, free books, and other fun stuff, sign up for the latest news here:

Website: www.annahackett.com

Printed in Great Britain
by Amazon